Taboo Desires
By Amanda Young

When his girlfriend demands he settle down and start a family, Cole Winchester has some hard decisions to make. Marry his girlfriend, or finally own up to his taboo attraction to other men.

Cole Winchester feels like a rat, boxed into a corner. Faced with the prospect of being trapped in a passionless marriage, he makes the hard choice to end his relationship.

A run in with an old friend on the beach, propels Cole's fantasies out into the open and forces him to confront his taboo desires. Before him, lies the choice of a lifetime—embrace his desire for another man and all the pitfalls that come along with it, or return to his girlfriend and live out the safe half-life he carved for himself.

Warning, this title contains the following: explicit sex, graphic language, and hot nekkid man-love.

D1522217

Custom Ride
By K.A. Mitchell

Life's not always about the journey, but who takes you on the ride.

A stint in the Air Force left Ryan MacRae with a bitter memory of life in the closet. Jeff Allstein is a mechanic who has too much to lose if his private life becomes public. The heat of their attraction boils over on a stormy summer night, but satisfying that need only makes them both crave more.

Their searing connection makes it hard for Ryan to understand the road blocks Jeff continually puts down. Ryan will have to buckle up if he's going to find love at the end of his custom ride.

Warning, this title contains the following: explicit male/male sex, graphic language.

Catching a Buzz
By Ally Blue

Can a straight-laced business student and an indie boy with a thing for extremely personal electronics turn one night's wild ride into a trip to last forever?

Adam Holderman isn't your typical twenty-something college boy. He prefers jazz to Goth, shuns body piercings and street-waif clothing, and despises the lack of vocabulary among his peers. Some call him uptight, but Adam doesn't see it that way. Just because he prefers his men articulate and well-groomed doesn't make him a stick-in-the-mud. He simply has standards, unlike most guys his age.

The new employee at Wild Waters Park, where Adam works, single-handedly throws a monkey wrench into Adam's orderly world view. Buzz Stiles wears eyeliner and black clothes, listens to emo bands, and talks like a teenage skate punk. He's the polar opposite of Adam's avowed "type". So why can't Adam get him out of his head?

When Adam finally agrees to go out with Buzz, he finds there's much more to Buzz than a hot body, a sharp wit, and a Goth fashion sense. Buzz is someone Adam can see himself being with for the long haul. But you need more than mind-melting sex to make a relationship last. Can they keep their hands off each other long enough to find out if they have what it takes?

Nut Cream

By Jade Buchanan

Two men and a bottle of nut cream...

Nut [nuht] noun, verb.

1. A dry fruit consisting of an edible kernel or meat enclosed in a woody or leathery shell.

2. Slang, Vulgar – a testis.

Cream [kreem] noun.

1. A soft solid or thick liquid containing medicaments or other specific ingredients, applied externally for a therapeutic, or cosmetic purpose.

2. Slang, Vulgar – to have an orgasm.

Toby Madison is coming into his mating phase, and is leaking pheromones all over the place. He is about to find out what happens to bad little wolves, in the best possible way. Cliff Bullen is more than ready to place his mark on the man he has always wanted as his mate – with a little help from a bottle of nut cream.

Warning, this title contains the following: explicit male/male sex and graphic language.

Temperature's Rising

A SAMHAIN PUBLISHING, LTD. publication.

Samhain Publishing, Ltd.
577 Mulberry Street, Suite 1520
Macon, GA 31201
www.samhainpublishing.com

Temperature's Rising
Print ISBN: 978-1-59998-776-7
Taboo Desires Copyright © 2008 by Amanda Young
Custom Ride Copyright © 2008 by K.A. Mitchell
Catching a Buzz Copyright © 2008 by Ally Blue
Nut Cream Copyright © 2008 by Jade Buchanan

Editing by Sasha Knight
Cover by Anne Cain

Taboo Desires, ISBN 1-59998-594-2
First Samhain Publishing, Ltd. electronic publication: August 2007
Custom Ride, ISBN 1-59998-590-X
First Samhain Publishing, Ltd. electronic publication: August 2007
Catching a Buzz, ISBN 1-59998-573-X
First Samhain Publishing, Ltd. electronic publication: June 2007
Nut Cream, ISBN 1-59998-582-9
First Samhain Publishing, Ltd. electronic publication: July 2007
First Samhain Publishing, Ltd. print publication: May 2008

Contents

Taboo Desires

Amanda Young

Dedication

In dedication to all the people out there, who stand brave and choose to be true to themselves.

Chapter One

Sunlight filtered in through the picture window in the dining room. Tendrils of gossamer light illuminated Karen's long, golden hair like a halo around her pixyish face. Her emerald eyes filled with fire, she stood in the partition between the dining room and kitchen, her hands on her slender hips. "What do you mean you aren't ready to get married?"

Cole Winchester swore under his breath and ran a hand over the stubbled, lower half of his face in exasperation. He really didn't feel like having this discussion again. After a long, unproductive day at the store, he was tired and cranky. The last damn thing he wanted to talk about was whether or not they should get married. It wasn't as if he'd changed his mind in the past twenty-four hours.

"Well?" she asked, her gaze pinning him down with a glacial frown that left him feeling two inches tall.

He sighed and decided then and there that something had to change. *Now.* He was sick to death of having to deal with being interrogated every time he came over. "I meant just what I said, Karen. We aren't ready to get married. Weddings aren't cheap and neither one of us has that kind of dough right now."

Karen glared and her lips parted, no doubt ready to lambaste him for saying something she didn't agree with. Luckily, she was interrupted by the shrill whine of the oven's buzzer. With a humph, she turned and stomped into the kitchen. Thank God looks couldn't kill, or he'd be a six-foot shish kabob.

The simple truth was he wasn't ready to settle down. He didn't think he ever would be, at least not with Karen. He cared about her—they never would have made it past the two year mark if he didn't—but he wasn't *in* love with her. Then again, she didn't seem to be very keen on him either these days. Which made her being so gung-ho to get married all the more strange. Up until the previous month, no mention had been made of getting married, and then all of a sudden it was the only thing she wanted to talk about. Or scream about, as the case may be.

Karen marched across the dining room, a glass pan full of steaming broccoli casserole between her oven-mitt-covered hands. "That's the dumbest thing I've ever heard. People get married every day without all the fancy trimmings." She punctuated her statement by slamming the dish down in the middle of the table and trudged over to her seat.

Cole watched as she bit into the rosy flesh of her lower lip, noting the way her skin turned pale around the edges of small, pearly white teeth. The action reminded him more of something a petulant teenager would do than a mature woman nearing thirty.

Where had the sweet woman he'd started dating gone in the last month? Marriage had become some kind of worry stone that shoved them further and further apart instead of bringing them closer together like it was meant to. The woman was obsessed. He didn't see what the big deal was. After all, it was only a piece of paper.

Tugging at the hem of his work shirt, a red polo with the words Winchester's Game Emporium embossed on the breast pocket, Cole pretended to pull at loose threads, while Karen silently filled her plate. Dinner smelled good, all cheesy and buttery the way he liked it, but his appetite had disappeared the moment Karen uttered the dreaded M word.

All they ever seemed to do was argue anymore. Sex was nonexistent, and though he'd never really understood what all the rave was about, he did miss the intimacy. His hand was fine for getting him off, but it didn't exactly keep him warm at night. More than anything else, he missed the cuddling and the kissing. He missed his best friend, Karen.

"If you're so worried about money, we could just go to the courthouse. Surely that isn't too expensive."

Cole looked up and met Karen's eyes from across the table. He felt trapped, like a deer caught in the headlights of an oncoming Mack truck. Tension mounted between them, almost palpable in the air. If he could just find the words to tell her the truth, he wouldn't have to worry about being browbeaten into a marriage he didn't want. Unfortunately, the prospect of explaining himself was scarier than wedding bells.

His mind drew a blank, no ready excuses waiting in the wings for him to placate her with. Lack of money was the best reason he could come up with and she'd just blown that defense all to hell. He swallowed over the lump steadily rising in his throat. "I just don't think it's a good idea right now, is all."

It wasn't as if he could tell her the truth. Not when admitting his lifelong fascination for men—hot, sweaty bodies and hard musculature instead of soft curves and feminine mystique—was growing stronger and becoming more of an obsession than a curiosity. He found himself picturing a man right before he stroked one off at night. As his inhibitions dissolved with his rising need, the same fuzzy, faceless image of a man flashed through his mind and propelled him over the

13

edge into orgasm. He tried to think of women, of breasts and smooth, pliant bodies, but somewhere between when he started jerking and when he climaxed, the images always transformed into hard pecs and rippling washboard stomachs.

He didn't want to be gay or bisexual, or whatever the hell he was. He wanted to stay in his safe little world, with Karen by his side, and live out the American dream—a beautiful wife and a nice home, maybe a Golden Retriever or two. But walking the straight and narrow line everyone else followed was becoming more difficult with every passing day. Like a drunk taking a sobriety test, he teeter-tottered on the brink of falling off the path.

Karen snorted in disagreement and pushed her long, straight blonde hair back over her shoulder. She took a dainty bite of food and made a big production of swallowing before she balanced her fork on the edge of the plate and glanced up. Cole sat immobile, sweat dampening the underarms of his shirt, while he anxiously waited to hear what she'd say next.

She huffed out a deep exhalation, the air swirling upward to ruffle her bangs. "So, you just don't want to get married, is that it?"

Shit. "What brought all this on, Karen? We've never even discussed getting married and now it seems like that's all you think about. I don't see what the big hurry is. Things are fine between us the way they are."

"No, things are not fine! I want to get married. I want to start a family. If you love me, I'd think you would want those things too. We aren't getting any younger, you know?"

Numb shock radiated through Cole's limbs. "Is that what this is about? Kids? We talked about that when we first starting dating. I told you I wasn't sure if I even wanted to have any of my own. You said you didn't either."

"That was two years ago, Cole. I changed my mind."

So that was it, she'd changed her mind, and now he was supposed to go along with it? "I'm sorry, Karen, but I haven't. I don't want kids. I thought you understood that."

Tears pooled in her eyes and broke his heart. He didn't want to hurt her, but he wouldn't lie to her about how he felt. If they got married and popped out a bunch of kids, they'd both be miserable. And that was no kind of situation to bring a child into.

"I'm sorry." He didn't know what else to say.

Karen pushed back her chair and stood. She walked past him, not meeting his eyes, and he rose to follow her. She stopped at the door, her hand on the knob, and finally met his eyes. "I'm sorry too. I love you, but I can't waste any more time on a man who doesn't want the same things I do." She yanked open the door and held it. "I think you should leave."

His chest burned, right along with the backs of his eyelids. He didn't want things to end this way, didn't want to lose her like this. "Karen—"

"No. Whatever it is you plan to say, I don't want to hear it. Just go."

Chapter Two

Cole ambled along the shoreline, his toes sinking into the cool, wet sand with each step. The hot midday sun scalded his face and shoulders. Sweat beaded and ran down his bare torso in wet little rivulets. High humidity made his skin sticky and his mind slow, the heat making him lethargic.

As far as the eye could see, families, couples and groups of teenagers frolicked in the sea or on the beach. A gentle wind carried the salty smell of the ocean and the giddy laughter of children at play. A bright red beach ball darted past him, quickly followed by a little boy in yellow swim trunks. A smile tugged at the corners of Cole's lips as he watched the kid scoop it up and sprint back to his family.

Cole buried his hands in the pockets of his jean shorts and continued down the beach. His gaze wandered out over the frothy blue-green water, where surfers sat perched upon their boards, waiting to catch the next big wave. It was a beautiful August day, the kind meant to be spent outdoors.

Other than escaping the monotonous cycle of waking up, going to work and then home to sleep, Cole hadn't had a destination in mind when he'd left his apartment. All he'd wanted to do was get away from his life for the afternoon and think things through. Meandering about on the beach, feeling small in comparison to the vast ocean, always had a way of putting things into perspective.

Two weeks had gone by since Karen broke things off with him. True to her word, she hadn't accepted any of his phone calls and had returned each and every bouquet of flowers he'd sent. Things were well and truly over between them. He simply wasn't sure how he felt about it.

Karen had been a part of his life for so long that he didn't quite know what to do with himself without her. A part of him was relieved she was gone—the same part that whispered in his ear about how wrong it felt to pretend to be someone he wasn't. The other half of him screamed for him to go crawling back to her on his knees and beg for forgiveness before it was too late. He knew she would take him back, if only so she could have the "Mrs." moniker before her first name.

While that would have been the easy, safe thing to do, he couldn't make himself give in to her demand. Simply put, he didn't want to marry Karen. Not now, not ever. And it wasn't fair to keep stringing her along so he wouldn't have to admit to things about himself he'd rather not face.

Loving someone wasn't the same as being in love with them, and that's what he wanted for Karen. He cared enough about her to want the best for her, and that wasn't him. She deserved someone better, a man who would love her the way he couldn't.

Cole shook his head, almost amused by how depressing his thoughts were. What he needed to do was go out and have some fun. Maybe call up one of his single buddies from poker night and see if they wanted to... *Oh, wait.* That wouldn't work. The last of his single buddies got married back in June, so getting anyone to go out with him on a Tuesday night was probably a no-go. Hell, it'd probably be out of the question on the weekend too. Did married people even go out with their single friends? He sincerely doubted it.

The tide hit the shore, washing in seaweed along with water. A slimy green clump of vegetation landed atop his foot. He stepped back, jiggling his left foot to dislodge it, even as the back of his right knee ran into something cold and hard.

"Hey, watch it!"

Arms swinging out, he tried to right his equilibrium, to no avail. His ass hit the ground, not really hurting anything besides his ego. Face flaming in embarrassment, he glanced up and around, trying to see who or what he'd run into.

The first thing he saw was the neon purple surfboard he'd tripped over. Right next to it sat the owner. Cole blinked and did a double take, seeing the flesh and blood version of his every fantasy sitting in the sand, smiling at him.

The man was the epitome of everything Cole had ever dreamt of. Sun-bleached blond hair, sheared close to the scalp on the sides and longer on top, fell into a face so classically beautiful it rivaled Michelangelo's David. Sharp cheekbones and a straight, tip-tilted nose led down to a full mouth the color of fresh strawberries. His neck was long and graceful, leading to leanly corded shoulders. His skin gleamed golden-bronze in the sunlight. His pecs and biceps were nicely defined, not too much muscle, just enough to broadcast health and fitness. Tiny copper nipples, pierced with silver barbells, sat above a chiseled, washboard stomach.

Heat rushed from his face to his groin, filling Cole's shaft with blood. He was damned glad he wasn't standing up. The pup tent in his shorts would have been mortifying.

Cool azure blue eyes, the color of the freshest mountain stream, met his and he could've sworn he felt the earth move.

So what if it was just the tide hitting the shore? It felt a hell of a lot more life altering than something that simple.

"Cole? Cole Winchester? That you, man?"

Cole's brow wrinkled in confusion. How did this kid know his name? He couldn't be more than twenty years old, if he was a day. Studying the man's face more closely, he saw a familiarity in his features, but was unable to place him as anyone other than the specter haunting his fantasies. "Uh, yeah, it's me."

"You all right?" the man asked, in a tenor voice that straddled the line between masculine and feminine. "You took quite a spill there."

"Yeah," Cole replied, still unable to figure out who the guy was, but not wanting to admit he didn't recognize him. He found it hard to believe that he could've met this guy and not remembered his face. "I'm good. Sorry about that, I didn't see you there."

"No problem. I know how it is. You look out into the water and you're miles away, right? It's cool." His smile kicked up a notch. "You have no idea who I am, do you?"

Damn. Busted. "Uh, well, not really. Sorry."

"It's okay. I think the last time you saw me I was about twelve and skinny as a light post, all teeth and limbs. I'm Eric Radcliff, Beau Radcliff's little brother."

"Oh, yeah, I remember you. Senior year, you used to tag along behind Beau everywhere he went. You followed him to all of the football team's home games and stuff. He was always bitchin' about how you ruined his chances of scoring with the cheerleaders."

Eric laughed. "Yep, that was me. I was a regular little buzz kill, the way Beau tells it."

"Oh man, how is Beau? The last I heard, he'd settled down with that Sherry chick he started seeing in college and was selling insurance or something."

Eric nodded. "Yeah, that's about right, except him and Sherry divorced a couple of years ago."

"Oh, I'm sorry to hear that." But he wasn't real surprised. Beau had always been a bit of a ladies' man, so it wouldn't exactly shock Cole to hear that marriage hadn't stopped Beau from getting a little action on the side.

The conversation tapered off and Eric turned away from him, glancing out over the incoming waves. Cole took that as a dismissal. He sat for a moment, giving his erection a chance to subside, before he climbed to his feet and brushed the sand off the seat of his shorts.

"Well, it was nice seeing you again, Eric. You take care and tell your brother I said hello." He turned to leave, but he didn't get more than a few steps down the beach before Eric's lyrical voice stopped him.

"Hey, Cole?"

"Yeah?"

Eric ducked his head, his gaze not quite meeting Cole's. "You want to maybe catch a drink tonight? There's a pretty good band playing over at The Razor, the grunge bar over on Eighth Street, you know, and the buddy I was planning to take bailed on me this morning. Said he had to work tonight or something. Anyway, if you want, you could go. You don't have to, mind you, if you have plans, but it might be fun. We could have a couple of drinks. Maybe catch up on old times or something?"

Though he wasn't into grunge music—so much so that he'd never even heard of the bar Eric named—he found himself wanting to go. It would be fun. They could kick back a few

Buds, catch up, and maybe scope out some chicks. Or, well, he could pretend to check out women.

Maybe this wasn't such a good idea after all. The last thing he needed to do was keep pretending. He needed to figure out who he was and what he wanted. Not put on another production of "Cole Winchester, straight guy extraordinaire".

Cole opened his mouth, intent on saying he had plans. "Sure, that would be fun," popped out instead. Well, shit, so much for erring on the side of caution. He'd just have to make sure he wore loose pants and a long shirt. Then maybe the boner he was sure to sport all night wouldn't be so obvious.

"Great!" Eric smiled, showcasing straight white teeth and a cute little dimple in his left cheek. "So, you wanna just meet me there, say around nine?"

"Yeah, that'll work."

Eric stood and bent over to pick up his board, giving Cole a full view of his firm ass covered by a thin layer of tight spandex. "Well, I, um, have some things to do, but I'll see you tonight, yeah?"

"Oh yeah," Cole replied, and then wanted to smack himself upside the head for sounding so eager. So what if the kid had an ass like two firm peaches, he was probably as straight as they came. For that matter, Cole wasn't even sure if he himself was bent, or just more naturally curious than the next guy.

As he stood watching Eric walk off, his pert bottom swishing from side to side, Cole wondered just how much trouble he was letting himself in for. One thing was for sure; it was bound to be an interesting night.

ꔷꔷꔷ

Eric whistled as he strode across the scorching sand toward where his jeep was parked alongside of the highway. What started out as a relaxing day at the beach, meant to curb his escalating boredom, had turned out to be the start of something he'd wanted for years.

Cole Winchester. Talk about a blast from the past. Eric shook his head and threw his board into the open backseat. Who would've thought he'd run into him again after all this time? Sure, they lived in the same general vicinity, but Tidewater was a big area, covering several counties and small coastal towns, plenty big enough that you never had to worry about running into someone you were trying to avoid.

Not that he was trying to avoid anyone, least of all Cole. That man, with his broad shoulders and fine ass, had single-handedly spawned more jack-off sessions during his adolescence than Blue magazine and porno combined.

He slid behind the wheel, the hot vinyl seat against his back making him wince, and started up the engine. Flipping through the CD case lying open on the passenger seat, he chose an old Stone Temple Pilots album, popping it into the player before pulling out onto the road.

He hadn't lied to Cole when he'd said he had plans. He'd just come out of the water and flopped down on the sand, trying to catch his breath after riding in one particularly awesome wave, and was preparing to haul his ass home, when Cole had sauntered by and almost stepped on him. Now he was running late for a lunch date with his brother.

Truthfully, he'd just as soon cancel the lunch and spend the rest of the evening daydreaming about his outing with Cole. Or speculating about whether or not the hunger he'd seen reflected back at him from Cole's chocolate gaze was real or imagined. He'd always had the notion Cole was straight, but a man's body wasn't designed to hide his needs and Cole's had been screaming, *do me.* Unfortunately, he didn't have time to ponder any of that. Ever since Sherry caught Beau banging their eighteen-year-old babysitter on the living room sofa, and moved herself and their four-year-old son, Bradley, into her mother's house across state, Beau had been a pitiful replica of his former self. The whoremonger Eric knew and loved was gone, replaced by an empty shell that moped and drank himself to sleep every night.

Eric turned into his parents' driveway and killed the engine. He stared at the home he'd grown up in, a two story Tudor with rosy bricks and hunter green shutters, and felt a nagging sense of suffocation. In two weeks, he would be back at school, and thank God for that. While his childhood had been a good one, it was filled with the typical teen angst, ramped up a few pegs because of his sexual orientation. With time, his parents had finally accepted him for who he was, but that hadn't stopped them from looking down their noses at him or referring to his homosexuality as a "rebellious phase". As if he sucked cock just to piss them off or something.

He jumped down from the jeep and marched up the cobblestone walk. The scent of the ocean and well-earned sweat clung to his skin. He needed a shower and a change of clothes before lunch. Sliding his key in the lock, he twisted the knob and shoved open the door. A rush of cool air hit his feverish skin and made him queasy as he climbed the stairs.

Stepping over the threshold into his bedroom was like taking a walk back in time. The same twin bed sat against the wall, plain white cotton sheets and puffy, navy quilt spread over the firm mattress. Pale blue wallpaper bordered plain white walls, littered with framed posters of his favorite metal bands. Mother had insisted on the frames when she'd caught him trying to tack the first one up when he was eleven.

That had been right around the same time he'd started lusting after Cole. A walking hormone on legs, he'd just begun to discover that while his pals were developing crushes on girls, he was more interested in hanging with the guys and sneaking curious peeks at their hindquarters. Eric grinned as he selected a pair of jean shorts and navy jersey from the closet and laid them out on the bed. Even back then he'd been an ass man.

By the time he'd been old enough to put a name to the differences he felt, Cole was long gone, already away at college. That hadn't stopped the fantasies though. Everything from down and dirty daydreams, where Cole cornered him in the guys' locker room and forced him to suck him off, to more gentle scenarios, where they held hands, kissed and made slow, sweet love to each other.

Plush cream carpet squished under the soles of his sneakers as Eric walked into the adjoining bathroom. He toed off his shoes and quickly stripped down to his skin. He dropped his clothes into a muddled heap on the blue tiled floor and bent over the tub, adjusting the shower thermostat to just this side of *boil you alive*, the way he liked it, and stepped in.

Just thinking about those dreams had his balls pulling up tight and his cock twitching in hopeful anticipation of the night to come. He resisted the urge to take himself in hand and relieve the ache thinking about Cole caused. Instead, he would wait and savor the buildup until later. Getting there was half the fun.

He wasn't entirely sure Cole swung his way, but he wasn't about to turn down the opportunity to find out. If he'd misinterpreted the signals, the worst that could happen was a punch in the face, but if he was right, well, then tonight would be the stuff dreams were made of. Only time would tell.

Chapter Three

After running some errands and basically just puttering around town for the afternoon in a bid to blow some time, Cole stumbled into his apartment. His hip hit the rickety table located inside the living room doorway and set off his answering machine, which was a touchy piece of shit. An automated voice confirmed what he already knew—he had zero messages.

Cole flopped down on his sofa and picked up the remote lying next to him on the side table. He flipped through the channels, passing by them all over and again, only to realize he hadn't actually seen a single thing. His mind was too wrapped up in what had happened earlier, on the beach, and what would happen later that evening.

The upcoming outing with Eric had Cole's balls tied up in knots. He didn't know whether to think of it as a date or just two friends hanging out. The word *outing* seemed like the safest box to categorize it in for the time being, at least until he knew whether Eric's overt flirting was normal friendliness, or something more. The image of the younger man's sparkling blue eyes and teasing smile popped into the forefront of his mind and lodged there, taunting him. Naughty thoughts of exactly what he'd like that mouth to do to him played out like a high definition movie.

Settling back against the cushions, Cole unbuttoned his jeans, shoved them and his boxer-briefs down over his hips, and let his wayward imagination have free rein over his psyche. Wound tight as he was, he needed to do something to relieve the tension. Fantasizing wouldn't hurt anyone and it wasn't as if someone would know what he thought about when he jerked off. Inside a world of his own making there was no one to placate, not a single soul who would be offended by something he said or did. He could do who and what he pleased without fear of recrimination.

Closing his eyes, Cole took himself in hand, the hot flesh of his semi-erect cock like a shock against the cool surface of his palm. Starting at the base, he stroked up and over the head, pulling his flesh taut along the way. With his other hand, he reached down and cupped his sac, giving it a little squeeze and rub. Soft skin wrinkled, his balls drawing up as his cock expanded and throbbed under his grip.

Using his mind like an empty canvas, Cole painted the picture he wanted. The hand kneading his balls became Eric's. The thumb he used to spread slick precome over the blushing cap and sensitive ridge morphed into Eric's tongue, those pretty blue eyes staring up at him over the thick jut of his dick, just begging for a taste.

"Mmm. Suck me," Cole muttered and bucked his hips, sliding his cock through the tight ring of his fist. Moisture leaked from the tip, dampness he used to pretend it was Eric's mouth covering him, bathing every inch of his shaft in hot, slick pressure.

The pace of his strokes sped up, phantom Eric swallowing him to the root. Cole squeezed the head, an imaginary throat compressing around the tip. His ass clenched and his balls jerked, liquid lightning jetting up the shaft of his cock. Come sprang from the slit, molten ropes of it splashing over his abs and the hem of his T-shirt. He rocked up into his hand, milking the last bead of come from his body, and wished Eric was really there to lick the seed from his fingers.

Cole opened his eyes and wiped his damp palm off on his shirt. He stood and headed into the bathroom, wondering how reality would measure up with his fantasy. At the rate he was going, he would never know. Even if the opportunity presented itself, he wasn't sure he would have the balls to go through with anything.

By the time he rushed through a quick shower and agonized over what to wear, Cole was running behind schedule. He hopped in his car and drove across town, breaking the speed limit half the time, while praying he didn't pass a cop.

Dusk began to darken the sky and change it into hues of lavender and pink as he made a left-hand turn onto Eighth Street. He slowed down, keeping an eye peeled for the club where he was supposed to meet Eric.

At the end of a strip mall, only three establishments wide, sat The Razor. He knew he'd found the right place before he saw the lighted black and silver sign bearing its name because clusters of young people loitered in groups outside the entrance, some waiting in line and some obviously just milling about, socializing.

Cole guided his pickup into the first parking space he saw. Nervous butterflies bit at the lining of his stomach as he got out and darted across the road to the opposite side. Making his way up the two blocks between where he was and where the club sat, he repeatedly second-guessed his motives for being there. It would have been so easy to stay home and stand Eric up. Not like he'd have to worry about getting an earful later on or something. The chances of running into Eric again, when they clearly ran in completely different circles, were slim to none.

And yet here he was, approaching a club he'd never heard of, to listen to music he didn't particularly care for, in the hopes of... In the hopes of what? That Eric was gay and would jump his bones? Drag him out of the closet and profess undying love? What a load of bullshit.

Agreeing to meet Eric, when he was so attracted to him, was a mistake. Which didn't explain why his feet walked him right up to the back of the entrance line, tapped impatiently while he waited, and then carried him through the club's door and into the dark and smoky interior.

Cole blinked as his eyes adjusted to the change in light. A classic Metallica tune, "Enter Sandman", blasted through unseen speakers, setting the mood as he swerved around groups of college kids and walked deeper into the cavernous room.

A black veneered bar with a cylindrical chrome rail decorating its lip, hugged the length of one dark paneled wall. In need of a stiff drink, he moved toward the bar, pushing and shoving his way through the quickly multiplying number of people. Wedging himself between two occupied stools, he waved the bartender over.

"Bud, in the bottle, and a shot of Jack, please."

The bartender, a skinny little man with enough piercings in his head to keep all the tattoo parlors in the county in business for a month, nodded and poured his liquor. While the man reached into the cooler beneath the bar for a beer, Cole threw back his shot, wincing as the stout liquor slid down his throat, and returned the empty glass. The bartender popped the cap off a longneck bottle and slid it across the counter in trade for the cash Cole held out. He accepted his change, dropped a five into the tip jar and wandered closer to the raised platform at the front of the room.

Along either side of the dance floor sat small tables, some with four stools and others with only two. He chose one of the smaller tables, butted up against the side wall, and sat down. From where he'd chosen to sit, Cole had a good view of the stage and the front entrance. He wanted to be able to spot Eric as soon as he came in.

Glancing down at his watch, he squinted in the low light, trying to make out the time. He silently chastised himself for not upgrading his watch to one of those with the luminescent numbers. Finally, he found a good angle and saw that it was five minutes till nine.

He looked up, having already decided he would only give Eric until half past nine to show up before he would leave, and saw Eric striding toward him. The anxious butterflies in his stomach began to do the rumba while his gaze wandered over Eric's svelte form, from the top of his sun-kissed hair to the tips of his white and blue sneakers. A snug white T-shirt stretched across his chest, the barbells piercing his nipples visible through the cotton. Faded denim, worn white and tissue thin around the pockets, hung low on his trim hips and hugged the long expanse of lean thighs.

Cole swallowed, the lump in his throat expanding right along with his dick, as Eric drew near. Sometime during the course of the day he'd managed to convince himself Eric's eyes weren't as blue as he remembered, that the attraction he felt hadn't been quite as electric as he'd thought. He was wrong. If anything, Eric's eyes looked more brilliant, his athletic shape more enticing, the attraction Cole felt more amplified.

"Hi," Eric said, sliding onto the stool across from him. He bounced a little and smiled, the single dimple in his cheek winking at Cole. "Thanks for grabbing us a good table. They fill up pretty quick some nights."

"Sure. No problem. This looked like as good a spot as any." Cole's gaze trailed from Eric's cute dimple to his full bottom lip, and then lower, to where Eric's nipples pressed against his shirt. He wondered how sensitive those piercings made Eric's nipples, if he preferred for his lovers to nibble or lick, and if he would get the chance to find out for himself.

"You didn't have any trouble finding it, did you?"

Cole's gaze shot back up to Eric's in confusion. "Huh?"

Eric laughed and patted Cole's hand where it lay upon the tabletop. "The club," he repeated. "You didn't have any trouble finding it, did you?"

Cole shivered at the feel of Eric's warm palm resting on his hand and resisted the urge to turn his hand over and intertwine their fingers. It was crazy, this inexplicable longing he felt for someone he barely knew.

Cole extracted his hand from beneath Eric's and used it to pick up his beer. He took a long, deep pull from the bottle before setting it back on the scuffed tabletop. "So," he said, "tell me about this band."

"Well," Eric drawled out, "Epoxy's Resolution is a great band. Their sound is sort of a mix between metal and grunge. It's kinda hard to describe to someone who hasn't heard them, you know, but they're really good. They do a lot of cover songs but the stuff they write themselves is the best."

Cole quirked a brow. "Sounds like a weird mix to me."

Eric laughed and scooted his chair closer, so they were both sitting on the same side of the table. His thigh brushed up against Cole's as he leaned nearer. "That's what everyone says. You'll like 'em, just wait and see."

Cole wasn't too sure about that, but he wasn't about to say so. After all, he was supposed to be there for the music, not to salivate over the guy sitting next to him. Hell, as long as Eric stayed where he was, the band could sound like cats screeching and he wouldn't move. He couldn't, not with his dick as hard as a tenpenny nail. Who would've thought just sitting beside Eric in the dark would have him ready to pop the seam out of his jeans?

Rows of white lights lit up at the top and bottom of the stage. The crowd hushed as the band ran onto the stage and the lead singer took the mike and shouted a welcome.

Cole sat motionless, listening as the band started their first song, the ear-splitting noise loud enough to drown out the pounding echo of his own pulse. He faced forward, trying to appear as if he were paying attention to the show, while watching Eric out of the corner of his eye.

Beside him, Eric wiggled in his chair, his excitement almost contagious. Every few seconds he would brush up against Cole, rubbing their shoulders or thighs together in a way that did nothing to help Cole's hard-on subside. It was as if Eric was intentionally trying to drive him insane.

Cole stared up at the stage, seemingly riveted on the antics of the lead guitarist as he swung his guitar wildly about. All of Eric's attention was on Cole. With him busy watching the stage, Eric finally had a chance to study the man without being obvious about his interest. Though the room was dim, light from the stage illuminated Cole's chiseled profile, highlighting just enough of Cole's features to make Eric's pants tighter than they already were.

He'd been half hard all day, just thinking about tonight, but the reality was even better. Either Cole wanted him just as bad as he wanted Cole, or the man had some strange fetish for metal, because Cole had been sporting wood since the band took the stage. He probably wouldn't have noticed, but he'd been rubbing up against Cole every chance he could without being too obvious and he'd been watching to see if he would have an effect on the man. Eric wanted to know if he was barking up the wrong tree before he actually put his ass on the line and hit on Cole. It wasn't that he was afraid of being rejected. Lord knew, he'd gotten used to that, being a single gay man. But he didn't want to freak Cole out, or come off as some slutty little twink who hit on every man he met. Whether they ultimately ended up as lovers or just friends, he still wanted Cole to like him.

The man in question glanced over at Eric and smiled. "You were right. They aren't half bad."

Eric's chest tightened. He nodded at Cole, too mesmerized to even pretend he wasn't gawking at him. Cole was a sexy man, but when he smiled, the expression lit up his whole face and made tiny, adorable crinkles pop up in the corners of his eyes. It transformed him from sexy to devastating.

He expected Cole to refocus on the band. He didn't. Cole stared right back, an odd look on his face, as if he couldn't decide whether to kiss Eric or kick his ass and run. He wanted to kiss Cole so bad he could taste it. All it would take was leaning forward the slightest bit and their lips would touch.

He acted on the thought before he even realized his intent. Cole's eyes widened and he jerked back, covering the hasty retreat by picking up his beer and taking a long gulp. Eric felt his face flame and dropped his gaze to his lap, embarrassed that he'd acted on the impulse to taste Cole and been rebuffed so amiably. God, hadn't he just decided he wasn't going to try and jump the man? And what did he do right after, but try to kiss the man. *Jesus.*

Eric swallowed his pride and looked up. "Listen, Cole, I'm sorry about that. It's just that you were looking at me, and I just..." God, he sounded mental, just blurting everything out loud like that. Eric tried to shrug it off with a laugh that came out a trifle too shrill for the carefree attitude he was trying to pull off. "Well, I acted before I thought, and I'm sorry."

"No sweat. Don't worry about it."

Cole's gaze lowered and Eric would have sworn the other man was staring at his mouth. He could actually feel his lips tingling from the attention and couldn't resist tempting fate by swiping his tongue over his bottom lip, just to see how Cole would react. Though he wasn't sure what to expect, the soft groan that spilled from Cole's parted lips wasn't it. That one tiny sound echoed through his bloodstream and shocked his balls like a cattle prod. His already snug jeans tightened further. The metal fly bit into his swelling shaft, making him squirm. As subtly as possible, Eric turned to face the wall and readjusted himself, trying to give his cock room to expand. He swallowed a whimper and idly wondered if he had masochistic tendencies he wasn't aware of.

Eric surreptitiously glanced back at Cole from around the rim of his drink. The pads of his fingers itched to rub over the surface of Cole's short brown hair and test its bristly texture. His gaze traced the expanse of Cole's forehead, the shallow dip where brow met nose, the straight bridge of his nose and bow of his thin upper lip. A full bottom lip and slight cleft in his chin softened the sharp cut of high cheekbones and his square jaw. The man was too damn hot for his own good.

The final strains of the song came to an end as he turned around. The lead singer shouted good night just as the lights around the stage dimmed and the overhead ones came back on. Finally, the concert was over. He loved the group, but being near Cole and smelling the intoxicating scent of his cologne and underlying musk—the tension of not knowing whether or not he had a snowball's chance in hell of being with him—killed his enjoyment. His little slip up didn't help matters any. Now he just felt awkward and dumb. He should've known better than to try to kiss Cole, even if the man *did* have a set of lips that appeared as if they were made to suck cock. He looked up from the lips in question and found Cole staring at him, another one of those curious expressions on his face. Eric felt his own cheeks go up in flames. He was busted. This could get ugly. "I, um." Damn, he needed to say *something*. "You have a nice smile." Eric winced. God, was that the best he could come up with? The man wasn't even smiling.

Cole quirked a brow. "Uh, thanks. Listen, I'm going to go get another beer. You want one?"

Relief, thick as syrup, slowed Eric's thundering pulse. "No thanks." He held up his coke. "I'm not much of a drinker." Eric paused, wondering if he should say something about the number of beers he'd seen Cole consume during the show. His conscience wouldn't let him stay quiet. He gave a pointed look at the near-empty brown bottle in Cole's hand. "Um, you aren't driving yourself home after the show, are you?"

"Aww, isn't that sweet. You're all worried about me." Cole smiled and winked at him. "Don't worry, I'll call a cab. I may have a nice little buzz going, but I'm not stupid enough to drink and drive."

"That's good to know. I'd hate to think someone as hot as you would be all brawn and no brains." *Open mouth, insert foot.* What was it about this man that turned him into a hormonal teenager again? And more importantly, what was going to pop out of his mouth next, *smell ya later?*

Cole chuckled, his laugh deep and husky, sexy as hell, just like the rest of him. "Well, I don't know about all that, but I'm glad you don't think I'm the dumb jock I was in high school."

"No fear of that happening." A hot empty shell was not the kind of man he would be attracted to. The ability to hold an intelligent conversation was just as important, more so, than being hung like a moose. And damn if that didn't derail his thoughts and bring them right back to what kind of package Cole could possibly be sporting beneath his pants.

Cole weaved his way through the crowd to the bar, where people packed in tight as canned sardines waited to give their orders. Eric trailed after him, his attention locked on Cole's ass as it flexed beneath worn denim. Now that was an ass worthy of writing home about.

Cole abruptly stopped and swung back around to face him. Unable to stop his forward momentum, Eric couldn't prevent his nose from smacking into the middle of Cole's sternum. His cheek pressed into the nubby cotton fabric of Cole's polo shirt, instantly surrounding him with his date's heat and scent. He could hear the fast thump of Cole's strong heart. The intoxicating smell of spicy cologne, soap and an underlying musky scent that was Cole's alone wafted up to his nose. Eric swallowed a whimper and fought the urge to bury his face in Cole's wide chest, wallow in his fragrance.

More than his next breath of air, Eric wanted to press closer, to rub his burgeoning erection against Cole's hip and let the man feel the powerful effect he had on him. Instead, he ducked his head and backed away, murmuring a hasty, "Sorry."

Calloused fingers, rough as fine sandpaper, slid under his jaw and pushed up, tilting his chin until he looked Cole square in the eye. For an instant, while he stared into those fathomless deep brown eyes, the crowd, the noise, all of it dissolved. Cole, the intense expression on his handsome face, the gentle press of warm fingers beneath his jaw, was all that existed. Electricity crackled in the air between them. His gaze dropped to Cole's mouth. Cole licked his lips, making them glisten, and Eric

35

whimpered. He took a step closer, needing to kiss, to taste Cole so bad it was like an addiction.

A woman with purple hair and enough eyeliner to make her resemble a raccoon turned from the bar, two frosty mugs of beer in her hands, and lurched into Eric. Cold, foamy beer sloshed over his arm and down the front of his shirt.

Cole dropped his hand and stepped away from him. Eric shot the woman a dirty look, more for ruining the moment between him and Cole than the accident. Beer would wash out. Other than the stench, it wasn't a big deal.

She handed the now-half-empty beers off to a friend—some guy whose shirt had more safety pins than material—and turned back to him. "Oh my God! I'm so sorry. I totally didn't see you there."

Eric waved off her concern. "It's no big deal. It'll wash off."

She apologized again and then wandered off after her friend. Eric returned his attention to Cole and found the man smiling down at him. "That was nice of you. To let her off the hook like that."

Eric shrugged. "Well, what was I gonna do, yell at her? She didn't mean to slosh beer all over me. The drinks here cost too much to waste them."

Cole snorted. "Isn't that the truth." He fidgeted a bit before continuing. "I was just thinking, I've had enough to drink, and... Well, I just thought maybe we could go somewhere quieter and get a cup of coffee or something."

Damn that sounded like a good idea. They could go somewhere and talk, or something better. Except now he was wet and smelled like a brewery. "Uh, that's probably not such a good idea."

A frown marred Cole's forehead before a neutral mask dropped down over his features. "Oh, well, that's okay. Maybe some other time, right?"

Disappointment flashed through Cole's eyes and disappeared so fast Eric wasn't sure if he'd really seen it or imagined it. Either way, he wanted to make sure Cole didn't get the wrong idea. "No, coffee sounds good, but I don't think I'm fit for going out anywhere smelling to high heaven and with a big yellow stain spreading out over my shirt. It looks like someone peed on me." He tucked his chin into his shoulder and sniffed, wrinkling his nose at the pungent smell. "Smells about like it too."

Cole snickered. "Well, you know what they say, it's better to be pissed off than pissed on," and then he was laughing again, harder this time. Eric joined in, both of them being loud in their mirth. People all around them shot weird looks their way, which for some reason only made it funnier.

By the time they were through laughing their asses off, the awkward moment from before was long forgotten. Eric was glad of that because he wasn't ready for this night to end yet. There was so much more he wanted to learn about Cole—everything really.

The most intriguing was the vibe he got from Cole. Usually, he would say that tingly gut feeling was his gaydar going off, but who knew what it was with Cole. Sure, the man had shot him some mixed signals—prolonged eye contact, lingering stares, and though he'd pulled back before Eric could kiss him, Cole hadn't exactly complained about being rubbed up against half the night. Then again, there was every possibility he was interpreting Cole's body language in the way he wanted instead of as it was really intended. Or maybe his brain was fried from being around an old crush and not being able to act out all the feverish fantasies he'd had about Cole over the years. That was as likely an excuse as anything else he could imagine. The urge he possessed to pounce on Cole and lick him from head to toe was his own problem to solve.

Eric glanced at Cole from beneath his lashes and tried not to sigh like a love-struck teenager. He hadn't been so torn up over a guy since he'd blown Tommy Morgan under the bleachers in the twelfth grade and ended up having to endure a month of ridicule before graduation because the little bastard told everyone he was gay and easy.

Cole glanced at his watch and Eric knew their time together was drawing to a close. If Cole had been anyone else, and Eric had still been at college, instead of home for the summer, he would've invited Cole back to the apartment he and two other guys shared and made a move on him just to find out which way he swung, but he couldn't exactly do that here. Just imagining the horrified look on Mother's face if she caught him sneaking a man into his room was enough to make his cock curl up and shudder. He wasn't a kid anymore, but he had enough respect for his parents not to bring anyone home with him. In the end, he didn't have to say anything.

Cole tapped his watch. "It isn't very late, only about eleven. I know you don't want to go out anywhere covered in beer, but if you're interested in a cup of coffee, we could go back to my place." He bit into his bottom lip and released it, looking cute and bashful all at once. "I make a mean pot of French Vanilla."

As if he was going to say no to that. "Sure, that sounds great. I'll drive."

Chapter Four

Cole pointed to the green exit sign. "Turn off up there, on the next exit."

"So," Eric asked, guiding his jeep off the interstate, "where to from here?"

"Take a right here and stay straight for about two miles, then turn left onto Magnolia Street. My place is about halfway down the street, on left. Just look for a big sign that says Winchester's Game Emporium and pull around back. My apartment's above the shop."

"Cool." Eric hit the gas and swerved around the corner.

Humid night air, pungent with the scent of freshly cut grass, whipped at Cole's face and stung his eyes. He latched onto the sides of his seat and held on tight. The ride so far had been interesting. Make that terrifying. Eric was sober as a saint, but drove like he'd thrown back a few too many drinks. Only his own hatred of side seat drivers kept Cole from commenting on Eric's haphazard driving. Especially since he was pretty sure the passenger side wheels lifted right up off the ground on one of those sharp turns a little ways back.

He had to wonder whether or not Eric always drove like a maniac, or if he was just in a hurry to get them back to his place. The thought made him smile, until Eric swerved sharply, barely missing a dog that ambled out into the street, and his death grip on the seat regained all his attention.

His old, two story brick building came into view. The neon yellow sign shined like a beacon out of the large plate-glass window. Cole had never been more grateful to be home in his entire life. He pointed the building out to Eric. "Right there."

"I see it. It's so cool how you live right above your store. Did I tell you that I'm majoring in business management at UVA?" The tires squealed as he maneuvered the jeep around the side of the building and slid into the small gravel lot behind.

Cole held his breath as the vehicle jerked to a stop, the bumper inches away from an old oak tree. Eric rambled on, unfazed. "That's what I want to do someday, own my own business. Maybe run a record shop or a bookstore, something like that. I'm even minoring in accounting so I'll be able to do my own books."

Cole glanced over at Eric and released his pent-up breath. "Yeah. That's what I wanted to do too, run my own bookstore, but there wasn't much call for one around here. There are already so many independent ones. Between those and the bigger chains, there was no way I could compete." He took a deep breath. "Man, do you always drive like that? Your license should come with a warning label."

Eric smiled, popped open his door and slid out. "Oh yeah, sorry 'bout that. I guess I can be a little heavy-footed on the gas sometimes." He shrugged. "I don't even realize I'm doing it. You should have said something. I can't really afford to get another ticket anyway. My insurance is high enough as it is."

Cole rolled his eyes and hopped down from the jeep. "Come on, let's go inside."

He strode across the lot, shooting a glance over his shoulder every couple of seconds to make sure Eric was following behind him. The rubber soles of his sneakers ate up the ground until he stood just outside the back door. The security lights, controlled by motion sensors, flashed on overhead and lit up the area around him. He dug through his pockets and pulled out his key ring, riffling through the dozen or so keys before he found the right one.

Eric stepped up beside him, yellow light spilling over his messy blond hair. "So, you like owning your own place? I bet it's great not having to answer to anybody, right? You know, being your own boss and all."

Cole unlocked the door and ushered Eric in ahead of him. "Oh, I still have to answer to people. IRS, the bank and customers; somebody always wants an explanation about something." He closed the door, plunging them into darkness, and relocked it. "It's good though. I always wanted to have my own place. Can't really imagine doing anything else."

He turned to find Eric right behind him, close enough to touch. Tension ratcheted up a notch, growing thick and palpable in the dark. His arms felt empty and longed to reach out, pull Eric to him.

"Sorry about the dark," he rambled nervously, while stepping around Eric. "I would turn on the lights, but by the time I get to the breaker box, we could be upstairs anyway."

Upstairs. Alone together. With a big comfy bed just waiting for us to make use of it. Cole gave himself a mental smack and, through determination alone, managed to keep his hands firmly at his sides.

Inviting Eric home with him was the equivalent of playing with fire. Oh, he'd noticed the sly glances the younger man had been shooting his way all night, seen him sporting wood more than once. And then that kiss—he didn't even want to think about what might have happened if he hadn't pulled away at the last second. He'd been so tempted to let Eric kiss him, to see what Eric's lips would feel like against his own.

Eric was interested, of that Cole didn't have any doubt. The real question was, was *he* interested? His cock shouted, "hell yeah", but the rest of him was torn. Eric was a cute guy, and they seemed to have a bit in common, but he didn't know if he was ready to take that next step, to go from fantasizing about being with a man to actually doing it. He could see him and Eric being friends, yes, but lovers? Oh, he wanted to fuck Eric, no doubt about that, but he wasn't sure if he could go through with it. Twenty-seven years of being conditioned to believe homosexuality was wrong stood a silent vigil between him and what he desired.

"This way," he said and headed for the private door leading up to his apartment. "Just follow behind me and I'll try not to steer you into a wall."

Eric's footsteps echoed on the stairs as he tagged along. "Yeah, that would be good. I'd hate to run my head into a wall and end up spending the night on your sofa."

Yep, Cole thought, that would be a tragedy. If Eric spent the night, he could think of a lot better places for him to spend time. Like sprawled out naked in bed, underneath him, or on top of him, or hell, even upside down would be okay.

Cole stopped on the last step and unlocked the door. Eric waited behind him, one step down. Any closer and Cole imagined he would feel the heat radiating off Eric's body, feel his hot breath on the small of his back. That instantly brought to mind a picture of Eric's pink tongue—the same one he'd coveted earlier in the night while it ran across Eric's pouty lower lip—peeking out to lick at the delicate skin of his lower back, drifting lower to explore territory no woman had ever touched. What would that bubble gum tongue feel like moving over his ass, licking, prodding his entrance?

The cheeks of his backside clenched in response to the taboo image. His pulse quickened and in the dark, silent corridor, he could hear the resonance of his own labored breathing. As he shoved open his door and reached a hand inside to feel for the light switch, he wondered if Eric had noticed it too.

His hand never made it to the light. Eric rushed him from behind and pushed him up against the wall opposite the open door. A hand wrapped around the back of his neck and pulled his head down.

"Fuck it. I may be way off base here, but I think you want this as much as I do," Eric whispered, hot puffs of breath caressing Cole's skin with every word.

Before he could utter a response, soft lips pressed against his, and a tongue slid over the seam of his mouth, coaxing him to open wide. His eyelids fell shut and his lips parted, allowing Eric in. The first touch of Eric's tongue gliding along his sent an electric current ricocheting through his body. He groaned and tilted his head, losing himself in the taste and texture of Eric's mouth.

His arms rose of their own will and wrapped around Eric's slim body, zeroing in on his firm little ass and pulling him closer. Their bodies flush, tongues dueling, Cole could feel everything. A hundred sensations hit him at once and short-circuited his senses. The whoosh of breath leaving Eric's body, the fast thump of blood rushing through his own ears, the ache of his balls drawing tight, the hard ridge of Eric's cock rubbing against his own through too many layers of clothes.

He wanted them naked. Now. Wanted to touch and taste with an intensity that should've frightened him, and probably would have if he'd been in the frame of mind to care right then. Luckily, he wasn't. He was too tired of all the bullshit, of hiding and pretending to be someone he wasn't. Though he wasn't sure why, Cole felt safe enough to let go and be himself around Eric. The only thing holding him back was himself, and for the first time ever, Cole was ready to ignore the persistent little whisper of his overactive conscience and throw caution to the wind for what he wanted. Nothing mattered but the man in his arms and the flame burning hotter between them.

Cole spun them around and pressed Eric's back to the wall. He sucked Eric's bottom lip into his mouth and nipped it, savoring the sweet whimper he got in response. His hands slid between their bodies and fumbled with the button of Eric's pants. The damn things were skin tight—he couldn't get them unfastened.

Eric shoved Cole's hands out of the way and undid them himself, yanking the front of his jeans open before going to work on Cole's. In a matter of seconds, Eric had both their cocks out, in his slender hand, and was rubbing them together. He leaned up on tiptoe, pressed his lips against Cole's and whispered, "Touch me."

He didn't need to be asked twice. Cole wrapped his fingers around Eric's dick and slid his palm from root to tip, stroking and caressing Eric with the firm grip he used on himself. The feel of Eric's dick, all hot flesh and throbbing need, was unlike anything Cole had ever dreamed of. So similar to taking himself in hand, but vastly different because it was Eric. Panting, Cole buried his face against the curve of Eric's neck, giving himself a brief second to calm down before he lost control and embarrassed himself. He listened to the rapid heartbeat under his ear, one that rivaled his own beat for beat, and inhaled the musky scent of Eric's skin.

He held another man's dick, the firm flesh hot as a brand and hard as iron in his fist, and he could scarcely believe how good it felt, how right. He couldn't remember another time in his life when he'd been turned on so easily, so fast. It was like every nerve ending in his body had been lit on fire and was tingling. Sensations bombarded him—the cool air against feverish skin, Eric's hot body against his own. It felt like he'd been waiting for this moment all his life.

Now that he'd had a small sample of what he'd been missing out on, he wanted to do it all, to experience everything. "Eric, I want..." God, he couldn't say it.

"What do you want, Cole?" Eric's voice was thick and hoarse, full of need. "Anything. Just please, God, don't stop now."

The desperation in Eric's voice boosted Cole's courage and gave him the balls to go through with what he wanted to do. He dropped to his knees and wrapped his hand around the base of Eric's cock, holding it down and in position for his mouth. He leaned in, took a deep breath full of the heady scent of warm skin and male musk, and swiped the flat of his tongue over the moist tip of Eric's cock, testing the taste to see if he'd like it.

The bittersweet flavor of Eric's flesh burst over his palate and made him groan. He ran his tongue around the spongy cap, exploring the shape and texture. When he flicked over the shallow groove beneath the helmet, Eric grunted and bucked his hips, forcing the blunt crown deeper into Cole's mouth. Cole accepted him, groaning at the alien sensation of Eric's dick sliding over his tongue.

Slender fingers wove through his hair, urging him to continue. "Oh yeah, Cole...suck me. Suck my cock."

Hearing Eric sputter those dirty words, feeling the smooth skin quiver under his tongue's manipulation, pushed Cole to take more, to hollow his cheeks and suck hard, while bobbing up and down over Eric's prick. He pushed down, trying to force the entire length into his mouth, and took more than he could manage. The bulbous head of Eric's prick butted up against the back of his throat and made him gag.

Sputtering and embarrassed at his lack of experience, he backed off and let Eric slip from between his lips. He glanced up at Eric, glad the darkness camouflaged the heat suffusing his face, but wishing he could see Eric's expression and know if he was doing a good job or not. Though he didn't want to mess this up, he had no idea what he was doing. It was harder than it looked. He was operating on pure instinct and the memory of what he liked done to him.

Eric's fingers tightened on Cole's scalp. His other hand reached down and petted Cole's cheek. "Don't stop, babe. I'm so close. Make me come." He grabbed his dick by its base and brushed the weeping tip over Cole's mouth. "Please, finish me off."

Cole's lips parted and he licked the salty ambrosia off the tip of Eric's cock. Surprisingly, it wasn't bad. A little bitter, maybe, but nothing gross, like he'd been half afraid of. His tongue dipped into the slit, searching out every drop. His hands rose and bracketed Eric's slim hips, pulling him forward, wanting Eric to take what he needed.

He slid his mouth off Eric's prick and looked up at him. "Do it. Fuck my mouth. Come for me."

Eric groaned and his hips bucked forward. With his hand still around the base of his cock, he set a fast rhythm, shuffling his length in and out of Cole's mouth.

His jaw began to ache, but he persevered, taking everything Eric had to give. He concentrated on keeping his teeth out of the way, his tongue moving along the firm shaft, keeping his jaw loose on the intake and his lips tight on the withdrawal. Saliva pooled in his mouth, making the slick glide of Eric's cock over his tongue more smooth. Just when he thought lockjaw was going to set in, Eric stiffened and cried out. His dick pulsed, growing impossibly larger, as spurt after spurt of creamy seed spilled into Cole's mouth.

The force behind Eric's release made Cole gag, but he quickly recovered and swallowed what he could, gently suckling Eric as he shook and shivered through the last of his climax. When Eric began to soften, Cole lifted his head and let Eric slip from his mouth. He sat back on his heels, feeling inordinately pleased with himself and horny as hell, all at the same time. His dick hung out of the front of his pants, hard enough to jackhammer concrete, and his balls ached like heavy stones hugging the base of a tree. While he sucked Eric, his own need to come was superseded by the desire to satisfy Eric and not fuck it up. Now that he'd accomplished what he set out to do— and judging by the strength of Eric's climax, he'd done a pretty damn good job even if he did say so himself—his own body was screaming for relief.

Wonder if it would be bad taste to ask Eric to return the favor. It didn't take much imagination to picture Eric's pretty mouth wrapped around his dick, swallowing his load and moaning to beat the band, like his come was the next best thing compared to Tom and Jerry's ice cream.

The downstairs lights blinked on, illuminating the stairwell and the foyer where he was still kneeling in front of Eric. Cole blinked, his eyes trying to adjust to the sudden change. "What the fuck?"

Eric gasped and hastily stuffed himself back into his jeans. "Who is—?"

A loud gasp sounded from below, right before he heard a shrill female voice scream, "*Oh my God!*"

He knew that voice. Cole turned, his movements slow as molasses, and saw Karen standing at the bottom of the landing, her eyes wide and a splayed hand covering the lower half of her face.

"Shit!" Cole scrambled to his feet.

Karen dropped her hand, her expression twisting from hurt to pissed off in the blink of an eye. "You *bastard*. How long have you been fucking him behind my back? No wonder you didn't want to get married."

"Karen, wait."

She shook her head, her long blonde hair whipping from side to side, and hurried away in the opposite direction. Cole started after her, only to be pulled up short by Eric's voice.

"Cole, what the hell is going on? Who is that woman?"

He looked back over his shoulder, his gaze connecting with Eric's guileless blue eyes, while his head filled with white noise. There was no fast and easy answer for that, so he said the only thing that came to mind, "That's Karen," before dashing down the stairs after her.

༄༄༄

Long after Cole disappeared downstairs and the loud crack of the back door slamming echoed up to him, Eric remained immobile. Cole's parting words replayed again and again inside his head. *That's Karen.* As if that was supposed to explain everything?

Anger, hot and heavy, pulled him from his catatonic state. Who the hell did Cole think he was, bringing Eric home with him, sucking his brains out through his cock, despite the fact that he had a girlfriend? Or was it fiancée? Hadn't she said something about a wedding?

Jesus. He sure knew how to pick men, didn't he? Unfortunately, this time around, he had no one to blame but himself. Cole had all the classic signs of someone locked in the closet, Eric just hadn't wanted to recognize them for what they were. He was a fucking idiot.

Eric leaned forward and flipped up the light switch. A bulb winked on overhead, illuminating the area around him, and cast dim fingers of light into the two adjoining rooms to either side.

To his left sat a small kitchen. He could only just make out part of the fridge and the corner of a waist-high counter from where he stood. He didn't care to see more of the kitchen, so he turned toward the room to his right. There he found an equally tiny living room, barely large enough to hold the matching black leather love seat and recliner, and a small black lacquered entertainment center.

Well, he had two choices. He could go into the living room and have a seat, or he could leave. Eric glanced at the door, still standing open, and considered leaving before Cole returned. He didn't know of any way out of the building except the one he'd been shown on the way in, where the happy couple were undoubtedly fighting right that very minute, so he chose to sit and wait. Facing Cole seemed like the lesser of two evils. Besides, running away smacked of cowardice and he wasn't a damn coward. He faced his problems head on and this time would be no different. He would stay, listen to whatever lame excuse Cole came up with, and then calmly tell him exactly what he could do with his wandering cock, specifically that he could shove it up his own ass and rotate on it until Hell froze over.

As much as he would've liked to give Cole the benefit of the doubt, the evidence was not leaning in his favor. Even if Cole hadn't been using him for some kind of bi-curious experiment, he was still a cheater and, as far as Eric was concerned, a slimeball.

Without his knowledge or consent, Cole had made him into the other woman...man, whatever. That pissed him off. He was not going to be someone's dirty little secret.

Eric stepped into the living room and bumped his hip on a shoddy-looking telephone stand just inside the door. An automated voice filled the air. "You have one message." The machine recited a time earlier in the evening, and then the message played. "Hey, Cole. It's me." The woman's voice paused. "I just wanted to let you know that I've been away for the last week at my parents' house, thinking things over. I've decided that maybe I overreacted by ending things between us so quickly." A man's voice sounded in the background, calling the woman in to dinner. "Listen, I won't be home until later tonight, but I was hoping we could talk. I'll swing by your place on my way home. Talk to you soon. Bye."

Eric stared down at the red light on the answering machine as if it had teeth and was going to jump off the stand and bite him. Chewing on his lip, he tried to shove down the overwhelming sense of hurt welling up inside him.

The message confirmed one of his questions, but it opened the door for so many others. Cole wasn't cheating on the woman, but it was obvious they'd just ended things. And she'd been the one to dump him, not the other way around.

Did Cole want her back? Was that why he'd run out of the apartment as if his ass was on fire?

Eric stumbled to the love seat and perched on the end of it. He slumped forward and rested his elbows on his knees.

Rubbing his hands over his face, he settled in to wait for Cole and the opportunity to give the man a piece of his mind.

Chapter Five

You're going to regret this, Cole. I swear it.

Karen's parting words rang in Cole's ears as he wearily trudged up the stairs, his head hung low. Any buzz he'd had earlier was long gone. A pounding headache had moved in to take its place.

Karen was furious. He'd tried to explain, but she refused to hear him out. Instead, she'd jumped to conclusions, choosing to believe he'd been seeing Eric on the side, even while they were together. That she could believe that of him, after two years of being together and his being nothing but faithful to her, hurt him more than he cared to admit. He cared for Karen, didn't want to see her hurt, but having her catch him with Eric, seeing her reaction, brought his latent feelings to the surface. It made him realize that although he didn't want to deal with the repercussions resulting from coming out, he couldn't put it off any longer. He wanted to step out of the closet and into the sunshine. Finally, he felt ready to embrace himself for who he was, without worrying about how it would affect anyone else.

No. That wasn't entirely true. He did care how his realization would affect one person.

Eric.

Standing next to Karen, seeing the woman he could have easily ended up spending the rest of his miserable life with, made him that much more aware of how lacking his attraction was to her. With Eric, right from the moment he'd laid eyes on him, he'd felt an inexplicable pull in his direction. The chemistry between them was real and good, so strong it was unsettling.

Cole paused in the doorway of his apartment. He pinched the bridge of his nose, stalling for time while he tried to steel his courage. He knew what he wanted. All he had to do was go for it. Lay it all out in the open and hope Eric wanted the same thing.

In time, he knew that he could fall for the younger man. It wasn't a question of if he could love him, more a question of when. If Eric could be persuaded—and Cole was going to try his damnedest to make sure he was—then Cole planned for them to share a lot more than a single night of passion. He wanted it all.

He stepped through the door and looked around for Eric. He found him in the living room, sitting in the dark, with his face buried in his hands. Cole cleared his throat, not wanting to startle him.

Eric's head jerked up. His gaze landed on Cole and narrowed. Damn, that didn't look good. He knew he had some explaining to do, but...

"Well, that was certainly quick. I guess your *girlfriend* decided not to stick around for an encore, huh?"

Cole winced at the sharp tone of Eric's voice, straightened his spine and crossed the room. He reached over and flipped on the lamp beside the love seat and plopped down on it next to Eric. Eric scooted over, practically falling off the other side in order to put as much space between them as he could.

Cole sighed. He didn't know why he'd expected Eric to be a little more understanding. Things never seemed to go as easy for him as they did for everyone else. "Could you maybe wait to hear me out before you start jumping to conclusions? I've had about enough of that for one night."

Eric arched one blond brow, his forehead wrinkled. "Why should I care what you want? Am I supposed to feel sorry for you now? Poor Cole, who has to deal with two pissed-off lovers in one night. Tsk, tsk, you really should have known better than to bring home a new playmate before you got the key back from your ex. You must have been absent the day they taught that lesson in 'How to be a Dog 101'."

Frowning, Cole wiped his damp palms on his pants. "It's not like that, Eric."

Eric rolled his eyes. "What's it like then, huh? Explain it to me. Make me understand because after what I've seen and heard, I'm having a hell of a time understanding."

"Karen is not my girlfriend. We broke up weeks ago."

Eric scowled. "Mm-hmm. I know that. She called and left a message. Said she was willing to talk about taking you back. That maybe she'd been a little hasty in dumping you."

"Shit." That explained why she'd shown up out of the blue. He'd been wondering about that.

"So...? You want to explain things, or what?"

Cole held Eric's gaze, imploring him to listen. Eric had no reason to accept his word for the truth, but that wasn't going to stop Cole from trying to explain. "Karen and I dated for about two years. There weren't any bells and whistles going off between us, but I was comfortable in the relationship, safe. As long as I was with her I could keep my head buried in the sand and ignore what my psyche, my fantasies, had been trying to tell me for years."

He paused, taking a deep breath before continuing. Now that he'd started, he wanted to get it all out. "Karen and I broke up two weeks ago. She wanted to get married and start a family.

I just... I couldn't live a lie anymore. Karen isn't what I want. She isn't what I need. You are."

Eric's eyes widened. "Cole, I—"

Cole held up a hand, cutting Eric off. "No, hear me out before you say anything. I know we don't know each other all that well yet, but there's something here, something between us. I felt it on the beach and I feel it even stronger now. If you're willing, I'd like the chance to get to know you better and see where things could lead for us."

As soon as the last words poured out of his mouth, Cole's gaze fell to his lap. Though he was anxious to hear what Eric had to say, he was petrified of being rejected. His pride dangled out on a line and Eric had the power to cut it in half.

When no reply came, Cole lifted his head, scared of what he would see on Eric's face. His gaze connected with Eric's. Cole was afraid to breathe, afraid he would blink and the soft, accepting look on his lover's face would dematerialize into one of scorn.

Coming up onto his knees on the love seat, Eric reached for Cole. A warm palm cupped Cole's cheek, but it was nothing compared to the heat he saw growing behind Eric's beautiful azure eyes.

His voice was feather soft when he spoke, "Do you mean that? I want to believe you. I just..." Large, expressive blue eyes searched Cole's face. "I've wanted you since before I knew I was gay. There was just something about you that drew me." He blushed. "I kinda feel like I'm going to wake up any minute, with wet sheets, and realize this was all a dream."

Cole grinned and reached out to swipe an errant lock of blond hair out of Eric's face. His fingers lingered over Eric's satiny skin. "I meant every word. I want to be with you, Eric. Only you."

Eric's attention dropped to Cole's mouth. His thumb swept over Cole's bottom lip, making him shiver. Before the shiver had time to work its way down his spine, Eric leaned in and replaced his thumb with his mouth, softly brushing his lips over Cole's.

Though the kiss began gently, there was a wealth of emotion behind it. Cole's heart warmed and filled with a sense of peace. This was right. The burgeoning emotions he felt for Eric were the real thing, not the glamour of lust. He wasn't sure how he knew, but as Eric sought to deepen the kiss, running his tongue over the seam of Cole's mouth, he believed it with every fiber of his being.

Eric was the one for him.

Cole tilted his head and parted his lips, allowing Eric inside. The fingers of one hand rose to wind in the silky hair at Eric's nape, while the other reached around Eric's back and pulled him in tight, pressing their chests together.

Eric moaned and the sweet sound vibrated along his tongue and into Cole's mouth. He inched the last bit forward and straddled Cole's lap, wrapping his arms around his neck. Their tongues twined and danced, mouths moving in concert with each other until both men panted, their chests rising and falling, pushing against one another in an effort to replenish their lungs with oxygen.

Though he didn't want to stop, Cole had to breathe. He pulled his head back a fraction and eased the kiss until their lips barely skimmed back and forth.

God, he was hard. Not having gotten off earlier with Eric, plus the additional torment of Eric's hard bottom pressing down into his dick, was working on his control. Too much more stimulation and he would be coming in his pants like a teenager.

That was not what he had in mind. No, tonight he wanted to come buried balls deep inside of Eric.

Cole's eyelids grew heavy and fell shut. It was so easy to picture pushing Eric backward and taking him over the arm of the love seat. All he'd have to do was yank those snug jeans down over Eric's tight little ass and shove inside, pump his way to heaven. He could almost feel the inviting grip of Eric's channel fisting around his cock.

"What?" Eric asked, his hot breath fanning over Cole's neck an instant before his lips pressed a moist kiss to the side of his throat.

Cole's eyelids slowly lifted. "Huh?"

"You whimpered."

"I did?"

Eric nipped at Cole's earlobe. "Uh-huh. What were you thinking about just now? Something good, I'll bet, by the way your hips jerked up."

Time to do or die. "Strip and I'll show you exactly what I'm thinking about."

"Thought you'd never ask." Eric pressed a quick, hard kiss to Cole's lips and scrambled off his lap.

Cole sat back and watched his lover quickly disrobe. Clothes flew in abandon as Eric yanked his shirt off over his head and shimmied out of his jeans. With every inch of skin that appeared, more blood rushed to Cole's prick, engorging him to the point of pain.

His tanned skin gleamed in the low light. Hands propped on his slim hips, Eric turned to face Cole. "This what you had in mind?"

Cole swallowed and nodded, his gaze riveted on the naked expanse of Eric's skin. The long, ruddy prick he'd seen before, but the rest... *Damn.*

Earlier, when he'd taken Eric in his mouth, it had been dark and he hadn't been able to see much. Now though... Now he wanted to make up for that slight. He wanted to touch and taste every inch of Eric's lithe body. Learn all the things that made him whimper and cry out.

He held his hand out to Eric. "Come here." Eric stepped forward and twined their fingers together. Cole pulled him closer, until Eric stood in the V of his open thighs. With his free hand, Cole ran an errant fingertip down the shallow indentation between Eric's abs and watched as the muscles tightened and flexed in response to his touch.

He looked up, his gaze roaming over the expanse of Eric's leanly muscled chest, and met Eric's eyes. "You're beautiful."

Eric's eyes shifted away and he blushed. "No, I'm not. Men aren't beautiful."

Cole thought how adorable it was that Eric could be so unconcerned with his nudity but be embarrassed by a simple compliment. He made a mental note to bestow them often and reached up to tweak the barbell piercing one of his plump pink nipples. "You are."

Eric made a pitiful little noise, half whimper and gasp, in the back of his throat and his hips jettisoned forward, riding air.

A bedeviled smile on his face, Cole advanced.

Chapter Six

Cole's hands moved to either side of Eric's hips and tightened. He spread his fingers and squeezed, holding Eric still. With his tongue, he flicked at Eric's innie bellybutton and moaned as the taste of clean, salty skin burst over his palate. Working his way up, Cole took his time licking and kissing every inch of smooth, tanned skin between Eric's navel and his pecs. He sucked and nibbled on one tender nipple, tugging on the barbell with his teeth, before moving to the other and lavishing the same attention on it. He switched back and forth, loving the way the tiny buds puckered under his tongue, until Eric's desperate pleas for more became too much for him to resist.

Letting go of Eric, Cole grabbed the hem of his own shirt and tugged it over his head. Eric dropped to his knees and began to work at the button of Cole's jeans. He popped the round metal disc through the hole and tore down the zipper. Anxious to be naked and feel Eric's skin against his own, Cole leaned back on his elbows and elevated his hips, easing the way for Eric to pull his jeans the rest of the way off.

He stared down, inflamed by lust at the sight of Eric kneeling at his feet, so similar to the fantasy he'd had earlier in the day. Eric grinned up at him and licked his lips, almost as if he knew what Cole was thinking. Eyelids at half mast, Cole watched as Eric's tongue extend and swipe a warm, wet trail over his balls. He sucked and lapped at Cole's sac, never taking more than the loose skin into his mouth. Breath whooshed from Cole's lungs, the feel of Eric's tongue too good for words.

He gaped down at Eric, fixated on the full pink lips as they moved upward and stretched wide around the flared head of his cock. Hot, wet heat engulfed him, swallowing half his shaft in one fell swoop, and his hips involuntarily bucked upward. Eric's cheeks hollowed and the suction intensified. Eric began to bob up and down, his mouth gliding over Cole's cock, taking him deeper with every pass. The nerve-rich tip of Cole's dick hit the soft wall at the back of Eric's throat. He held still, so damn still, not wanting to push and take the chance of hurting Eric, but goddamn it felt good. Their gazes connected, and at that moment, the muscles at the back of Eric's throat began to flutter and gave way, allowing the tip of his cock to pop through. Eric groaned around Cole's cock, making his mouth vibrate, and then his throat compressed around Cole's knob, sucking him into a vise of hot, almost impossibly tight pleasure.

Cole's balls drew up and hugged the base of his dick. His body screamed for him to thrust, to give in to the pleasure and spill himself down Eric's throat. His heart, *his damn contrary heart*, screamed no. The orgasm would be spectacular, no doubt about that, but when he came, he wanted Eric to be right there with him. A one-sided climax wasn't enough.

With a touch of reluctance, Cole fisted his hands in Eric's hair. "Eric..." Eric backed off of Cole's cock a couple of inches and used the tip of his tongue to fuck the slit of Cole's cock. A moan forced its way out of his mouth, undermining what he was trying to say. "Stop, baby, that's enough."

Eric gave Cole's cock one last, good, hard suck and released him. He leaned back on his heels, his pretty, pink dick bobbing up against his washboard stomach. "Party pooper. I was enjoying that."

Cole grinned at the fake pout Eric sported. "Yeah well, so was I. A bit too much, if we're going to do what I think we are." *Please, let Eric want the same thing I do.*

"Oh yeah?" Eric teased as he crawled up into Cole's lap and straddled his hips. "And what would that be?" He wiggled his ass over Cole's groin and shuffled around until Cole's cock slid back and glided between his ass cheeks.

Cole grunted and fought his body's natural inclination to thrust. "You keep doing that and this will be over before we even get started."

Eric chuckled and wrapped his arms around Cole's neck. He brushed his lips over Cole's and kissed him.

With Eric clinging to him, their bodies pressed close, Cole found himself unable to think. His body took over and demanded satisfaction. The insistent throb and ache in his balls swept away all his insecurities and allowed him to float on pure sensation. He was carried away by the power of Eric's kiss, the tender hands petting his chest and sides, the small whimpers spilling from Eric as he rocked to and fro. Over it all, the heady scent of lust and testosterone rose in steady increments, skyrocketing right along with the desire to take that last final step and make love.

Cole slid his hand between his and Eric's bodies and took hold of Eric's cock. He pumped up and down, thumbed the weeping tip. They were both ready and impatient for more.

Blindly, with one hand stroking Eric's cock, he reached over the arm of the love seat and into the drawer of the end table. He divided his attention between kissing Eric and searching for the bottle of lube he knew was somewhere in the drawer. After he fumbled through pamphlets, magazines and more odds and ends than he remembered being in there, his hand finally landed on the dented plastic bottle he sought.

Eric chose that moment to back out of their kiss. He looked up with huge, slightly foggy blue eyes and noticed the bottle in Cole's hand. "Thank God. We'll need that. It's been a while for me."

"Yeah, about that. Um, I haven't exactly done this before. So you might need to guide me through things. I don't want to screw up and do something that might hurt you by accident."

Eric smiled softly and cupped his cheek. "You won't. I'll walk you through all the steps later on. For now, hand me that lube and I'll get myself ready for you. I'm too revved up to wait. I'll lube up while you squeeze that huge cock of yours into a rubber."

Cole butted his head back into the cushion. "Shit, I don't have any. I'm sorry, I didn't plan this far ahead."

"Good thing one of us was more optimistic for tonight's outcome. I have one in the pocket of my jeans. Hold onto my hips and I'll get it. I don't want to get up."

Cole was about to ask what he meant when Eric's thighs tightened around the outside of his and he twisted backward. Cole's hands flew down to Eric's hips, holding on, while Eric reached over his head and grabbed his jeans up off the floor. The image of Eric splayed back, his body displayed like a wanton banquet, burned into Cole's retinas.

All too soon, Eric propelled himself upright and began to rifle through his pants pockets. He came up with a small, square foil packet and held it out to Cole with a triumphant smile. "Got it."

Cole accepted the condom and tore it open. He positioned it over the wide flare of his cock and only then noticed how bad his hands were trembling. Heat suffused his cheeks.

Eric covered Cole's hand with his own. "Here, let me." Nimble fingers took up where Cole left off and quickly finished unrolling the condom down Cole's hard shaft.

Eric picked up the bottle of lube lying next to Cole's thigh and squeezed out a giant dollop of slick liquid. He rested his head on Cole's shoulder and reached around behind himself.

Whatever he was doing caused Eric to stiffen up and moan. Cole could well imagine those slender fingers working lube into his hole but he had to see it for himself. He craned his neck and glanced down over Eric's back. What he saw caused his cock to jerk, the already hard length stretching impossibly longer. He goggled at the sight of Eric preparing his own ass. Slim, graceful fingers, first one and then a second, plunged in and out of Eric's ass. The tiny opening was flushed a dark, angry shade of pink as it was forced to stretch beyond its natural size to accommodate Eric's manipulations.

Eric eased his fingers out and grabbed for the lube. He spread more slick liquid over his crease and added a third finger. He shoved them deep and hissed, "Almost ready."

Cole had had enough of being a spectator. Watching was fun, but he wanted to touch and play too. He kept one hand on Eric's back and with the other palmed Eric's balls, rolling the heavy sac in his hand. The tips of his fingers reached back to rub over the sensitive skin behind, and he could feel Eric's hand at work. A strong flame of lust incited him to grip Eric's wrist. Together, they set the speed of Eric's fingers until Cole was well past the point of turned on and couldn't wait another minute to be inside Eric.

His hold tightened around Eric's wrist. "Enough. I can't wait any more, Eric. I need you. Please." Cole didn't like the way his voice sounded, all pleading and desperate, but it was too late to call it back now.

Eric sat up and braced one hand on Cole's shoulders. He leaned in for a kiss, while his other hand traveled down to grip the base of Cole's cock. Angling Cole's penis into position, Eric began to lower himself down.

Tight, hot heat kissed the tip of Cole's dick. He felt snug pressure shoving down on him. He was just about to tell Eric to stop, that he feared Eric was too small to take him, when he felt the restricting ring of muscle give way. Eric's body flowered open and the crown of Cole's dick popped through. Cole gasped and Eric cried out as the snug ring of muscle snapped closed around the blunt head. Eric began to push down, taking more of Cole's shaft inside him, one excruciating inch at a time.

Cole gritted his teeth and held his body rigid, afraid that if he moved, he would force too much of himself inside Eric and hurt him. It took all his willpower to stay still. The muscles of Eric's channel rippled and caressed every inch of cock fed into it. It felt like he was being devoured by the hottest mouth on earth.

Finally, after what seemed like hours, but couldn't have been more than a few minutes, Eric's buttocks rested firmly on Cole's thighs. He was in, buried all the way inside Eric's body. Cole could hardly believe it.

"Oh God, Cole. So good... You're so deep inside me... You feel so *damn* good."

Beyond the point of being able to speak, Cole grunted and enfolded Eric into his arms. His hands immediately sought out the firm mounds of Eric's ass and squeezed. He smashed his lips down over Eric's and thrust his tongue into Eric's mouth, swallowing down the smaller man's moans as their tongues slip-slided against one another.

Eric's hips began to swivel, rocking slow, but moving all the same. Cole took that to mean he was free to move and pushed up with his hips. He thrust into Eric with small and concise movements. The wet drag and pressure of Eric's channel pushing against him on the outstroke and then blossoming open to allow him right back inside on the upstroke was almost too much for him to take.

Eric's neck arched, pulling his mouth away from Cole's. His head fell back and his eyes closed, a string of whimpers and obscenities falling from his mouth. "Fuck me, Cole. Harder. Please."

Hearing his lover's strangled cries, Cole plunged upward. He put everything he had into each hard-driving thrust and hoped like hell it was enough to send Eric over the edge. The sound of ragged breathing and the soft thump of damp flesh thudding together filled the air. Cole was seconds away from coming. The telltale tingle of impending orgasm started in his balls and plumped his cock beyond endurance.

Whimpering, Eric sped up the pace, riding Cole fast and hard. "Fuck, Cole, I'm gonna..." His ass clamped down on Cole's dick, released, and clamped down again. Come spewed from his dick and splashed against Cole's abdomen.

It was too much for Cole. The tension building deep down in his balls reached a crescendo and exploded. The skin of his shaft tightened, almost to the point of pain, before his balls clenched and released, the first spurts of his climax jetting into the condom.

"*Eric...*" He threw his head back and howled, no longer able to control himself as his climax ripped through his body and drained him.

Eric fell forward, his weight a blessing against Cole's damp chest. He pressed his lips to Cole's cheek and snuggled closer. "I'm so glad I was on the beach this morning."

The wealth of meaning behind his words rang out loud and clear. It was too soon to make declarations of love, for either of them, but Eric's words told him he was cared for all the same. "Me too. I didn't even know what it was I wanted until I tripped right over it."

Eric laughed. "Well, thank God you're a klutz."

Cole grinned and rubbed his cheek into the curve of Eric's neck. "Yeah, thank Heaven for that."

Happenstance may have led him to Eric, but perseverance and time would cement the bonds between them. In Eric, Cole found all he'd been missing and more. He wasn't sure where the road of life would lead, but he was confident that no matter what tribulations awaited them, they would face them together.

About the Author

Amanda Young spends her days basking in the sun by the seashore and her nights surrounded by dozens of serenading male strippers whose only desire is to make her happy.

Yeah, right.

In real life, my husband would chase away all the hot men, right before asking me what I'm going to fix him for dinner and reminding me to do the dishes for the umpteenth time.

Always an avid reader of romance, I was thrilled when I discovered erotic romance. For a long while I toyed with the idea of writing my own but could never find the time.

When I found myself unemployed, I decided that it was high time I gave it a shot. I sat down at my trusty computer and, according to my very patient husband, haven't moved since.

To learn more about Amanda Young, please visit www.amandayoung.org. Send an email to Amanda Young at AmandasRomance@aol.com.

Look for these titles by
Amanda Young

Now Available:

Missing in Action

Shameful

Sins of the Past

Custom Ride

K.A. Mitchell

Dedication

For all of you who didn't let me give up, especially B.F.S.

Chapter One

Ryan didn't do random hookups.

But try telling that to the hand around his dick.

Okay, so maybe sometimes he did do random hookups. But not on a single beer and five club sodas, and certainly not in public—or as public as the space between the cigarette machine and the wall under the strobing lights of the Playhouse. It was dark, and the guy behind him was pretty big so he wasn't exactly providing everyone on the dance floor behind them with free porn, but still this wasn't exactly Ryan's style.

Which led him straight back to that hand on his dick, the hand belonging to the guy behind him. Ryan was six-foot-one and this guy was still tall enough to rest his chin on his shoulder as he licked and mouthed the spot under Ryan's ear. Even if he didn't do random hookups, it was Gay Pride weekend, and Ryan had come down to Minneapolis for the party, so he wouldn't have objected if the guy wanted to move this somewhere private. That had been what Ryan had been hoping when the guy had started dancing with him, grinding into his ass from behind while keeping him pinned with an arm around his waist.

After steering them to this little space, the hand had undone both their jeans before pulling Ryan's dick out through his fly. Ryan couldn't deny some curiosity about the rest of the guy. The stranger jacked Ryan's cock like it was his own, knew the perfect strokes, timing and twists, dragging him to the edge and making him bite his lip to keep in the moans before backing off when Ryan was a breath away from coming.

Ryan looked down as the flashes of light revealed the wet, red slide of his cock through those fingers, the bunch and shift of muscles in the forearm beneath the swirling inks of his tattoo. The design roped around, ending in an open-mouthed dragon's head at the base of his thumb, the tongue curling to the first knuckle, a knuckle that was rubbing right under the head of his dick, while the other fingers kept up their long hot pulls. Ryan's hips bucked, and the guy's dick caught the top of his ass. Ryan pressed in closer, giving that thick wet head more friction as the guy rocked them, plastered them together with sweat and need.

The stranger's voice rasped in his ear, a deep rumble that vibrated against the skin made wet by his mouth. "Bet your ass feels even better inside, huh? And this hair"—his free hand tugged—"bet it'd be perfect for pulling when you suck me off."

If Ryan knew his name, he'd have told him to stop fucking with him and get him the hell off, then he'd show him just how good his mouth and ass were. A sense of self-preservation that had helped him survive four years in the Air Force told him this was crazy—if not dangerous—letting some guy whose face he'd never seen jerk him off in a crowded bar, but his dick told that part of his brain to kindly fuck off. Ryan reached behind him, his hand curling around the back of the guy's neck, fingers brushing the fuzzy edge of a military buzz cut.

The stranger's mouth landed on his neck again. A groan vibrated against his skin. Ryan ground his ass back into the guy as he finally finished him off, his hand blurring on Ryan's cock. Ryan's muscles locked as the jolt pushed that first burst out of him, the hand on his dick moving faster, better with the slide of come. That knowing hand pulled every last shot out of his dick, as Ryan's head dropped back, unable to strangle the sound that came out of him with that last rope of come. Seconds later, wet heat splashed against the small of his back in time with a hard suck at the base of his neck.

A tongue soothed the bite, a hoarse voice murmured, "Sorry. So fucking hot," and something rough swiped at the stickiness on his back. Then the hand keeping their hips together was gone. By the time Ryan had tucked himself back into his jeans and turned around, the guy had disappeared into the crowd.

ᏜᏜᏜ

As soon as the drive-in marquee got close enough for him to read the title, Ryan turned to glare at his brother. "Another penguin movie?"

David shrugged. "Hey, you'll like it. There's a subplot with two male penguins raising an orphaned chick. A very gay-positive message."

"Penguins!" was the happy cry from his niece.

"Yes, honey," Ryan said with another glare at his brother. "Penguins."

David ignored his daughter's pleas and parked his Land Rover toward the back.

"We'll be able to see just fine, honey. Daddy's car is very tall." Ryan coughed into his hand, muttering, "Overcompensation."

"You could walk home, you know."

"You're the one who dragged me here." Not that Ryan would have turned him down. Ryan loved spending time with his niece.

David fished a juice out of the built-in cooler and handed it back to his daughter. "You didn't have other plans, did you?"

"No." He'd been plan-free since last weekend and the hookup he hadn't been able to get out of his head. Yeah, it had been hot—okay really hot—but hardly something he should have spent a week thinking about. The guy had probably gone on to do three more strangers that night.

"It's been awhile since Paul, though, hasn't it?"

"What are you, my therapist?"

"You in therapy?"

"Daddy, I'm hot."

"I'm sorry, honey." David turned the car back on and powered down the windows. There still wasn't a breath of air. The sticky night wrapped the car in a wool blanket.

"Here, Holly, you don't have to be belted in." Ryan crawled back and unfastened the belt holding her in her car seat. "I'm going for soda and popcorn."

David reached for his wallet, but Ryan popped open his door.

"I think I can spring for it, big brother. I do have a job, even if it doesn't pay like yours."

The air outside the Rover was a bit thinner than the air in, and Ryan decided to take his time. The previews were running before he'd crossed a few rows.

Three rows from the concession stand, he saw it. A forearm dangling from the window of a pickup, that dragon tattoo twining around it, and he knew the tongue would curl right to the first knuckle of the thumb.

He stopped, his sneakers digging into the gravel. It was ridiculous. The odds were damned slim that he'd run into the same guy who'd jerked him off in Minneapolis last weekend up here in St. Cloud. But the hair was the same as he'd pictured, a grown-out buzz, and with the light of the opening Antarctic scenes glowing white on the screen, he could see that it was a light brown. He deliberately cut in front of the pickup, trying to get a glimpse inside the cab, and saw a blonde girl a couple years older than Holly in the passenger seat.

Fuck. Ryan's stand on random hookups could get a little fuzzy, but he was really clear on not messing with people who were married, or considering his basket-case of a brother, recently divorced. And he sure as hell didn't want to be anyone's maybe-I'm-gay test case.

The concession stand was lit with those god-awful yellow bulbs that supposedly didn't attract mosquitoes, but as Ryan swatted one of the bloodsuckers on his arm he couldn't see that it made much difference. The line was still full of impatient parents and whiny kids. By the time he'd paid the cashier, the guy was standing at the entrance, and Ryan could see everything he'd only been able to feel.

Nobody should look that good in piss-yellow light. His T-shirt clung to a broad chest and tight abs. His eyes were a piercing blue, so clear Ryan thought they must be contacts. Light stubble covered a jaw he could almost taste, the line sharp, chin broad. Those blue eyes raked over Ryan's body, and the smile that pulled on the corners of the guy's mouth made blood pulse in Ryan's cock.

That impulse got checked the second the blonde girl from the truck came up and grabbed the guy's hand. "Dad, I want some ice cream."

Ryan stepped around them on his way back to the Rover, but he took the time to walk past the pickup again and read the "Connor's Custom Rides" lettering on the door—which was useless information in spite of what his dick thought. Even another hookup was out of the question if the guy was married or playing straight. He wasn't stepping on that land mine.

He felt a breeze lift his hair and heard it start to snap in the trees around the screen. He smiled. It was going to storm, and he'd be spared an evening brooding over the wasted potential of Custom Ride guy with no distraction but anthropomorphized penguins.

ᏬᏬᏬᏬ

Ryan's phone rang at seven-forty-five Tuesday morning. David. Of course.

"What?"

"I need you to pick me up at work at noon."

"Why?"

"Because the car had work done, and I'm picking it up then."

"Why is it that your car always needs to be picked up on Tuesdays?"

"Because it's your day off, and you can drive me."

"I hate you. Noon? And it's at the dealers?"

"No, this is the Mustang. It's at Connor's. You've been there before."

Ryan almost dropped the phone. "You know, now that I'm awake I just remembered the other tech is on vacation and they need me to cover in the Sauk Rapids office."

"This is because Dad left the Mustang to me and not to you, right?"

"No, David, it's not. I told you before, I didn't care and I certainly don't need something shiny and red to prove I've got a dick."

"Rye, I really need the ride."

It was a garage. There were probably a half-dozen mechanics, and he wouldn't be there long. "Fine."

☊☊☊

Yeah, he probably wouldn't be seeing tattoo guy, and if he did there were reasons why Ryan couldn't get acquainted with more than the guy's talented left hand, but he still changed his T-shirt five times before settling on the green one that even Paul had grudgingly admitted looked good on him.

David insisted Ryan drive around the back so he could transfer his briefcase to the Mustang more easily. When Ryan rolled his eyes, his brother punched his arm.

"What? It's hot out."

"It's July. It gets that way every year." So much for just slowing down long enough to drop David off.

"Well, some of us have to wear ties to our job."

Ryan wondered if it had been a mistake to come back to St. Cloud. Every time he and David were together, they acted out the same sibling drama, and it was even worse with Mom in the mix.

"Some of us were smart enough to go into a field where we can wear comfortable clothes all day." He stopped as close as he could to where the Mustang was parked.

David left his briefcase and suit coat in the car as he got out. "Wait for me. I want to make sure everything's all set." He slammed the door shut before Ryan could answer.

He felt like an idiot sitting out here with the a/c running, would feel even dumber wandering around the lot. It wasn't as if he didn't like cars, especially classic cars, but if he got out, it would be like he was looking for an excuse to run into tattoo guy; if he sat in the car, it was like he was avoiding him.

He shut off the car. Heat hit him instantly. After two minutes, the air was impossible to breathe. He opened the door. A bike was between his car and the back entrance to the garage, and he examined it as he passed, chrome blinding in the sunlight.

With the shimmering heat, the dark opening was too tempting to resist, and Ryan ducked inside the garage. It was cavernous, cluttered without being messy. David was off in the far corner at some kind of counter and even at this distance, Ryan could see the light brown brush cut on the mechanic settling his brother's bill. He went back out into the heat and glare.

Ryan checked out the bike again, tried to picture himself on it, laughed and walked down past a line of cars in the back lot. He stopped between a gleaming late 60's Camaro and a disintegrating car from a 1930's gangster movie. The car looked like it had given birth *Alien*-style, with a gaping hole exploding out from the roof. He tried to figure out what caused it.

"Thanks, Rye!"

He glanced up in time to see his brother peeling out of the lot in the Mustang. He ought to head back to his car, but the sun baked in a lassitude that kept him looking at the rusted-out car. Maybe it was a relic from a real gangster, taken out when police had launched some kind of explosive into the backseat. He was reaching a hand toward the fragmented metal when a voice said, "Tree."

"Huh?" He turned. Tattoo guy had come up behind him.

"A tree did it. Grew right through the floor and tore right through the roof. It's going to be gorgeous when we get her fixed up though. A '37 Buick." The guy's voice curled over Ryan's ears like smoke, a deep graveled edge hugging the words.

The guy was definitely not taking gay for a test spin. He was subtly teasing the edge of Ryan's space, his eyes holding his a little too long to be misinterpreted as anything but interest. Ryan wondered if he even remembered him from that night.

He returned the look, watching the way the unbuttoned grey work shirt stretched across his shoulders, framing a grease-smeared white undershirt, sweat-stuck to hard pecs. Ryan wished mechanics still had names stitched above the pocket.

As if he were reading his mind, the guy stuck out a hand. "Jeff."

He reached for Jeff's hand, but before he could offer his own name, Jeff was saying it in that husky voice. "Ryan, right?"

"Yeah, how—"

"Your brother."

"Oh." He couldn't wait to get *that* phone call.

Jeff shook his hand firmly, but not in some kind of out-to-prove-who's-butcher way, and then didn't let go, leaving them fused at the palms.

"I remember you." Jeff broke the ice, but Ryan felt hot all over. "From the club."

"Oh..."

"Or should I say, I remember your ass a hell of a lot better." Jeff's grin was all sharp white teeth, and he took another step closer. The dense summer air squeezed between them, every breath syrupy and thick. Ryan felt the heat in his cheeks and was relieved he was too tan to show much of a blush.

"I'd still like to," Jeff said suddenly.

"What?"

"Find out if my dick'll feel better in you." Jeff leaned in and dropped Ryan's hand, fingers skimming the ends of Ryan's hair. "I can get out of here by six, if you want to meet me," Jeff offered, his breath licking hot against Ryan's cheeks.

"Okay."

As Jeff filled the last bit of space between them, Ryan balanced himself with a hand on the searing hood of the Camaro. Ryan had never had a guy come on this strong before; his dick felt like a pike shoved down his pants. Jeff was close enough to feel it too, he had to. Ryan wondered what Jeff would do if Ryan turned and bent over the burning hood behind him, let Jeff fuck him as the heat took them over, turned them boneless and liquid until they slid onto the ground in satisfaction.

Jeff's words jarred him out of his fantasy. "If you bring beer, I'll bring pizza."

"Sure." He met Jeff's eyes, holding his gaze, hoping he sounded as self-assured as he felt. Jeff peeled away from him, eyes hot, his hands subtly adjusting himself in his jeans.

Ryan headed toward his car.

"Ryan?"

He turned back, surprised at the way his gut tightened.

Jeff winked. "What do you like on your pizza?"

Chapter Two

Ryan had barely been home long enough to shower when the phone rang. He was still toweling his hair dry as he picked it up.

"So, dude. Garage guy."

He'd known David would call. Sometimes Ryan wished David had actually had an issue with his sexuality. It was embarrassing to have his big brother tease him about hot guys. Then he thought of the way his mother was constantly making the sign of the cross over him and remembered how nice it was that someone in his family didn't believe he was touched by Satan.

"Something wrong with your car?"

David laughed. "Yeah, good one. Man, I never would have pegged that guy and I've been bringing the car there for at least two years. My gaydar must be on the fritz."

"You don't have gaydar. You're straight. And what makes you think that guy"—he managed to avoid saying Jeff's name at the last second—"is gay?"

"Dude. The way he asked about you—Rye, the guy was practically drooling."

Ryan caught himself before he could blurt out an excited, *Really?* "Was there a point to this call, or are we just revisiting high school? And you still can't come to my tenth reunion as my date because you want to score Katie Thatcher."

"Katie *Stacker*, man, I wonder if she's still hot."

"David."

"Okay. So do you think there's any chance you could get me a discount the next time the Mustang needs an oil change or something?"

"Okay, I'm hanging up now."

"Wait—Mom wants you to come to dinner Sunday."

"And there's something wrong with her phone?"

"Rye—"

"I'll think about it."

But he didn't. Because pretty much all he could think about was tonight. He thought about it during a second shower, thought about the thick length of cock against his ass and grabbed an extra three pillow packs of lube from the drawer next to his bed. He thought about Jeff's blue-eyed wink and splurged the extra bucks for a six pack of Sam Adams, thought about how that gravelly voice could make even pizza toppings sound sexy and bought a twelve-pack of prelubed condoms.

When he got to the garage, the Camaro was parked in front, and Ryan couldn't resist getting out to check the edge of the hood for his handprint.

"Might need a touch up." There was amusement in the smoky voice that spoke behind him.

Ryan turned and leaned back against the hood. "Think the owner will mind?"

"Don't know. Doesn't have one yet."

Ryan looked back over his shoulder at the glow of wax, the shine on the windows.

"It's a junker I fixed up to sell. I saw you looking at it before, thought you might want to try it out."

The activity Ryan had had in mind involving the Camaro wasn't anything that could be done in the front of the lot, but before he could explain, Jeff tossed him a key.

"Want to drive it? I'll be right back."

Ryan transferred the cooler to the backseat of the Camaro, and Jeff came back out with a pizza box and a wide smile. Jeff had changed into a plain blue T-shirt, one Ryan was sure he knew set off his eyes and hugged the definition of his biceps and pecs and—Ryan bit his tongue back into his mouth— lickable abs.

Ryan wanted to tell him he really didn't have to try this hard considering Ryan could already taste that thick head sliding over his lips, but it was kind of sweet that Jeff was making the effort.

"You can drive, really. We've got insurance that covers cars taken off the lot."

Ryan eased into the leather seat, the trapped heat warming his ass and thighs through his worn-thin jeans like skin-to-skin contact. "If you're that worried about my driving…"

Jeff swung in and leaned over to murmur in his ear. "I thought you might like the chance to drive—at least for now."

Ryan's dick seemed to catch Jeff's double meaning before his brain did, a quick kick of warmth spreading out from his balls. He turned the ignition and was startled by the deep rumble of the engine. "Where are we heading?"

Jeff's directions took them out to the state park, the car responding so smoothly and powerfully beneath him that Ryan could finally understand why people viewed cars as something besides a way to get from one point to another. Power vibrated up his spine, tingled in his fingers.

They didn't talk on the way, just let the force of wind through the open windows and the purr of the engine fill the car. Ryan was almost disappointed when he pulled off in an out-of-the way picnic area after more than an hour.

Three slices of pizza and two beers later the sun had faded, leaving behind a comfortable heat to match the growing one in his stomach. Jeff was good company even without their dicks involved. Ryan was kind of surprised to find Jeff cared little about any of the popular sports—even racing—but that they shared a passion for martial arts movies, the good, the bad and the idiotic.

"If I ever have time to get back into a dojo, I'm going to see if I can finally finish my brown levels." Jeff set his empty down on the picnic table and tapped his foot where it rested on the bench.

"I still say Pai Mei in *Kill Bill* could handle Tony Jaa." Ryan reached back into the cooler for a third beer.

"Because you're an old man yourself."

"Do not insult the master. I'd hate to think of you losing one of those beautiful eyes."

"Beautiful?" Jeff's lips twitched.

"Uh—" He shouldn't have been so stupid on just two beers in a little less than two hours.

"You think I'm pretty, is that it?" Jeff leaned in, brows raised over the eyes in question. In the dark those eyes shone like a lake in starlight.

"Can I change my answer?"

"To?"

"Hot."

"Depends."

"On what?" Ryan forgot about the beer in his hands until the cold wet shock hit his stomach, and he shoved the bottle to the other side of the table.

"Which one gets me laid?"

Ryan licked his lips. "Pretty." He caught Jeff's head in his hands. "Beautiful." He leaned in until his lips were resting against Jeff's. "And hot."

Jeff laughed against his mouth. "Guy's gotta have all three, huh? And here I was hoping you were easy."

"Try me."

The kiss warmed slow and deep, buzzing along his nerves like the summer night around them. Jeff's tongue flicked the corners of his mouth before stroking his, sharing and blending the rich malty taste of the beer.

Ryan slid his hands into Jeff's hair, the short spikes softer than they looked. Jeff's thumb traced his jaw, rubbed behind his ear while his other hand pushed his T-shirt out of the way to get his warm hand on the skin of his back. He followed Jeff's push to deepen the kiss, bringing their chests together, pressing forward until Jeff was stretched out along the picnic table beneath him.

When his hands slid under Jeff's shirt, finally brushing the hard muscles he'd been dying to touch, Jeff broke off the kiss. "Maybe we should move this to the car."

They ditched their shirts on the way. Ryan hadn't made out in a car's backseat in...well, ever. Cramming two six-foot-plus frames into the backseat of a car was an adventure. He got an elbow to the ribs and bruised his shin on the seat edge before he managed to get Jeff back under him, all those long muscles pressing hot and hard into his skin. Jeff's hands cupped his ass.

"I've been wanting to get my hands on this ass for more than a year."

"Huh?" Ryan arched up.

"I've been watching you since you started bringing the car in."

Realization hit him like a bucket of cold water. David, of course. "I think you're with the wrong brother."

"Nope." Jeff's hand slipped past the loose waistband of his jeans. "I'd never make a mistake about an ass like this. Your brother's been bringing the car in for two years. You started picking him up the May before last."

That was when he'd moved back to St. Cloud. And Jeff had been checking him out since then?

"Why didn't you say something before?"

"I'm shy."

"You gave me a hand job in the middle of a club because you're shy?"

Jeff laughed, belly shaking against him. Ryan was really starting to like that sound. He liked the kiss that followed even more. He couldn't remember laughing through kisses before.

They were both still laughing as Ryan tongued his way across Jeff's jaw, down his neck, over his Adam's apple.

Jeff pulled his mouth up and kissed him hard, hand on his ass, fingers working toward the crease. Ryan's dick ached, trapped in his jeans. Ryan shifted until he could pull one of the pillow packs out of his pocket, and Jeff's hand reached for his fly.

The opening chords of "Sunshine of Your Love" rang through the car.

"Son of a bitch." Jeff pushed up; Ryan hit his head on the ceiling as he sat up.

"Are you on call, like with a tow truck?"

"No." Jeff flipped open his phone and looked at the display. "This better be fucking good. Yeah?" he said into the phone.

The one-sided conversation was easy to follow.

"Jesus Christ, what the hell for?... How the hell did she fall out of bed?... Damn it, Val, were you even home?... Yeah. I'll be there as soon as I can... About an hour... Because I am the fuck an hour away." He snapped the phone closed. "I'm sorry."

"Is your daughter all right?"

"Yeah. She might have broken her collarbone. I'm really sorry about this."

"No. It's fine. Do you want me to come with you?"

"No. I'll drop you at the garage for your car."

As they got out, Ryan tossed him the key before dumping their trash and collecting his cooler from the picnic table. Jeff had already turned the car around when Ryan slid in next to him.

"Ex-wife?"

"Wife?" Jeff's tight laugh was nothing like the ones he kissed him with. "No. We made Anna. And that was the extent of it."

The light from the dash was enough to see that Jeff's expression had closed off. Ryan didn't press. They were back at the garage in forty minutes. Ryan hopped out.

"I'll call you."

Well, Ryan hadn't expected to hear that until after they'd fucked. "Let me know how she is. Oh, wait let me give you—"

"Got it from your brother." Jeff flashed a crooked smile and sped off.

ᏒᏒᏒ

Ryan's phone rang at quarter of two. Fuck. He grabbed it and took a deep breath. "Yeah."

"Sorry to wake you. Maybe this was a bad idea."

Ryan shook off the sleep and dread. "Jeff?"

"Yeah."

"How is she?"

"Fine. It was her collarbone. Doc says it's not a bad break. She's a little pissed she didn't get a cast, just a sling. I stayed with her until she fell asleep."

"I'm glad she's all right. And I'm glad you called."

"Well, I did feel kind of bad. I don't want to get a reputation as a cocktease."

"Huh?" Sleep and sudden arousal at the shift in conversation deteriorated Ryan's vocabulary.

"I hate to leave a guy hanging."

Ryan was getting pretty familiar with that teasing smoke and sex tone in Jeff's voice, and the tingle it sent to his balls. "And exactly what were you going to do about it?"

"Get you off."

The tingle turned into a rush of blood. "Oh, really? I don't hear anyone at my door."

"Well, I think I could do it from here, if you're up for it."

"Could be." Ryan slipped his hand through the slit in his briefs.

"Good, because I really like that sound you make when you come."

Ryan's breath hitched.

"That's a nice sound too."

Ryan slapped blindly at the nightstand, digging for one of the pillow packs he'd tossed there after tonight's disappointing ending.

"What's that?"

Ryan figured Jeff was perfectly familiar with the sound of a top snapping off a pack of lube, but he answered him. "Lube."

"Mmm. You hard?"

He had been since the word *come* had rasped over the phone line, but he wasn't sure he was ready to admit it. "Getting there."

"Get there faster."

"Hey, if you started without me..." He heard Jeff's breaths speed up, imagined the slide of his hand on his cock, pictured the dragon tattoo snaking around his forearm as the head of his dick popped past that tongue-wrapped thumb. God, he wanted it to be his tongue.

"Ryan." His name in Jeff's voice, the sound so deep he might have been choking.

"Yeah?"

"Make that sound again."

"Make me."

"Want you in my bed. Wanted you so long."

Ryan tucked the phone under his chin so he could get both slick hands on his dick. "Jesus." His own voice was getting harsher.

"Want to fuck you until you can't stand it, finish you in my mouth and then come all over your sweet ass."

Ryan couldn't stop the jerk of his hips, the moans rolling from the back of his throat as he thought about Jeff inside him. "Don't stop."

"How close are you?" Jeff's voice had gone impossibly deeper. The sound rumbled through him like the purr of the Camaro's engine.

He felt the warning tingle in his balls. "Close. Really. Close." He panted between breaths.

"Finish it. Get a finger in your ass."

Ryan rubbed the skin below his balls, his other hand still fast and hard on his dick. He barely had the tip of his finger in him before the explosion that had been building all day burst through him.

"Yeah, you gonna make that sound when it's me in there?"

The words pressed the last shudders from him, slowing his hand to soothing strokes as he listened to Jeff go.

"Oh fu-uck." The deep voice got tight, squeezing from his throat until it dissolved into moans hard and fast as Tony Jaa's punches.

Post-come lassitude hit him hard, and he was fighting the weight of his eyelids as he listened to Jeff's breathing slow.

"Night, Jeff."

"Good night. I'll call you."

This time Ryan believed him.

☙☙☙☙

Ryan skipped his morning run in the park on Wednesday, muscles heavy and eyes bleary when his alarm sounded. Jesus, Jeff could make a fortune if he hired himself out for phone sex. As Ryan headed out of the park gates at seven-forty-five the next morning, he heard a motorized growl and turned to see the bike he'd admired at the garage pacing him. The rider didn't need to tip the visor for Ryan to recognize Jeff.

Jeff followed him the quarter mile back to his apartment, parking the bike and kicking down the stand. He tugged off his helmet.

"So you and my brother had a lot to talk about, huh?" Ryan pulled the sweat-soaked shirt away from his torso as he stretched his legs and paced a little.

"He might have mentioned you liked to run and where." Jeff stepped off the bike. "You know, you're a little distracting on the phone."

"And in person I'm easily ignored?"

"Well, I was hoping I might be able to demonstrate better control in the middle of Bradford Street. Doing anything after work tonight?"

"I get out at four."

Jeff straightened from his lean against his bike. He glanced up and down the street and then leveled an intense blue stare at Ryan. "I thought if you weren't busy, I'd come over and we'd fuck."

The desert-dry condition of Ryan's mouth had to do with more than just panting through his five-mile run, but at last he managed enough spit to say, "What time?"

"I'll be here by eight."

Jeff put his helmet back on and swung a leg over the bike. Ryan watched him ride off. Jeans, boots and a grey T-shirt, not a leather chap or silver stud in sight, but the lingering heat from that gaze made Ryan feel like Jeff had just slapped a dog collar on him. He had to jerk off in the shower before he could think about making it in to work.

Chapter Three

"Hey."

Jeff slid his helmet onto the table Ryan used to hold his mail. "Hey."

"You rode over? I thought it was supposed to rain tonight."

"It's going to clear up by morning, and I didn't plan on being done before then."

Ryan had never had a guy want him, look at him with that kind of intensity, as if he wanted to inhale him, could never get enough of him. He felt that invisible collar tighten around his neck.

Jeff's hand came up and his tattooed thumb rubbed across Ryan's lips. "Is that a problem?"

"No." Ryan crushed him back against the door.

Jeff tasted like wintergreen, the cool flavor fading under the heat of Ryan's tongue. He could smell the promise of a warm rainy night on Jeff's skin, lying just over the soap from his shower. He pushed up Jeff's shirt, desperate to get at those hard warm muscles. His teeth caught on the curls sprinkling his breastbone.

Jeff's hand slipped through his hair and held him as he tried to drop lower. "I like the hall, but I kind of hoped for bed."

Ryan couldn't resist another lick under the ridge of his left pec.

"If you want to be fucked standing up here, keep right on going." Jeff's voice was a growl, and Ryan raised his head.

"Maybe later." He stepped back far enough to peel off his shirt. "This way."

Jeff dropped his clothes as he followed; both of them shucking their jeans and shorts as they hit the bedroom. As Jeff turned, Ryan caught his arm to study the newly revealed tattoo on Jeff's back. Another Asian-style dragon sat upright on his shoulder, one vibrant jade eye open over a reptilian grin. The rest of his scales were in red, green and yellow. Ryan ran a finger over the marks, feeling the raised bumps the colored inks left in the skin. He repeated the action with a wet, open mouth. Jeff drew Ryan's arms around his waist, and they pressed together, Ryan's cock snugged up against the small of his back.

"I like your bed."

"I like your car."

"We'll get back to it sometime." Jeff lifted Ryan's arms and turned to face him. "I've got to be at work in eleven hours." He pulled them forward onto the bed. "And you don't know how many ways I've thought of having your ass."

Ryan's cock twitched and leaked against Jeff's thigh. He rolled onto his hip and licked his way down that flat furred belly, tugging a little with his teeth.

God, Jeff had a gorgeous cock, thick and cut and curving against his stomach. Ryan dragged a nail lightly down the vein on the underside all the way to the root. The muscles of his ass tensed. Jeff was a lot bigger than his last lover. He stretched his lips over the head, letting spit ease the way until he could slide him over his tongue.

Jeff rolled onto his back, cradling Ryan's head in his hand. Ryan took him deeper, swirling his tongue around the head, tightening his lips as he went. Jeff's fingers threaded through his hair, a sharp sound breaking from his lips. Ryan eased back, let him slide free and mouthed and licked the length all the way down to the balls. He worked his thumbs into the deep grooves inside his hips, stroking up the cut to the narrow sharp bones. Jeff tugged at his hair. Ryan lapped the salty drop on the slit and took him back in his mouth. The fingers in his hair pulled painfully.

He looked up. Jeff crooked a finger on his free hand.

"You're too good at that. I don't want this to be over before it starts."

Ryan let Jeff pull him back up his body until they were kissing again. Jeff rubbed his back, long strokes sweeping down toward his ass. Jeff licked beneath Ryan's ear, and as his finger slid along the crease, Ryan's hips jerked.

"You do bottom, right?" Jeff's rough voice purred in his ear.

"Yeah." But saying *I'm a little nervous because you're huge and it's been six months* sounded at best lame and at worst desperate so he kept his mouth shut after that.

"How do you like it?"

Ryan thought for a minute. He wasn't ready to let Jeff watch his face. "On my knees." He rolled on his belly, dragging a pillow underneath him. "There's stuff on the nightstand." He'd left the box of condoms out. "I—uh—don't go bareback."

"Neither do I."

Ryan stretched out as he felt the press of Jeff's body over his, the prickle of chest hair against his back, the weight of his dick and balls rocking between his legs, strength and power and heat wrapped around him. Jeff kissed his way down his back, hands making deep caresses of the tense muscles around his spine.

Jeff rumbled against his skin as he wet the base of his spine with his mouth, tongue dipping lower. Ryan barely had time to process his intention before Jeff's hands pressed him wide and Jeff's mouth zeroed in on the opening of his body. His tongue teased the rim, slicking the muscle, thumbs holding him open as he flicked inside.

"Jesus." Ryan couldn't catch his breath. Jeff was making deep groans of satisfaction as he licked him, then his tongue was inside, hot and flexible in a way even fingers could never be. Ryan fisted the sheets, twisting his head until he could find a way to breathe against the sudden stabbing pleasure.

Jeff's thumbs drove a little deeper, playing with the ring of muscle until they slid in next to his tongue. Ryan's head rolled back on his shoulders, the groans tearing, burning his throat.

"Fuck me."

Jeff stroked faster with his tongue, worked his thumbs in to the knuckle.

"God, now, please."

Jeff's hands and mouth traveled back up to his waist. "Just getting started," he breathed against his skin.

Ryan's heart was hammering high up in his throat. "Shit."

He thought his whisper was inaudible, but Jeff laughed against his skin again, that deep vibration shared between them.

Jeff's hands lifted him higher on his knees, reached between his legs and slicked his cock, deep comforting pulls that took that *now-now-now* edge off. Ryan's hips rocked back toward him.

"Yeah." Jeff dropped kisses on his back again, and just as Ryan thought he might get his heart rate under two hundred, Jeff slid two fingers into him.

"Christ, you're tight." Jeff twisted his fingers, and Ryan panted into his forearm. "Gonna feel so good. Can't wait to get my dick inside you."

Ryan felt the cold slick of lube, and then Jeff drove him forward on three twisting fingers. Ryan could feel Jeff's groans as much as he could hear them, Jeff's body stretched over his as Jeff fucked him open and ready.

It took Ryan a couple of tries before he could scrape together enough brain cells to pant, "Now."

He heard the tear of foil. His pulse pounded everywhere now, sharp at the tip of his dick, a deep tingle in his balls, thick and hard in his ass. He braced himself up on his arms and waited.

He knew what to expect, knew it took a minute for that fiery protest of muscles being forced open to turn sweet and good, but when Jeff started to press inside him, it might as well have been his first time. He jerked away, body tensing, locking down. Jesus, it felt like Jeff was trying to shove a baseball bat in him.

Jeff's hand stroked his dick again before wrapping around his waist and holding him steady. He pressed in again, slowly. A bead of sweat rolled into Ryan's eye from his temple and he blinked it away. Jeff's hands stroked his back, his ass, waiting, and Ryan could feel the tremble in Jeff's thighs as he held himself still.

"Need me to back off?" Jeff's voice was hoarse with thick breaths, but he spoke softly.

"No." He wanted it, God, he just—

"Push back on me when you're ready."

Ryan knew how hard it was to hold yourself in check like that, when everything inside you wanted to fuck into that tight clinging hole, and he didn't think anyone had ever kept him waiting as long as he was making Jeff.

He arched his back and eased down a little. It wasn't good yet, not by a long shot. His body protested, and his muscles fought every inch, but he managed to work himself back until he could feel the prickle of hair against his ass.

Jeff made a rough groan as Ryan stretched himself back that last inch and brought them together. "Christ, you're tight. Jesus, Ryan. Feel so good." His hand wrapped around Ryan's hips and pulled on his flagging dick until it was full and hard.

"Go," Ryan whispered, his head hanging between his shoulders, his whole body trembling.

The first stroke was a tearing scrape. The second burned. The third ripped through him like summer lightning. His body shuddered, surrendered to the force of that deep possession. He rocked back, and every screaming nerve lit up with pleasure. Jeff increased his pace, grabbing Ryan's hips and slamming forward, quick and deep.

"Yeah." Jeff's approving groan had Ryan arching for more.

Jeff shifted his angle, swiveling his hips and rubbing against that sweet spot inside him until Ryan couldn't support his weight on his arms. As Ryan collapsed onto his face, Jeff fucked him forward until his head was jammed into the headboard. Jeff grabbed his shoulder and held him steady against his thrusts, kept him tipped at that devastating angle so that every stroke of Jeff's cock forced an explosion of pleasure out of that swelling knot of nerves.

Ryan's knees slid wider until his hips came down on the pillow. He reached for his dick, and Jeff stretched out over him to whisper in his ear.

"Can you go longer?"

"Oh, yeah." Every fucking atom in him was singing the hallelujah chorus now, and it was fine with him if that went on all night.

Jeff hooked his arm under Ryan's knee and dragged it up toward his shoulder. He licked behind his ear and murmured, "This good?"

With his leg up, he was more open, and Jeff went deeper. He alternated gut-deep thrusts with that roll, blending sizzling friction with a touch that milked every inch of his ass for pleasure so bright it hurt.

Jeff's breath was wet and hot on his neck, and Ryan tipped his head back for a sloppy, musky kiss full of moans. Jeff fucked his tongue into his mouth in rhythm with his dick in his ass until Ryan ran out of breath and turned his face back into the sheets. Jeff's hand pressed his shoulder down again as he rode him into the mattress, driving thrusts that slapped against his ass.

Their bodies slipped against each other, slick from sweat and lube. Ryan could feel Jeff everywhere inside him as his blood pumped thick through his muscles with every stroke.

"How hard's your ass gonna squeeze me when you come?" Jeff hooked his leg higher, pulled on his shoulder and rolled him onto his side.

Ryan locked his foot behind Jeff's knee as Jeff rocked forward in sharp tight thrusts that hit him dead on.

Ryan was pinned under the weight of too much pleasure, crushing the breath from him, burning through his blood until he had to come or die. Jeff's hand landed on his cock before Ryan could find the muscle control to move his own.

The rush hit him. "Don't stop, don't stop, Jesus, don't—"

Jeff's wrist twisted just right around his cock and he couldn't keep it back another second. The first burst ripped through him, ten thousand volts through his pipes, shooting from his dick. Jeff fucked him right through every shuddering blast until he had to cover Jeff's hand with his to slow his strokes.

Jeff kissed him back down, soft and wet on his mouth, holding himself still inside him.

"Christ, Ryan, you are so fucking hot."

Ryan knew he should be able to come up with some kind of quip, but his brain had just been poured out his dick and the return of verbal skills seemed pretty far off in the distance. His arm ached and he realized he'd had the headboard in a death grip. He shook his hand free.

Jeff rolled him back onto his stomach and started to ease out.

"'S'okay," Ryan managed. "You can—"

Jeff buried a groan in the skin of his shoulder as he started thrusting again, his hips snapping so fast Ryan thought he'd break the sound barrier until he stiffened and took one long deep stroke, almost sliding out before slamming back in and jerking against him.

Ryan had been so lost in the sounds of their sharp gasps and the thick clash of flesh slamming together that he hadn't noticed that the rain had started until a wet breath blew through the screen, cutting through the smell of sex. Thunder rolled, adding ozone to the scent of freshly washed streets. He really ought to get up and close that window, but he couldn't remember how to move.

"Rug's getting wet," Jeff mumbled in his ear.

"Uh-huh."

Ryan felt a little ridiculous. His muscles were still shaking, his pulse throbbing behind his closed eyes like he'd run a marathon. It was as if Jeff had fucked him inside out, and he couldn't get everything back together the right way. He pried his eyes open.

Jeff rolled off the bed, ducked into the bathroom and came out to close the window.

"Uhm, there's beer in the fridge."

"Great."

He watched the play of muscles in Jeff's ass and hips as he stalked out of the bedroom. The guy was gorgeous, fucked like a jackhammer and seemed genuinely nice. There had to be a catch.

Ryan managed to get a towel spread over the wet spot on the bed before Jeff came back with two cold bottles. He twisted the cap off one and handed it to Ryan. Yeah, there *had* to be a catch.

Jeff sat on the edge of the bed and took a long pull on his bottle. Ryan matched him, pouring half the bottle down his burning throat.

Jeff looked at him for a long minute then licked his lips. "Tony Jaa."

Ryan felt the knot in his stomach dissolve as a grin spread across his face. "Pai Mei." He leaned over and grabbed the *Kill Bill Volume 2* DVD off the bookshelf and tossed it to him.

"Wait until you see *The Game*," Jeff countered and slipped off the bed to examine the bookcase. "You don't have *The Protector?*"

Ryan got up and pulled out the case. As soon as the DVD slid in, they sprawled on the bed to watch.

Tony Jaa had just taken out seven guys, feet and hands slamming into skin with a rapid rhythm when Jeff turned his head on Ryan's lap. Warm breath teased his dick.

"That makes it a little difficult to concentrate," Ryan said.

"On?" Jeff breathed on him again.

"The movie."

"I'll tell you how it ends." Jeff leaned forward and pressed a kiss on the head of his cock.

He licked him until Ryan was lightheaded from the loss of blood as it flooded his dick like cement. Jeff kissed his belly, circled his navel, thumbs flicking hard against his nipples as he made his way up to his throat. Jeff lifted his head and looked at him, only a thin rim of blue showing around pupils blown wide with arousal.

"Look. Don't think I—I mean—I do—" He swallowed. "Christ. Ryan, I want to fuck you again."

The muscles in his ass tightened in protest but his mouth said, "Yeah."

⁊⁊⁊

When he woke up, it was just light and he was alone, but he could hear the shower running. He rolled out of bed, muscles protesting the movement. He winced as he made his way to the kitchen to start the coffee. No matter how this ended, he'd be feeling Jeff all day.

Jeff had left the bathroom door open so Ryan took it as an invitation, stepping inside and digging out a clean towel.

Jeff slid the shower door open. "Do I smell coffee?"

"Yup."

"Thank God." He waved at the shower. "I didn't think you'd mind."

"Not at all."

"I'm willing to share."

Ryan edged in next to him, and Jeff turned to share the spray. Ryan leaned forward to rinse his mouth and reached around Jeff for the soap. Jeff took it from him and lathered his hands, trailing soap across Ryan's chest.

"I've got the DVD of *The Game* at my house. You could come over tonight if you want to watch it."

Ryan watched the soapy hand dip lower. "Come over and watch a movie, huh?"

"I make really good popcorn."

"I'll need directions, since you don't seem to have an over-sharing brother."

Chapter Four

Ryan spent the weekend at Jeff's. They fucked until their dicks were too raw to enjoy it and talked about nothing and made inroads in Jeff's martial arts DVD collection. Sunday night, Ryan was sprawled in a contented heap on Jeff's couch, Jeff on the floor at his feet, mouth still wet from Ryan's come.

"Man, I really do not want to go to work tomorrow." As soon as Ryan said the words he knew he was in trouble, because what he really meant was that he wanted to spend a long stretch of days in this house, doing nothing but hanging out with Jeff.

"Long day?" Jeff asked.

Ryan seized the out he'd been given. "Mondays always are."

Jeff got up and came back with two cans of soda. He dropped down on the couch after handing one to Ryan. "Look. I know how this is going to sound."

Ryan felt the soda burn all the way down his throat. Here was the brush off he'd been waiting for. Well, it's not like he'd had much of an expectation going into this.

Jeff turned on the couch and looked at him. "I want to see you again."

That was unexpected.

"I do," Jeff added. "But I can't until next Monday."

Ryan wondered if a why would make this conversation even more awkward than it felt, but Jeff went on without the question.

"I'll have my daughter next week."

"I like kids."

Jeff looked away, focusing his attention on the soda he still hadn't opened. "I just need it to be this way. If you don't want to get together again, that's fine too."

"I want to," Ryan said, maybe too quickly. Jeff's reasons made sense. He could see Jeff not wanting to introduce him to his daughter. They'd just started whatever it was they'd started, meeting family ought to wait, but he couldn't help feeling shut out. They'd spent so much time together that Jeff's closed expression jarred, like he'd become a stranger again.

Jeff nodded and opened his soda. "So, I'll call you."

Another burst of resentment burned his chest. He couldn't be the one to call? He'd think the interest was all one-sided, but Jeff was the one sitting on the couch with his dick tenting his shorts while he washed Ryan's come down with soda. Not all one-sided, no, but definitely on Jeff's terms. Ryan wondered exactly how much of that he was willing to put up with. He didn't like his answer.

෨෨෨෨

When the phone rang at ten-thirty Thursday night, Ryan didn't need caller ID to know it was Jeff. The second his "Hey" came over the phone, Ryan felt blood pump south.

"Hey."

Jeff asked him about work, which took all of a minute. Then Ryan heard him shift the phone around, and Jeff said, "You want to know about Anna?"

"If you want to tell me."

Jeff took a deep breath. "I was eighteen and despite the fact that I'd been jerking off to pictures of guys for years, I really didn't want to admit it, you know?"

Ryan had admitted to himself that girls weren't really his thing by the age of fourteen, but coming out was never easy so he murmured an acknowledgement.

"Val—Val was—we dated for a month, and damn, when I found out she was pregnant I didn't even want to believe it was mine, but when Anna was born, when I saw her—I just—well, I got the job at Connor's and as soon as I'd saved up some money I petitioned for joint custody.

"I've got four sisters and two brothers, but Anna, she's my whole family."

Ryan heard him swallow hard.

So Jeff loved his daughter, how was that a bad thing? Ryan liked kids. He'd just never really thought about them for himself. Cold realization washed over him. He was thinking about the long term with this—with them, on the basis of what? An extended weekend?

"I saw her at the drive-in," he said. "She's adorable. How's her collarbone?"

"She's upset because she hasn't been able to swim at day camp. She can still do crafts, though. It's a good thing she's a lefty like me."

The love and warmth coloring Jeff's voice reminded him of every other proud parent. Ryan realized he was wishing he knew what it would sound like if Jeff turned that warmth on him. He was so screwed.

Jeff's voice turned husky enough to make the blood throb in Ryan's dick. "So, we still on for Monday?"

"Sure."

"If you want to meet me at the garage after work we could take the Camaro."

"Sounds good."

Before he fell asleep, Ryan jerked off to thoughts of Jeff fucking him over the hood of the Camaro.

☙☙☙

As soon as the doors shut on the Camaro, there was no question of driving back out to the state park or anywhere they could get private with the car. They needed the safety of walls around them before the heat of *need, want, now* shattered into frantic touches and kisses. Time was frozen on the drive out to Jeff's house, but the second they were inside it sped up again.

Once inside the kitchen Ryan managed one deep breath of the charged air before the tension snapped in a crash of hard bodies. He couldn't remember the steps but it seemed like seconds later he was naked and holding on to the column framing the breakfast bar, riding three of Jeff's fingers, while Jeff kissed and licked at his neck.

"There's a condom in my shirt pocket," Jeff breathed against his ear.

Ryan let go with one hand to fish out the package and tore it with his teeth. Jeff pulled his fingers free to lift him with both hands under his ass.

Ryan rolled the condom down on Jeff with shaking fingers and grabbed back onto the column behind him as Jeff lifted him right off his feet.

"Get your legs around me."

Jesus, Jeff was strong, but Ryan doubted they could—holy shit, Jeff was in him. Ryan wrapped his legs around his hips and hung onto the pillar behind him as Jeff pushed him up and back.

"God, I missed…this," Jeff panted in his ear, lowering his head to nip at Ryan's shoulders, never hard enough to bruise.

He rocked them slowly at first, and then started to pull Ryan down on him as he pushed up.

It wasn't enough. Not after a whole week of not having him.

"Harder."

"Can't get deep enough like this."

Jeff eased him to the floor and spun him so that he was bent over one of the barstools. He filled him again in one long thrust, and Ryan gripped the counter before he went flying off.

"Shit…wanted…watch you."

Ryan reached back and grabbed Jeff's thigh, pulling him tighter. "Don't stop."

Never stop. It was only the endorphin rush. He'd taken enough biology in college to know that the chemicals released in your blood during sex made you want to get attached. But knowing didn't stop feeling, and Ryan'd never felt like this with anyone. He'd never felt this quick connection, known that it felt so good, so damned good because it was *him.* Jeff's arm wrapped around his chest, and his mouth kissed his shoulders over and over, broken only by sandpaper moans in his ears.

"Sorry, I can't—oh fuck."

Ryan recognized Jeff's about-to-die noises and the increased speed of his hips. He tightened himself around him, and Jeff went off, deep spasms that shook his whole body.

"Man, I am so sorry," Jeff murmured against his neck when he got his breath back.

Ryan shifted his hips, and Jeff groaned.

"It's actually kind of flattering."

"Well, I'm just embarrassed." Jeff slipped from him, and Ryan turned to face him. Jeff was looking down. "I haven't lost it like that since..."

"Your first blow job?" Ryan suggested.

"Something like that. If we can make it to the bed, I'll try to make it up to you."

Jeff had a king-sized bed with a metal frame that Ryan had discovered was strong enough to anchor him against Jeff's thrusts. The frame, the firm mattress and the size made it perfect for fucking, and Ryan wondered exactly how many other guys had had fun finding that out then shoved that insane jealousy down deep inside him. The room was stifling after being closed up all day, so Ryan pushed open a window before stretching out on sheets that smelled like Jeff. Only Jeff.

Jeff was naked when he joined him, rolling up on his side and cocking an elbow behind his head.

"So, on a scale of one to ten, how pissed would you be if I just fell asleep?" Jeff's hand slipped down his chest and paused just above Ryan's swollen, leaking cock.

"Forty-two," Ryan snapped, the ache spreading from his cock to his thighs as he tried to tip his hips toward that teasing hand.

"You could do it yourself," Jeff suggested.

"This is your idea of making it up to me?"

"Not quite." Jeff rolled away and came back with a condom and lube. He made his fingers into a tight ring around the base of Ryan's dick. "I want you in me."

Despite the grip Jeff had on him, Ryan's dick went harder at his words. Jeff leaned down and teased the skin behind his ear with his tongue. "I want to ride you until we both come."

It took every bit of control Ryan had not to shoot from just that dirty whisper in his ear. He grabbed for the condom and Jeff pulled it out of reach.

"Let me." Jeff tore it open and stretched it around the head of Ryan's cock before leaning over.

"Shit." Ryan hissed as Jeff's mouth took over the operation. That took a lot of practice, and again Ryan felt that irrational stab of jealousy before the heat and the pressure of soft lips sliding down his shaft shorted out his brain.

Jeff lifted his head and crawled over him, and Ryan reached for the lube, pouring the gel over his fingers. Jeff kept up a distracting amount of kissing and licking and nipping, right up until the moment Ryan pressed his finger inside him. Jeff gasped and his head snapped back against his neck.

Ryan licked the exposed tendons as he worked his finger deeper. The smooth tight heat crushed his finger, making his cock just about vibrate with eagerness. He squeezed in a second finger, making Jeff arch away and then back as he adjusted to the stretch.

He was starting to wonder if this was a good idea, maybe Jeff didn't like to bottom, was only doing it because he felt bad about shortchanging him, and then Jeff's eyes snapped open and there was no mistaking the pleasure burning in them. Ryan curled his fingers up to find the swell of Jeff's prostate. Jeff's hips bucked as his cock started to fill again. Despite the choking need in Ryan's balls and the sharp agony in his long-denied erection, he wanted to keep finger-fucking Jeff for hours, just to watch Jeff's face tighten and relax in that sweet blend of pleasure and pain. Ryan stroked and rubbed him into desperate, tight jerks of his hips.

When his fingers were sliding easily, he slipped free and urged Jeff higher on his body. He gripped the base of his cock, half for leverage, half to prevent the orgasm boiling in him from spilling over as that first bit of perfect pressure swallowed the head. He let Jeff set the pace, releasing his grip as Jeff sank down to his thighs with a gravelly moan. Jeff held his shoulders as he shifted, squeezed Ryan's dick until light burst behind his eyes, and he had to clamp down with every muscle to keep from fucking up, driving into Jeff until he lost himself in mindless pleasure.

Jeff's breaths were coming in quick pants, his tongue wetting his lips as he rocked a little. Then his eyes opened again, and he levered himself up and down. So good, such perfect slick-hot friction, but so slow. Ryan kept his hips pinned against the mattress until Jeff released his shoulders, his fists dropping to the sheets next to Ryan's ribs. Ryan grabbed Jeff's hips and gave into his body's demands. He arched up into that burning channel of muscle, dragged Jeff down to meet each thrust.

The stream of sexy filth from Jeff's mouth each time Jeff had fucked him had driven Ryan insane, but he almost lost control when he realized that the best Jeff could manage with Ryan's dick up his ass were strangled *fucks* and frequent *yeahs*. Jeff was slamming down on him now, his features so dazed Ryan couldn't help leaning up to taste his slack lips. Jeff responded with a hungry, forceful kiss that had Ryan rolling them over, slamming back inside and pounding him into the mattress. He moved so long and deep that Jeff's rim squeezed his crown at the top of each stroke. He braced himself on his arms, watching everything play out across Jeff's face, the way his eyes turned to slits shut when Ryan went deep, the sound he made when the thick ridge tugged on that ring of muscle on the upstroke.

Jeff grabbed his cock and started pulling, the sounds getting deeper. Ryan's breath tore at his lungs and he was certain an aneurysm was one heartbeat away when he watched Jeff break, pumping thick streams across their bellies. Ryan lowered his head and let the contractions around his dick finish him, send him off like fireworks inside Jeff's body.

His pulse was still loud in his ears as he looked down at Jeff, whose face had gone intent, his gaze focused on his. He didn't care if it was the oxytocin or whatever post-orgasm high that pumped in his blood. He wanted this, wanted this man, wanted it as long as he could make it last. He hoped to God that's what that look on Jeff's face meant too. He lowered his forehead to Jeff's and breathed.

"Damn." Ryan's voice sounded strange to him, not the fucked-out hoarseness, but the amazement coloring that one word.

"Yeah."

And then he knew what it sounded like when Jeff turned that affection on him.

♋♋♋

Ryan woke up alone.

He could hear a TV on in another room, but it was faint, it couldn't have woken him up. Then he heard the voices outside the open window.

Jeff's bedroom faced the front of the house and the long front lawn. The house was small, but had lots of yard space. Ryan didn't have to ask; he knew he'd bought it with Anna in mind. The voices must be right at the front door.

Jeff, and based on what he heard, a woman who must be Anna's mother Val.

He climbed off the bed and realized his pants were still in the kitchen. He found a pair of Jeff's jeans and slid them on. They were loose but should stay up. He pulled a T-shirt over his head as he crept toward the window.

"Because I need a day or two," Val said.

Jeff was silent for a minute. And then, "For Christsake, are you blown? Tell me you didn't drive her like that."

"Craig drove."

Ryan peeked through the screen and saw a red two-door out on the street.

"And I'm supposed to believe he's sober?"

"I don't give a fuck what you believe. I'll pick her up in a couple of days."

"If I find out you're putting Anna at risk like that—"

"If you thought you'd win, you'd have done it years ago." She laughed.

"So what is it this time? Craig doesn't like kids, is that it?"

"Not everybody wants to live like a monk." She paused. "Or a fag like you."

Jeff laughed, so bitter that Ryan felt his stomach churn.

"Try a new one, Val. Every guy who doesn't want to screw you isn't a fag."

"Yeah, well you'd better hope I never find out you're one. You'll never get near another kid, especially not your own."

The morning was already warm, but Ryan felt a chill on his skin. Jesus. Jeff was living with that kind of threat over his head?

He waited until he heard the car start up and then slipped into the hall.

When he got to the kitchen, he could see Anna parked in front of the TV. The clothes from last night were gone. He waited but Jeff didn't come back inside.

He decided to make breakfast. In his limited experience, kids were usually hungry, and he doubted her mother had fed her.

He checked the fridge, found it stocked and started to make French toast.

As soon as the bowl hit the counter, the blonde head in front of the TV spun around.

"Dad?" She had her father's eyes, sharp, bright blue. "Who are you?"

"I'm Ryan."

She got up and came a little closer. Her right arm was still in the sling and harnessed to her body. "There are two Ryans at my school."

"I'm a friend of your dad's."

She looked at him for a minute. "Did you have a sleepover?"

Given the conversation he'd just overheard, he wondered what she thought a sleepover was. But since he was standing in Jeff's kitchen at seven a.m., it didn't seem like a good idea to lie to the kid. "Yes."

"I like to sleep over at my friend Jessica's house."

"Oh?"

"Her mom makes *pancakes*." Using her one good arm, Anna clambered up onto one of the stools and looked at the bowl with pointed emphasis.

"I can make pancakes." Ryan hoped Jeff had a mix somewhere around here.

Taking it upon herself to assist, Anna pointed at one of the cabinets. He was still scanning the shelves when he heard Jeff come in. With his face as blank as he could make it, Ryan turned around, not sure how Jeff wanted to play this.

"Dad." Anna jumped down and ran to hug her father.

Jeff met his eyes over his daughter's head, and Ryan shrugged. Jeff lifted Anna onto the stool again and came over to the cabinet. "She talked you into pancakes, didn't she?" He grabbed a box from the top shelf and set it next to the bowl.

Anna giggled.

"Anna would eat pancakes for breakfast, lunch and supper." Jeff put a hand on her head and went to fill the coffee machine.

"But they taste better at supper," she said. "Did you and Ryan have fun?"

The coffee carafe hit the counter hard. Glancing over, Ryan saw how dark Jeff's cheeks had gotten. He raised his eyebrows in apology.

"Yes," Jeff finally said.

"Because you never have sleepovers. Is Ryan your best friend now?"

"Boys don't usually have best friends, honey. But Ryan is a good friend."

The mention of friends launched Anna on a monologue about her friends at camp and school. Ryan decided that the best thing he could do was concentrate on the pancakes. Jeff stepped around him to get to the sink, making him conscious of every inch of space between them. The measuring cups were hanging next to the stove, which meant he had to go around Jeff again. He felt Jeff's jeans start to slide on his hips and he tugged them back up. This was going to be one hell of a dance.

Anna packed away an astonishing amount of pancakes into her small frame, politely declaring that his pancakes were good, but not as good as Dad's. "My birthday is in two weeks. Can you come to my party?"

Ryan looked at Jeff. "I'd like to but..."

"But my friends will be there and I want Dad to have a friend there. He never has friends."

At eight, Jeff sent Anna out to his car.

"I've got to take her to day camp. If you want to go, the key to the Camaro is on the hook and your clothes are under the sink." Jeff tugged on the jeans sagging over Ryan's hips and then yanked his hand back as if he'd been burned. "But you don't have to go." He looked out the door and then back at Ryan. "Will you be here?"

"Yeah."

♋♋♋

He drank a second cup of coffee while he cleaned the kitchen, digesting a whole lot more than pancakes. Anna was sweet, her mom was a bitch and Jeff—Jeff was caught in the middle. There had to be some lawyer who could take on this case. He couldn't believe anyone would give Val a goldfish to raise after spending five seconds in her company. He thought of all the news stories he'd read of parents losing their children because they were gay. But this was Minnesota, not Georgia, and that was years ago.

He knew now why Jeff had been the one to call, why he'd said he couldn't see him while he had Anna. The realization sat like a cold hard lump in his stomach.

When Jeff got back, Ryan was sitting at the breakfast bar and the lump hadn't gone away.

Jeff poured himself coffee and sat next to him. "Sorry about that."

"Why? She's great. I told you I liked kids."

"Yeah."

Ryan turned to face him. "I heard."

Jeff put down his mug. "I kind of figured you did."

"Exactly how many people know?"

Jeff didn't have to ask what he meant. He looked at his coffee. "I assume anyone who's had his dick in my mouth figured it out. Other than that, it doesn't come up."

Ryan got up and went to lean on the counter. "I did four years in the Air Force. You don't have to explain 'don't ask, don't tell' to me."

"So?"

"And it sucked. I was miserable. Have you even discussed it with a lawyer?"

Jeff shook his head. "I can't risk it. I can't lose Anna."

"What about your family?"

"I don't know that my mother or sisters wouldn't try to take her from me if they knew. It's why I've never tried for full custody."

Ryan ran his hands through his hair. "There are lawyers who—"

"You don't understand. I can't risk it."

"I understand. Believe me. My mom's been telling me for years that having a gay son is what drove my father to an early grave. But I couldn't stand lying anymore."

"Your brother?"

"David's great. But don't think it's been easy for me."

Jeff looked at him then and his voice was soft, the way it had been last night. "I never said it was."

The look was the same, too, blue eyes so intent on his, so open, like Ryan could reach inside, and everything he'd felt last night was still there, no post-orgasm chemicals, nothing but a bone-deep knowledge that he should shut his mouth and walk over there and kiss him.

Ryan pushed away from the counter and the lump in his stomach did a queasy roll. "I just don't think I can live like that again."

"Did somebody ask you?"

"No. I guess not." He went to the spot where he'd stashed his phone.

"What?"

"I'm calling a cab."

Jeff got up and walked over to the door. He stepped back and slapped a key on the counter next to him. "Take the fucking Camaro."

If Jeff had stood there in front of him a second longer, Ryan would have given into the instinct that was telling him to grab him, make them figure out how this had gone so bad so fast. But Jeff stepped away and went in to sit on the couch. Ryan looked at the key. If there was anything he wanted less than to drive that goddamned car he couldn't think of it, but he doubted he had enough for cab fare in his wallet.

Ryan picked up the key.

ᏕᏕᏕ

On Friday Ryan's car wouldn't start. No grinding, no whine of a dead battery, nothing.

He called David.

"You're dating a mechanic and you call me when your car won't start?"

"I'm not dating a mechanic."

"You broke up already?"

"I never said—we were never dating."

"You had *plans* and couldn't come to Mom's for dinner that Sunday."

Tony Jaa on TV and Jeff's homemade popcorn and Jeff taking the bowl from his hands as he slid from the couch, hands on his fly.

"So can you help me?"

"I can give you the name of a good mechanic."

"Thanks a lot."

ᏕᏕᏕ

The warranty had expired a year ago. Between a dealer's prices and a tow, Ryan could see his bank account emptying. He opened his phone again and realized he didn't have Jeff's number. Not his cell, not his work, not his home. That connection had clearly been all in his head, but at least maybe a couple nights of great sex would be enough to get his car running without leaving him bankrupt. He found Connor's in the phone book.

"Connor's."

It wasn't Jeff, and he wasn't sure if that made things better or worse. He gave the guy his information, and the guy told him they'd tow it and Ryan could call to check on it at four.

"Do you want me to wait with you?" David asked as they pulled up to the garage at five-thirty.

Ryan squinted into the dark opening. There was no mistaking Jeff's tall frame moving around.

"I'm just picking up my car. I think I can handle it."

He stepped down from the Rover. The sun was bouncing off the glass in the garage windows, making it hard to see anything beyond the dark opening. The voice that came out of the shadows was easy to recognize.

"We closed at five."

Ryan hesitated in confusion. He didn't hear anyone else moving around. Was Jeff going to pretend he didn't even know him? He looked back. David was still waiting.

"The guy on the phone said—"

"But as a favor..." Now Jeff was close enough for him to see the white of his teeth as he smiled. "C'mon."

Now that his eyes adjusted he could see his little silver Altima in the corner. He followed Jeff farther into the cool darkness and heard David drive away.

"What was wrong with it?"

"I hit that switch." Jeff led the way to the counter in the back.

"What?"

"The switch in your engine that makes you need a mechanic."

Ryan looked at him.

"The alternator," Jeff said.

"Sounds expensive."

"It can be. Especially if it's a rush job."

"I never—"

"Ryan, I'm kidding. I'd have done it for free but I had to buy the part."

"Oh." Where the fuck was his sense of humor? Gone the way of his self-control. His pulse was jumping and his lungs felt as tight as if he were making the last sprint on a 10K. He reached for his wallet.

Jeff was holding a pink receipt in his hands. "You know, I couldn't believe it when Tony gave me the address for the tow. I kind of thought this would be the last place you'd call."

"Yeah."

He tried to focus on the receipt Jeff had handed him, tried to look anywhere but at Jeff's eyes, his throat where his Adam's apple bobbed as he swallowed. Tried to think about anything but how that skin tasted, how powerful that body felt against his own.

"Your wipers are kind of shot. I could see if I've got some that would fit."

Ryan didn't care if that was an invitation or not, he followed him into the back room. In contrast to the order in the main garage, this room was chaos. Boxes everywhere, shelves littered with parts, but Ryan's gaze just focused on Jeff. He breathed in metal, grease and exhaust and wanted to bury his nose in Jeff's neck, fill himself with the smell of his sweat. Jeff pulled a package off a hook on the wall and turned back to him.

"Ryan, hey—" Jeff grabbed his elbow.

Startled, Ryan jerked free.

Jeff's jaw got hard. "You were going to trip."

That touch had snapped something loose inside Ryan, and he stepped around the box as he pushed Jeff back against a shelf. Jeff's hand came up to tear into his hair, tugging so hard Ryan thought he'd rip it out as he crushed their mouths together with a groan.

Jeff kissed him like he was starving, a hunger Ryan felt in his own gut, a craving to feel his skin under his hands. He shoved his shirt out of the way, struggled with the fly of Jeff's jeans, but Jeff's hands on his head and ass had them smashed together so tightly he couldn't work the button.

Jeff's tongue tangled around his own, the sounds vibrating between them so that he couldn't tell who was moaning. The slam of blood into his cock had Ryan desperate for friction. A groan of frustration burned his throat, and Jeff worked his hand around to Ryan's fly. The kiss hauled the breath from him as Jeff's hand finally got his cock free, pulling it from his briefs with a long stroke that made him want to swallow Jeff's tongue. Ryan braced his hands on the shelf behind Jeff's head, bucking into the touch he'd been dying for.

Jeff's thumb spread drops of precome over his head, down the shaft, his hand tightening as Ryan panted into his mouth. Ryan finally managed to get Jeff's fly open, and Jeff's dick pressed against his belly, leaving a wet trail.

But he shoved his hand away as Ryan reached for him. He used his grip on Ryan's hair to lift his head. "Just come for me, can you do that?" Jeff whispered into his mouth.

Oh, he definitely could.

Jeff's cock slid against his stomach, his hand slid over his dick, twisting, calluses catching just under the rim as he sped up his strokes. Jeff dragged him back into a kiss, tongue hot and demanding. Ryan stretched his jaw open for him. They rode together on that shared breath, shared sweat, the shared want slicking their cocks.

Ryan hit the point of no return, fucking into that tight grip, heat bursting from him to pool between them. Jeff pulled his head into his shoulder as he shuddered through the aftershocks of pleasure, legs shaking, mouth hunting for skin under Jeff's work shirt. Jeff dragged him in closer as he rocked against his stomach, breaking into those sounds that made him wish he could go again because just the sound of Jeff coming could send him right over the edge.

Jeff kissed his neck, lifted the wet strands of his hair out of the way and sifted through them, soothing the burn on his scalp.

"Why do you wear it so long?"

"I had to keep it so short in the service."

"Rebel." Jeff laughed and combed it through his fingers again. "I like it." He kissed him again, a soft caress against his swollen lips.

The hand on his ass shifted to his hip, and Ryan realized how much of his weight he'd had on Jeff. He straightened, and Jeff let him go with one last kiss of his lower lip. With a grin that lit up his eyes, Jeff scrubbed at their stomachs with a rag from one of the shelves.

The aggression that had had Ryan pushing Jeff into that shelving had faded, leaving Ryan wondering exactly what happened now. He couldn't imagine being with Jeff and not being with him, pretending to be buddies instead of lovers, worrying that a casual touch could cost Jeff his daughter.

He backed away, just remembering to avoid the box on the floor before he ended up on his ass. Every time they got together it got that much harder to think of not having this again. Even now he wanted to step back into Jeff's body, despite the thick heat in the airless room. He looked away, tucked himself back into his clothes and zipped up.

"What?"

He had the feeling Jeff's eyes could see right through to the back of his head, see through all the reasons why he was practically backing into the far wall.

"I should probably go."

"A guy could feel a little used." Jeff hitched his jeans back up on his hips. "Just came by to get off and your car fixed for free?"

Anger stirred his pulse as hot and quick as desire had moments before. What the hell did Jeff want from him? He wasn't the one making things so goddamned complicated. "What do I owe you?"

"What a fucking pussy."

It was a mutter, but Ryan knew he was meant to hear every word. His hands tightened into fists. "What?"

"You heard me." Jeff made that bitter laugh that hurt just as much as his other laughs felt good against his skin, his mouth. "You know, when your brother said you liked to run I didn't realize how much."

Ryan had been on his way out to the counter and Jeff's accusation brought him up short. "And you're not running?"

"I'm right here. You're the one who keeps leaving, who won't even stick around to see where it goes."

"But you're running from who you are."

"Oh Christ, don't try that psychobabble shit with me. I know who I am." Jeff pushed past him.

"And no one else does."

"So you want me to take out an ad or something?"

"No, but I can't go back to hiding who I am."

"And you think I'm asking you to? I just have to be careful."

"Careful? You never even gave me your number."

"Did you ever fucking ask me for it?"

Ryan heard the hurt in his voice and stared at him.

Jeff shook his head. "Ah, forget it. It's obvious you've got your mind made up. It's all black and white. If I'm not wearing a T-shirt declaring my sexuality, I'm in denial." He stepped behind the counter and grabbed the receipt. "The part was $97.38 with tax. You can have your brother drop it off when you've got it."

Ryan reached into his pocket. "I—I've got it." He pulled five twenties out of his wallet and laid them on the counter. "Thanks for—" The glare Jeff shot him made him stop. "Thanks."

It had to be the heat of the sun slanting in through the garage that made it so damned hard to breathe.

"Goodbye, Ryan."

And even then he knew he could fix it. *Say something,* he told himself. Or just pin him up against the counter and kiss him, but maybe they were past sex being able to fix things. *Tell him you understand. Tell him you don't want to say it.*

"Bye, Jeff."

Chapter Five

Ryan's car ran perfectly. Life, on the other hand, sucked.

David called him Saturday, ostensibly to ask about the car. Ryan ended up hanging up on him.

He skipped his run on Monday, which didn't improve his mood. People started to avoid him at work. He ran the rest of the week, and that didn't help either. He knew he'd fucked up, but that didn't make it any easier to fix. He lay in bed Thursday, trying to decide if he should drive down to the city tomorrow and see if a night in the bars could get his mind off Jeff, when his phone rang.

His heart rate kicked up at the familiar *hey*, and Jeff went on without giving him a chance to respond.

"Look. I'm sorry to bother you, but Anna's birthday party is Saturday and she's got this thing in her head about me having a friend there and she's decided it's you."

He couldn't stop the smile at knowing how tightly Anna had her dad wrapped around her finger.

"I realize this is kind of fucked up," Jeff said when he didn't answer.

"No. I'm—" *I'm glad you called? I'm kind of freaked out because I may be falling in love with you?* "I'll be there. What time?"

ᏙᏙᏙᏙ

After a quick consultation with his ex-sister-in-law, Ryan ended up with a Polly Pocket play set and a multi-piece sticker and coloring package. He'd had to guess at Anna's age, and was relieved when he saw the big eight stuck in the cake on the picnic table in the back yard of Jeff's house. The yard seemed full of screeching girls, running around the swing set waving iridescent ribbons on sticks.

He'd attracted the gaze of the two women standing next to the picnic table and hoped that neither of them were Val. Anna jumped off the swing and ran up to him. "Hi, Ryan."

"Happy Birthday." He held out his gifts.

Anna's greeting turned the women's scrutiny into smiles and one of them came to take the gifts from him.

"Dad's in the kitchen," Anna said before running back to the swing set.

Jeff met him at the door, his hands full of a box overflowing with things in pink wrapping paper. "Glad you made it. You mind?"

"No." Ryan took the box and brought it to the picnic table. Jeff came back out with another two bags.

It was a little girl's birthday party, but just watching Jeff come down those stairs hit him like a shock rolling right down his spine. How was he going to get through the next two hours without staring at him, touching him, some kind of betraying action?

As it turned out, it wasn't that hard. Four adults and eight—God, were there only eight?—girls should have made things manageable, but Ryan had never realized what organization was necessary for an eight-year-old's birthday party. It was grueling enough to be a required part of basic training. There were games to be played, the adults trying to insure that each girl got at least one prize, a few crying fits to be placated, snacks, drinks and ice cream and cake to be disseminated, no easy task since every girl insisted on a piece with a pink and green flower on it. Ryan barely had time to catch his breath let alone think about Jeff.

Anna was just starting to tear into her presents when a car door slammed and heels clicked up the driveway. Ryan didn't need the murmurs from the two other women or the heavy sigh from Jeff to get the message. Val was here.

She was so thin she made x-ray technology redundant, hair that might have been blonde was pulled into a sloppy knot on her head, and her reddened nose showed the signs of her choice of recreation. But there was still a beauty to be reckoned with in that face. Despite the hardness in her light eyes, they held an exotic tilt and the lips were full, features in perfect symmetry.

"Wasn't anyone going to invite me to my daughter's birthday party?"

Ryan busied himself gathering the remnants of wrapping paper.

"Val." Jeff's voice held a warning note.

She ignored him. "Anna, sweetie, Mommy brought you a present."

Anna slid off the picnic table and stood half-behind her father as she looked up at Val.

Val held out a small box.

Anna took it as if it might bite her and peeled back the paper. Ryan couldn't see her face as she opened the box, but he could see Jeff put a reassuring hand on her shoulder.

"Anna doesn't have pierced ears, Val. You know that."

"Yes and it's time she got over that fear. Mommy will take you to have them done on Monday."

"I don't want a shot in my ears."

"It doesn't hurt, honey. All pretty girls wear earrings. Don't you want to be a pretty girl?"

He could see Jeff pull Anna in against his side. "She is a pretty girl."

"Of course she is," Jessica's mother added. "Val, did you see this? Isn't it adorable?" She picked up the game Anna had just unwrapped, but Val refused to be distracted.

"Mommy will take you today, if you want, honey. Look at how pretty these earrings are."

"I don't want needles in my ears."

Ryan could hear the quaver of tears in her voice.

"Val, will you come in the kitchen with me for a minute?" Jeff's voice was quiet but there was no mistaking his anger.

"Can I at least have a piece of my daughter's birthday cake?"

As Val staggered closer to the picnic table, Ryan could smell the fumes on her breath. "Val." Jeff's hand was on her arm, pulling her back.

"Jesus fucking Christ." She jerked free and stomped up the steps.

With the windows closed, the words were unintelligible, but the volume of the voices was perfectly clear.

"How about one more game of Statues?" Jessica's mom suggested and turned on the portable CD player.

The kids went into wild gyrations that were supposed to be dances, until they froze when the music went off. Over the blare of pop music, the woman murmured, "She's quite a piece of work. I feel so sorry for Anna."

Ryan nodded.

"Have you known Jeff and Anna long?"

"Not long."

"I wish—I try to have her stay as often as I can—I worry—" She stopped the music and the kids froze. "Oh, Marisol, you're still moving."

Marisol went to sit on the bench. There was a crash from the house, and the front door slammed.

"Don't think you can scare me with that!" Val screamed as she stomped to her car.

Ryan found Jeff in the kitchen, picking up the shattered pieces of the popcorn bowl. He bent down to help. "Jeff, I—"

"Not now. Can you just make sure none of the kids come in until I get this cleaned up? Most of 'em have sandals on." Jeff's voice was hoarse.

"Sure."

He went back outside. He stayed through the presents, stayed through the handing out of goodie bags, stayed through the clean up.

As part of the celebration, Jessica was spending the night. As soon as they bid Jessica's mom goodbye, Jessica and Anna tore upstairs with the pile of brand-new toys Anna had received. The downstairs was relatively quiet when Ryan finally cornered Jeff as he was dumping a load of jeans into the washer.

"God, Jeff, I'm so sorry."

Jeff turned around and leaned on the machine, face closed, arms folded across his chest. "For what?"

"I've been an asshole."

Jeff's eyebrows went up, but he didn't contradict him.

"I understand. If Anna didn't have you... I get it."

"Just like that, huh?" The corners of his mouth lifted, but his eyes never changed.

Jeff wasn't going to make it easy. But then there was no reason why he should. "And I still want to..." He swallowed. "I want to see where this goes."

"Really? And now all of a sudden you can put up with those restrictions that you couldn't deal with a week ago?"

"If that's what it takes."

Jeff pushed past him, and Ryan's stomach sank as he realized it was all too late. But Jeff just pulled the folding doors shut on the alcove and pressed back into him.

"If that's what it takes for what?" Jeff put his hands on the machine on either side of his hips.

Ryan couldn't think with the heat of Jeff's body crowding him against the machine, his mouth so close to his. He took a breath, dryer sheets and detergent and Jeff, then went for broke. "To have you." He leaned forward and kissed him.

Jeff grabbed his hips and kissed him back, brought every inch of them together as his tongue curled hot and deep around his own. Ryan's hands pressed in at his back, slid through the soft spikes in his hair. He swallowed back the moan building in his throat and arched closer. Just that long, hard kiss sent blood pumping through him slow and thick as honey.

Jeff broke off the kiss with a gasp. "I'm sorry. I want to, Christ, I want to, but..." His eyes flicked upward.

Ryan tugged on his suddenly too tight jeans.

Jeff stepped away. "If you want to run, now might be a good time. It's just going to get worse."

"What?"

"I may be getting full custody of Anna."

"But that's great."

"One of the hospital workers reported that Val was under the influence when she brought Anna in. There's a hearing on Wednesday. I may be walking out of there with Anna permanently."

"Why is that a problem?"

"There's going to be home studies and social workers and lawyers and not a lot of time for this."

"I'm not fifteen. I can keep it in my pants."

"I'm not just talking about that. I may not be able to see much of you for awhile." Jeff turned away and braced his hands on the machine as if he expected him to leave again.

"You suck as a salesman, you know that?" Ryan covered his body with his, running his palms down the length of Jeff's arms. He rested his head on his shoulder. "It's a good thing you're pretty."

Jeff laughed and turned in his arms. "Back to that, are we?"

That laugh acted like a hand on Ryan's dick. "I know you said it was going to be awhile but there can be phone sex, can't there?"

"Sounds good to me." Jeff hooked his fingers in Ryan's belt loops.

There was a squeal and a thud overhead. Jeff listened for a moment, body tense. Pounding feet and giggles followed, and he relaxed again.

He brought up a hand to Ryan's neck, his thumb stroking his jaw. "Last chance. It's more than just my dick involved here, Ryan. If you pull that crap again, something's going to break and it's not going to be pretty."

Something clamped hard and tight inside of him. For a second it hurt, but then he looked at Jeff, and it felt damned near perfect. "Yeah." He smiled.

He could do this.

About the Author

K.A. Mitchell discovered the magic of writing at an early age when she learned that a carefully crayoned note of apology sent to the kitchen in a toy truck would earn her a reprieve from banishment to her room. Her career as a spin control artist was cut short when her family moved to a two-story house, and her trucks would not roll safely down the stairs. Around the same time, she decided that Chip and Ken made a much cuter couple than Ken and Barbie and was perplexed when invitations to play Barbie dropped off. An unnamed number of years later, she's happy to find other readers and writers who like to play in her world.

To learn more about K.A. Mitchell, please visit kamitchell.com. Send an email to K.A. Mitchell at authorKAMitchell@gmail.com.

Look for these titles by
K. A. Mitchell

Coming Soon:

Hot Ticket

Catching a Buzz

Ally Blue

Dedication

To Jesse, for sending me the link that gave me the idea in the first place, and to the girls of J_A_W_breakers for helping me hammer it into shape.

Chapter One

Planting a foot on the rim of the rubber raft, Adam shoved it over the edge of the waterfall.

"What time is it?" he asked, watching the raft swirl out of sight down the blue plastic tunnel, the three young children and their sunburned dad whooping all the way. Adam wished *he* could still enjoy Thunder Falls that much.

That's what two months of working in a water park'll do to you, he thought sourly.

"It's four-forty," Marcy answered, glancing at her watch.

Adam wrinkled his nose. "Shit. I can't believe our shift's only half over. It seems like we've been here all day."

"Adam, language." Shooting a stern look at Adam, Marcy caught the next raft coming off the conveyor belt and steadied it in the entry pool. "I have to leave early today. As a matter of fact, someone should've been here to replace me ten minutes ago. They better get here soon, or I'm in trouble."

Adam stifled a groan. He wished, selfishly and not for the first time, that Marcy didn't have kids. Or could at least find a reliable babysitter. She was the only person at Wild Waters he particularly enjoyed spending time with, probably because she was ten years older and at least twenty years more mature than the rest of the mostly college-age staff. He'd never gotten along well with people his own age, preferring the company of those

Ally Blue

whose every fourth word wasn't "like" and who did not insist on calling him "dude". His mom, of course, interpreted this behavior as "antisocial" and declared he would never find a nice girl to settle down with if he didn't make an effort.

Adam sighed and rubbed the bridge of his nose, which still tended to turn pink in spite of the deep tan he'd acquired over the summer. The thought of the hysterics his society-belle mother would have when she discovered he didn't swing that way made his stomach turn flip-flops. Which was why he hadn't told her yet.

God, he didn't want to think about that right now. Later. Tomorrow, maybe.

After all, he thought, in the Scarlett voice that tended to plague him at times like this, *tomorrow is another day.*

A sharp smack on his arm brought him back to the present. He winced when he realized Marcy had been forced once again to get physical in order to interrupt his runaway thoughts. "Sorry."

Marcy shook her head. "Honestly, how do you make such good grades when you daydream so much?"

Adam shrugged and kept his mouth shut. He had a natural head for figures and for the classroom environment in general, which kept his grades in the B range, but he'd only majored in business to make his parents happy. He hadn't told them—or anyone else, for that matter—about his pie-in-the-sky dreams of becoming a famous novelist. His dad would lecture him about "responsibility" and "optimum career choices", and his mother would have an attack of The Vapors.

Dear God. *I'll think about that tomorrow.*

He snickered, earning him a glare from Marcy. Blushing, he leaned over the edge of the tall tower. The raft carrying the dad and the kids hit the exit pool with a splash. He waited until all four were safely out of the way, then beckoned to the next group in line. Three giggling preteen girls shuffled over, their arms linked. They wore matching bikinis in blinding pink. Adam thought they looked like a three-headed Barbie. Only without the huge plastic boobs and impossible proportions.

Give 'em ten years. He mentally berated himself for the uncharitable thought, and summoned a smile.

"Sit with your legs crossed," he instructed the three, ignoring the renewed burst of giggles. "Keep your arms and legs inside the raft, and stay seated at all times. You with the shades, take 'em off and hold them in your hand."

The girls climbed into the raft. The blonde removed her heart-shaped pink sunglasses and gave him a prepubescent version of a come-hither look. *Christ, not even if I was straight,* he thought, horrified, and shoved the raft rather harder than was necessary.

A husky laugh at his right shoulder made Adam jump. "Dude, that little chicklet was *totally* into you."

Adam whirled around and found himself staring into a face that would definitely be lobster-red within the hour. A fall of glossy black hair streaked with crimson partially obscured the milky pale face. Adam would've bet his last dollar there was black eyeliner under those wraparound sunglasses.

Goth, Adam decided. He jerked his thumb toward the line of people trailing down the wooden steps to the ground a couple hundred feet below. "Line's there. No cutting."

"Naw, I'm here to replace Marcy." The boy stuck his hand out, evidently unfazed by Adam's back-off attitude. "I'm Buzz. Pleased to meet you."

Adam took the offered hand and shook it, hoping he'd heard wrong. "You work here?"

Buzz grinned, and Adam scowled. *Why'd he have to have dimples? And such pretty lips? Shit, shit, shit.*

"First day, yeah." Buzz let go of Adam's hand and reached for Marcy's. "Hey, sorry I'm late. I had trouble getting away from Neil."

Marcy laughed. "No problem, I understand. Neil's a good boss, for the most part, but he does get long-winded. Have you been shown what to do here?"

"Nope," Buzz said cheerfully. "But it's okay. Happy Boy here can show me how it works. I'm a quick learner."

Happy Boy. Great. Adam drew a deep breath and forced himself to smile, ignoring Marcy's snicker. "My name's Adam Holderman. I'll show you what to do, sure. There's not much to it."

"Well, I'm off, you boys have fun." Marcy slipped on her flip-flops and headed for the stairs, giving Adam's arm a squeeze as she passed. "Nice to meet you, Buzz."

"You too." Buzz hooked both thumbs in the waistband of his black-and-red trunks, which hung dangerously low on his slender hips. "So. Happy. Gonna show me how this operation works?"

Adam bit back a groan. It was going to be a long afternoon.

☞☞☞☞

The next two hours proved a couple of things to Adam. One, Buzz really was a quick learner. He had the routine down within the initial few runs. Not that it was all that hard, but most newbies were a little more awkward to start with. Two, Buzz must be in possession of the strongest sunblock known to man, because his skin remained flawlessly alabaster except for a faint rosy glow painting his cheeks, nose and shoulders.

Adam still remembered the sunburn he'd gotten on his first day. Anyone who had the audacity to keep his ghostly complexion intact after spending a couple of hours in the southern Alabama sun deserved to be hated.

The problem was, Buzz was impossible to hate. The incessant "dude"ing aside, he had an open, friendly and easygoing personality that drew Adam like a beetle to a porch light. Of course the hard, lean body didn't hurt any. Neither did the full lips, or the dimples, or the frequent laughter. And his hair was sexy as hell, razored short-short in the back and falling over his face in the front.

I do believe you're gettin' sweet on that boy, the Scarlett-voice declared.

"Am not," Adam muttered, catching the raft coming off the conveyor belt.

"Not what?" Buzz asked as he beckoned a pair of teen girls over.

"Nothing." Plastering on his best Customer Service smile, Adam gallantly held out a hand to help one of the girls into the raft. "Keep your arms and legs in the raft and remain seated at all times."

"Thanks." The girl gave him an appraising look. "Can I come back later and give you my number?"

Adam stifled a sigh. Girls were always coming on to him, though he could never figure out why. He'd always thought women liked the square-jawed, no-neck, Alpha-dog type, but his own experience didn't bear that out. They seemed to find his baby face and perpetual bedhead irresistible. His female friends assured him girls fell all over him because of his slim, athletic build and the enormous eyes his sister had once jealously dubbed "aquamarine". Adam privately thought all women were on a mission to flirt the gayness out of him.

"No, thank you," he told the girl as politely as he could.

Her eyes widened. "No? Why not?"

Adam blushed. He hated telling perfect strangers he was gay. "I...um..."

"He's seeing someone," Buzz interjected, flashing a dimpled grin. "Now, if you could just sit down, please?"

The girl huffed, but sat in the raft with her friend. Buzz shoved the raft over the edge, waving at the girls as they whirled off down the tunnel.

"I'm not seeing anybody," Adam said, and instantly wished he hadn't. *Real smooth, Casanova.*

"Excellent." Buzz lifted his sunglasses, revealing a pair of smoky blue gray eyes rimmed in—*yes! I knew it!*—black eyeliner. "Wanna go out?"

Adam's jaw dropped. "What?"

"You. Me. Go out." Buzz slid his shades back into place. "You know, like a date."

"A date?"

"Yeah. Dinner. A movie. Making out in the backseat. Or haven't you ever been on a date?"

"I...uh..."

Buzz crossed his arms and cocked his head to the side. "You *are* gay, right?"

"Um, yeah. Er..." Adam felt the conversation slipping out of his control. *You mean you had control at some point?* He licked his lips, trying to think of something to say that wouldn't make him sound like a complete idiot. Nothing came to mind.

Chuckling, Buzz shook his head. "Dude, chill. It's no big deal if you don't want to go out with me. We can still be buds, yeah?"

Not waiting for an answer, Buzz leaned over and grabbed the handle of the next raft. Adam caught the scent of sunblock and sweat and spicy cologne under the ever-present chlorine smell, and felt a sudden rush of desire.

Shit. Fuck. Fuck, fuck, fuck.

"Um. Yeah, sure." Adam bit his lip. *Naked grandmas,* he thought, desperate to rid himself of the tent forming in his trunks. *Neil and his wife having sex. Preteen girls coming on to you.*

That did it. He let out a grateful sigh as his cock deflated.

"Cool." Buzz clapped him on the shoulder, then turned his megawatt smile to the next person in line.

Adam brushed off the twinge of disappointment. He did *not* want to go out with Buzz. He didn't date Goth-surfer-skate-punks, or whatever the hell Buzz was with his striped hair and eyeliner. He didn't.

Watching the play of lean muscles in Buzz's back, Adam wondered how much trouble he was going to have convincing his libido of that.

♋♋♋

Buzz asked him out again the next day, while they were working the side-by-side water slides in the children's area.

"We don't have to, you know..." Putting a thumb and forefinger together in a circle, Buzz made a decidedly lewd gesture with his other hand. "We can just catch a show or something."

A blush crept up Adam's neck and into his cheeks. "Good grief, Buzz. Do you have to do that?"

"What?" Buzz lifted a towheaded toddler into position at the top of the slide and nudged him down the yellow plastic slope. "Are you worried about the kids? C'mon, they don't know what that means."

"Doesn't matter. What if one of them goes home and shows their parents the neat hand gesture they learned from the guy on the slide? You'd get fired."

"Good point." Buzz waited until Adam sent a little girl in a SpongeBob swimsuit down the slide, then leaned close enough for Adam to catch his sun-and-sweat scent. "So what about it? There's a poetry slam at Darkshines tonight, wanna go?"

He's courtin' you, Scarlett purred. *You're not going to turn him down again, are you? Such an attractive young man.*

"No thanks," Adam answered, ignoring Scarlett and her prodding. No way was he spending his evening listening to a bunch of emo kids recite their overwrought odes to misery, even if he *did* want to go out with Buzz. Which he didn't.

Really.

"We don't have to—"

"Yeah, you said that," Adam interrupted before Buzz could make it even clearer. "I'm not really a fan of poetry slams."

Buzz shrugged. "Suit yourself, dude."

He turned back to his work, seemingly unaffected by Adam's refusal. To Adam's annoyance, part of him felt stung by the fact that Buzz didn't continue the pursuit.

Stop it, he admonished himself, helping a gangly preteen boy settle his baby sister on his lap for a trip down the slide. *What are you, an eighth-grade girl? You don't want to go out with him anyway. He's not your type.*

Inside his head, Scarlett chuckled. *Honey, that boy's hotter than blacktop in July, and he's got a hankerin' for you. Tell him you changed your mind.*

"But I didn't," he blurted. "I don't want to."

Shoving his sunglasses on top of his head, Buzz shot Adam a puzzled look. "What'd you say?"

Adam cringed. When would he learn not to answer Scarlett out loud? "Nothing," he mumbled. "Just talking to myself."

Buzz laughed. "You're weird."

You have no idea. Adam kept that thought to himself.

Chapter Two

In the weeks that followed, Adam and Buzz fell into an easy routine. They were assigned together more often than not, and on the days they weren't, they would meet up on their lunch break and talk. Topics of conversation were nothing particularly thought-provoking—movies, sports, gossip about their coworkers—but Adam found himself looking forward to their time together.

It was surprising, and a bit disconcerting, to realize how comfortable he'd become with Buzz. He'd known the man for only a month, but he felt more relaxed with him than he did with people he'd known for years. He figured it was mostly due to Buzz's easygoing nature. The man accepted Adam's idiosyncrasies with a Zen sort of calm like Adam had never encountered before. It was nice to spend time with someone who didn't constantly tell him he should do this, or be that, or act this other way. He got more than he could stand of that from his parents and other friends.

Ironically, the fact that Buzz had asked him out every single day since they'd met made it easier to not take him seriously. It had become sort of a game between them, with Buzz inviting Adam to the most outrageous events—like drag queen mud wrestling, which Adam still maintained Buzz had made up—and Adam turning him down with a smile and a shake of his head.

Of course, every time Buzz sidled up to him and requested his company for the evening, it became a little harder to say no. It threw Adam completely off kilter to think about that, so he tried not to.

Not that the ignore-it-and-it'll-go-away approach had ever worked in the past.

He didn't want to think about that either.

"School's starting back next week," Buzz observed through a mouthful of veggie burger one day at the end of August. "You gonna keep working after you go back?"

"No, I have a full class load. Next Saturday's my last day." Popping a corn chip into his mouth, Adam crunched it up and swallowed. "What about you? The park closes for the winter at the end of next month, do you have something else lined up?" He already knew Buzz didn't attend college. Not that he held that against him. Adam wanted the security of a business degree, but he'd never held to the notion that a college education was necessary for everyone.

Buzz nodded, taking a long swallow of the mango-flavored water he always drank. "I already work part-time at Best Buy, I'm just gonna go full-time."

Adam laughed. "Geek Squad, right?"

"Right you are, Happy Boy." Grinning, Buzz stole one of Adam's Fritos. "I'm damn good with computers and stuff."

They fell silent. Adam shoved the last bite of his chicken sandwich into his mouth, watching Buzz drag a clump of fries through the God-awful ketchup, mustard and salsa concoction he always ate. Something about the way the sun glinted off the red streaks in his hair made Adam's insides twist.

As Buzz tilted his head back and crammed the entire handful of red-and-yellow smeared fries into his mouth, Adam realized the days of low-key flirting and banter over lunch trays were about to come to an end. And he didn't want them to. His throat constricted.

Buzz frowned, took his sunglasses off and pinned Adam with a keen look. "Dude, you okay? You look like your dog just died or something."

Don't say it, Adam warned himself, but the part of him which always got lost in Buzz's eyes had already seized control of his tongue and wasn't about to let go. "I was just thinking how much I'll miss hanging out with you."

Buzz's eyebrows shot up, and Adam groaned inwardly. *Why, why, why can you not keep your big mouth shut? Now he'll get the wrong idea, idiot.*

Seems to me it wouldn't be the wrong idea at all, Scarlett chimed in.

Adam ignored that. He didn't much like how true it felt.

For a few heartbeats, Buzz didn't say a word, just stared hard enough to bore holes in Adam's skull. Adam hunched his shoulders and dropped his gaze to the corn chip crumbs littering the red tabletop.

"We don't have to stop hanging out just because we won't be working together anymore." Buzz's hand closed around Adam's wrist, his fingers warm and slightly damp, and Adam had to fight off the urge to jump across the table and rip Buzz's swim trunks off. "Hey. Look at me."

Adam reluctantly obeyed, both wanting and dreading what he figured he'd see. The uncharacteristically serious expression on Buzz's face surprised him.

"Go out with me?" Buzz asked, his voice devoid of its usual teasing tone.

148

"Okay." Adam blinked, as stunned by his own answer as he'd been by the grave manner in which Buzz had asked this time. "You still want to go out with me?"

"I've been asking you every day for a month. What do you think?"

"Okay, yeah, but I've been turning you down every day. Most people would've given up by now."

Buzz's face broke into a smile that promised all sorts of sin. "I am not most people."

"You got that right." Adam let his mouth curve into a grin. "So. What are we doing?"

"Don't know. I hadn't really thought about it, since you never said yes before." Tilting his head sideways and thus baring a stretch of throat Adam desperately wanted to bite, Buzz scratched his chin. "Want to hook up after our shifts are over and just see what happens?"

"Okay, sure."

They stared at each other. *I will not molest him in the middle of the snack bar,* Adam chanted to himself. *I won't, I won't, I won't.*

With a look suggesting he could read minds, Buzz stood, walked around the table and bent down so that his lips brushed Adam's ear. "You can ravage me later, Happy," he whispered, and flicked Adam's earlobe with his tongue. "I've been dying to spread for you since day one."

All the blood drained from Adam's brain, making a beeline for his crotch, and he groaned.

Buzz let out a throaty chuckle that did nothing to lessen Adam's desire to bend him over the table, sandwich wrappers and Frito crumbs be damned. "Come on," Buzz said, straightening up. "Gotta go back to work now."

Adam had to wait a couple of minutes before he could stand without scandalizing everyone in a fifty-foot radius. Buzz laughed, and Adam wondered what it meant, exactly, that he'd still rather kiss Buzz than hit him.

♋♋♋♋

Four hours later, Jane and Rita came on shift, and Adam and Buzz were free to go. Buzz took Adam's hand as they made their way through the throng of sunburned families and teenagers on dates. A hot flush crept into Adam's face. He could sense everyone staring at them. It was uncomfortable as hell, but not enough to make him let go. The feel of Buzz's long, slim fingers laced through his was too good to give up.

Adam's Inner Scarlett chuckled. *Why, sugar, I do believe you might get lucky tonight.*

Why, Scarlett, I do believe you may be right. He grinned, ridiculously pleased with how well things seemed to be going.

They strolled toward the locker room hand in hand, not talking, but smiling at each other from time to time. Buzz had pushed his sunglasses up on top of his head, making his long bangs stick up in a way Adam found enchanting. Every few seconds, those pretty eyes would rake down Adam's body. Adam swore he could feel the warmth of those hungry looks, and wondered idly if Buzz had heat vision or something. *Like Superman,* he mused, picturing Buzz in blue spandex and a cape.

The mental image was more amusing than arousing, and Adam stifled a laugh.

"What's funny?" Buzz asked, pushing open the door to the men's locker room.

"Nothing." Adam let go of Buzz's hand and crossed the room to his locker. "Can I ask you something?"

"Sure." Buzz went to his own locker and started dialing the combination to his padlock. "What?"

"Is Buzz your real name?"

"Took you long enough to ask."

"Yeah, well, I'm asking now." Turning around, Adam leaned against the bank of lockers and crossed his arms. "So is it?"

"Nope."

Adam waited, but it seemed Buzz was content to leave it there. Adam was not. "So, what's your real name? And why do you go by Buzz?"

Sighing, Buzz rested his forehead against the wall. "Promise you won't laugh?"

"No," Adam answered, not wanting to lie since he had no idea what Buzz was about to say. *If his name's Priscilla, there's no way I'm not laughing.* "But I'll try not to. Will you still tell me?"

One corner of Buzz's mouth lifted in a sly smile. "Myron Stiles."

Adam blinked a couple of times, then threw his head back and laughed until tears rolled down his cheeks. In all his life, he'd never seen anyone who looked less like a Myron.

"Dude, come on," Buzz—*no, Myron! hahaha!*—grumbled. "It's not that fucking funny."

"Okay, okay, I'm sorry." Adam wiped his streaming eyes on a mostly clean towel from his locker. Buzz stood with his arms crossed, glaring daggers at Adam, and Adam felt a twinge of guilt. "It's just that Myron doesn't suit you. You look more like a... I don't know. Something sexier than Myron."

Instantly, the hurt in Buzz's eyes vanished, replaced by a hot lust that made Adam's prick sit up and take notice. Leaving his locker open, Buzz crossed the room and pressed his body against Adam's.

"You think I'm sexy?" Buzz asked, his voice low and rough and practically dripping with seduction.

Oh, honey-child, he's good, the Scarlett-voice chortled. *I bet he gets more cock than the last hen in a barnyard full of roosters.*

And tonight he's getting mine. In his ass and in his mouth, though not necessarily in that order, because, ew. Unless we fuck in the shower, because there's soap and I can wash my dick after I fuck him and then it wouldn't be gross for him to suck me off after. Of course maybe it's not gross to him anyway, how do I know?

Scarlett tsked at him. *Honey, you'd best pay attention. You don't want your daydreamin' to cost you your chance with this pretty li'l thing, hm?*

As usual, she was right. A hint of uncertainty had crept into Buzz's eyes, and Adam wanted—no, *needed*—to make it go away.

Sliding his arms around Buzz's waist, Adam gave a tiny thrust of his hips, pushing his rapidly stiffening prick against Buzz's thigh. Buzz's lips parted on a soft gasp, and Adam felt like emperor of the universe. "Yeah. I think you're sexy."

Buzz licked his lips, his gaze flicking lightning quick to Adam's mouth and back to his eyes. "Dude, the feeling is *totally* mutual."

Oh, sugar, he's gonna kiss you. From her floral-print chaise in Adam's mind, Scarlett clapped her hands in delight. Adam ignored her, because she was right and he wanted his full attention on Buzz and those gorgeous lips. He leaned forward at the same time as Buzz.

Their noses bumped, then Buzz tilted his head and his mouth covered Adam's and it was amazing.

Adam closed his eyes and lost himself in the kiss. Buzz tasted like French fries and salt and a surprisingly appealing mixture of condiments. His hands came up to frame Adam's face, thumbs caressing his cheeks. It was oddly tender considering how little they really knew about each other, but Adam wasn't about to complain. Now that he'd made up his mind to give in to his attraction, he wanted to enjoy every second. Sliding his hands down to Buzz's ass, he got a double handful and squeezed, making Buzz moan in the most wonderful way.

The locker room door banged open, and Adam nearly jumped out of his skin. He groaned when Kevin, Ross and Connor—the three most homophobic lifeguards ever spawned—sauntered in. Their shifts hadn't intersected with Adam's in weeks. Wouldn't it just have to be *now*.

Land's sake, I do believe they saw you boys kissin'.

No fucking kidding, genius.

Before Adam could say a word, or even let go of Buzz, Kevin pointed at them and bellowed, "What the fuck, Adam? Were you and him just *kissing?*"

For a heartbeat, Buzz's eyes blazed with anger. Then he seemed to shake himself, and turned a blandly friendly smile to the three lifeguards.

He strode forward with his hand out. "I've seen you guys around, but we've never been introduced. I'm Buzz, nice to meet you."

Adam watched with interest as Kevin, Connor and Ross all shook Buzz's hand and introduced themselves, the expressions of shock and disgust still plastered to their faces. He wondered if it was some sort of Pavlovian response. You see a hand held out in greeting, you shake it and introduce yourself, in spite of the danger of catching Gayness.

Mindin' their manners, like their mamas taught 'em.

Adam grimaced. *And thinking me and Buzz are evil and going to hell. Just like their mamas taught them.*

Ross crossed his burly arms and scowled at them. "We don't want you fags doing your fag business in here."

Fag business? Adam snorted, earning him a glare from Ross.

Tilting his head to the side, Buzz gave Ross a considering look. "I guess this means you wouldn't be willing to accept the position of Fag/Non-Fag Liaison."

Ross's thick eyebrows drew together in confusion. "Huh?"

"Whores," Connor hissed, his face an angry red that clashed violently with his carrot-colored hair. "Filthy fag whores! Don't try spreading your seeds of evil here."

"Of course," Buzz continued, not missing a beat, "there are many other excellent opportunities for enterprising young people such as yourselves at Filthy Fag Whores, Incorporated. Give my secretary your number. My people will call your people, we'll do lunch. Now if you'll excuse me, Happy Boy and I are in the middle of a meeting of the Committee for Spreading Seeds of Evil. You'll have to come back later."

To Adam's immense surprise, all three lifeguards turned around and filed out of the room. At least they were heading for the showers. If they actually went back outside, Adam would've been forced to conclude that either they were even dumber than he'd thought, or Buzz had mind-control powers.

Actually, Adam was inclined to believe the latter. How else was he supposed to explain the fact that he was now dating a "dude"-spouting, eyeliner-wearing, apparently three-quarters insane Goth boy? That was so *not* his usual type.

"Get your stuff," Buzz ordered, snatching his ubiquitous black T-shirt and baggy shorts out of his locker and slamming it shut. "We should probably leave before they figure out how pissed they are at me."

Removing the duffle bag with his clothes and toiletries in it, Adam shut his locker and clicked the padlock closed. "How the hell did you do that?" he demanded as they left the locker room.

"Best way to deal with the 'phobes, dude. Confuse 'em." Buzz grinned. "It's usually not too hard."

"Not with those three, for sure. They are *collectively* dumber than a bag of hammers." Adam let out a chuckle. "Filthy Fag Whores, Incorporated. You're crazy."

"Hey, I'm just pimpin' the fag business."

Adam laughed loudly enough that people stared as they passed by. For once, he didn't care. So what if Buzz made him laugh? It was no one else's business, and it was nothing to be ashamed of.

Acting on a whim, Adam looped his arm around Buzz's shoulders. He was going for cool and casual, but he had a feeling it came off as desperate and horny instead. Not that Buzz seemed to mind. His arm went around Adam's waist, his hand slipping into the back pocket of Adam's trunks to gently squeeze his ass.

They both turned their heads, their eyes met, and a tingle went up Adam's spine. He felt like he was back in high school, sneaking a kiss with his first real boyfriend at the church picnic. The giddy thrill of it was the same, only better because he no longer felt the need to hide it from the rest of the world.

Not here, anyway. In his own environment—at work, at school, in his apartment in a building full of college students being rebellious—he could be himself, and no one would fault him for it. No one he gave a damn about, anyhow. However, if his mother saw him right now, walking hip to hip and arm in arm with another man, he'd have to break out the smelling salts.

I won't think about that right now. I'll think about that later.

"So," Buzz said, tightening his arm around Adam's waist. "Got any ideas where to go?"

Adam pursed his lips, thinking. A crowd of dripping children ran past, shrieking with laughter, pursued by a hefty woman in a flowered one-piece and bright orange flip-flops. Her matching flowered miniskirt ruffled around her dimpled thighs as she trotted after the youngsters, grumbling under her breath.

"Let's go clubbing," Adam suggested, watching the flowered woman swat a recalcitrant toddler on the butt. "I think I've had my fill of families for one day."

Buzz snickered. "I hear you. I want to shower and change first, what about you?"

"Yeah." Leaning closer, Adam nuzzled Buzz's hair. The glossy locks smelled like coconut. "Where do you live? I'll come pick you up."

"Sounds good." Buzz tilted his head up for a quick kiss as they reached the front gate and went into the small office to punch out. "You got something to write on? So I can give you my address?"

"Yeah, in my glove compartment."

After they clocked out, they left the office and crossed the parking lot. On the other side, the westering sun flung long shadows from the pines edging the asphalt. Adam's car sat in deep and blessed shade, which was why he always parked here. Sitting out in one-hundred-degree heat for six to eight hours, he'd quickly discovered, nearly melted his leather seats. Snagging a spot which would be in the shade for most of the afternoon made for a much more comfortable ride home.

Buzz let out an admiring whistle when they reached Adam's car. "Dude, sweet! A Viper." Pulling away from Adam's side, Buzz ran his fingers over the smooth curve of the midnight blue hood. "Wish I'd asked to check out your ride sooner. Ninety-seven, right?"

Adam puffed up a little. He couldn't help it. He fucking *loved* his car. "Yeah. Got it cheap from my parents' next-door neighbor. Her husband left it when he ran off to Italy with some girl he met online. I think she sold it just to get back at him. She knew what she had, but she just wanted to get rid of it."

"Lucky for you." Buzz sidled up to Adam and wound both arms around his neck. "You know what?"

"What?"

"Muscle cars make me horny."

Adam grinned. "Yeah?"

"Yeah." Buzz rubbed his crotch against Adam's thigh, sending a dizzying wave of lust through Adam's brain. "You know what I want right now?"

"Um. No." *But God, if it's what I think it is, I'm gonna come in my pants.*

"What I want," Buzz murmured, lips brushing Adam's ear, "is for you to bend me over this fucking sweet hood and fuck me."

Oh my, Scarlett tittered, furiously fanning her nonexistent self. Adam closed his eyes and conjured an image of the flowery mother to keep from shooting like a virgin on prom night. It worked, thankfully. He licked his lips, trying to find his voice.

"I'd love to fuck you across the hood of my Viper," he said, with absolute sincerity. "Later. When it's dark, and we're not in the Wild Waters parking lot."

"Deal." Snaking a hand between Adam's legs, Buzz gave his crotch a squeeze. Adam squealed, and Buzz laughed. "Get your little black book and write down my address, Happy Boy, before I lose it and have to sit on your cock right here."

Now, that's mighty temptin'.

Mighty tempting, indeed. Tempting enough to get them both fired and/or arrested. Resolutely ignoring the Scarlett-voice telling him to drag Buzz into the trees for a quickie, Adam fished his car keys out of his bag and opened the door. The sooner he got Buzz's address, the sooner he could peel the man out of the Goth-boy clothes he was sure to be wearing later.

He was halfway home, already daydreaming of pounding his cock into Buzz's ass, when he realized the sneaky bastard had never said how he got the nickname "Buzz".

Damn.

Sugar, you got all night to sweet-talk it out of him. Once you start lovin' on that boy, he'll tell you anything you want to know.

One thing about his inner Scarlett was she was almost always right. He grinned. The night was definitely looking up.

∽∽∽∽

While he showered, dressed and made the requisite vain attempt to tame his hair, Adam pondered the possibilities for the night ahead. There were lots of clubs in downtown Mobile, including a wide variety of gay spots. He could picture Buzz in a place like Bela's, with its black walls and earsplitting death metal music, but he hated Bela's and really hoped Buzz didn't want to go there. On the other hand, Buzz would be sadly out of place in Adam's favorite club, The Top Hat. Somehow, he didn't think Buzz went for smooth jazz and a Rat-Pack-cool atmosphere.

Honey, you ever met a beau at that place? Scarlett arched a phantom brow at him. *Let your young man decide. Let him take charge. Use your feminine wiles.*

"Whoa, wait just a fucking minute." Adam pointed a stern finger at his reflection in the bathroom mirror. "You, missy, are overstepping your bounds. I don't have any stupid wiles. I am not a girl."

Except for the girl who seems to be stuck in your brain, he reminded himself sourly as he turned away and went to get dressed for his date.

Part of him still couldn't believe he was actually going out with Buzz. It galled him that he'd gone loopy for a guy who painted his toenails black and knew the words to every Joy Division song by heart. How, he wondered, could he take someone like that seriously?

His long-neglected sex drive pointed out that he didn't need to take Buzz seriously in order to fuck him blind. Adam nodded to himself and decided that made perfect sense.

He ignored the part of him which insisted he wanted more than sex. *I can't think about that right now. I'll think about that tomorrow.*

The phone rang just as he was about to leave. Grumbling, he snatched the receiver from the cradle. "What?" he barked.

"Adam, mind your manners."

He groaned. "Mom, I was just getting ready to go out."

Her long-suffering sigh set his teeth on edge. "I won't keep you long. I know you don't have time for an old woman like me."

"You know that's not true," Adam answered through clenched teeth. "It's just that I have a date. I need to leave or I'm going to be late."

"Do your father and I get to meet this one?"

Jesus, I hope not. "Mom, did you need something?"

She sighed again, and Adam barely stifled the urge to bang his head on the wall. "We're having a little get-together with the Taylors tomorrow night. Sharon's going to be there, I thought you might want to come and keep her company."

Adam grimaced. George and Eileen Taylor were his parents' oldest friends. They were decent enough people, in their own clueless way. But their daughter Sharon was, in Adam's opinion, a complete skank and he couldn't imagine any man wanting her unless he had a herpes fetish.

"I sort of promised Megan I'd go to church with her tomorrow night," he lied. His mother adored his friend Megan, and what kind of mother would complain about her son going to church?

"Oh, I see. Well, tell Megan hello for me. Such a nice girl."

Adam bit back a laugh. He could practically see the gleam in his mother's eyes. "I will. Talk to you later, Mom. Love you."

"Love you too, baby. Have fun on your date."

"Oh, I will. Bye." Smiling, Adam hung up the phone.

Chapter Three

Fifteen minutes later, he pulled his Viper up in front of a house that looked like it ought to be condemned. Frowning, he flicked on the overhead light and checked the paper in his hand, then stared at the lopsided number nailed to one of the front porch pillars. 147 Poinciana Street. This was the place, all right. At least there were signs of life. Light poured from every window of the two-story structure, and he thought he could hear the pounding bass of someone's stereo turned up too loud.

"Good grief," Adam muttered. Shaking his head, he killed the engine and climbed out of the car.

The porch steps squealed alarmingly under his weight. He breathed a sigh of relief when he got to the front door. Glancing behind him to make sure no one had stolen his car while he wasn't looking, he knocked on the door.

Just when he was starting to think Buzz hadn't heard him and he should knock again, the door flew open. The bass grew abruptly louder and defined itself into a song Adam vaguely recognized, but he forgot all about the music when he saw Buzz.

Adam's mouth fell open. It was the same gorgeous face and sexy body which had starred in his masturbatory fantasies for the last month, but everything else had changed. The black hair was now dark auburn and cut close to the scalp. The eyeliner was gone, making him look both older and younger. He wore khaki shorts and a dark blue T-shirt.

It was such a shocking change, Adam had no idea how to deal with it. He felt strangely disappointed.

"Wow," Adam managed. "You look... I mean, I didn't expect... Um..." He winced. *You're blowing it, dumb-ass, say something not stupid now before he tells you to go away.*

The man at the door laughed. "You must be Adam. Come on in, Buzz'll be right down."

Adam blinked. "What? But, but you're Buzz. Right?"

"Wrong." Flashing a very familiar dimpled grin, the man held out a hand. "I'm Jordan. We're twins."

The light bulb went on in Adam's brain, and he sagged with relief. Smiling, he took Jordan's hand and shook it. "Nice to meet you, Jordan. Yes, I'm Adam."

Jordan walked over to the foot of the stairs. "Buzz!" he shouted. "Adam's here, get your ass down here." His eyes twinkled as he ushered Adam in and shut the door. "Buzz hasn't shut up about you ever since he started at Wild Waters. I can see why."

"Are you gay too?" Adam blurted before he thought about what he was saying. Mentally smacking himself, he gave Jordan a sheepish smile. "Sorry. I've never known twins before."

"That's okay. We've gotten weirder questions before. No, I'm not gay. Me and my girlfriend, Tanya, are getting married in a couple of months. But hey, I'm secure enough to admit when a guy's hot. Buzz always did have good taste."

Blushing, Adam stuck his hands in the back pockets of his jeans and ducked his head. "Thanks." He glanced around, casting about for something to say. "This place is pretty nice inside."

"Thanks. Buzz has been living here rent-free since I bought it last year. He's been helping me fix it up. The outside's still shit, but at least it's livable where it counts."

"Yeah." A sudden thought struck Adam, and he went with it. Leaning closer to Jordan, he dropped his voice to a whisper. "How did he get the nickname Buzz? I asked earlier, but he...um, distracted me, and I never found out."

Jordan shot him an amused look. "I just bet he 'distracted' you. Hey, you seem like a great guy, but I can't tell you that. I like my balls right where they are, thanks."

"Dude, don't be telling my date about your balls. I don't want him thinking about any balls but mine."

Startled, Adam turned toward Buzz's voice. Buzz bounded down the stairs, looking like a wet dream in low-slung black jeans and a tight red Dirty On Purpose T-shirt that bared a strip of flat, creamy belly. His eyes glittered with something undefinable that made Adam's heart race, and his pale cheeks were flushed.

Adam wanted to lick him all over.

"Hey, Happy Boy." Buzz strode over to Adam, threw both arms around his neck and planted a wet, open-mouthed kiss on his lips. Taken by surprise, Adam went with his gut and let himself respond, pulling Buzz close and opening his mouth for Buzz's tongue. A sharp thrill shot through him when he realized Buzz was semi-erect in those snug jeans.

That's for you, honey, Scarlett purred.

I know. Adam thrust his pelvis against Buzz's, just to hear his faint, lusty moan.

Beside them, Jordan cleared his throat. "Maybe you guys should just skip the going-out part and head on up to Buzz's room."

Buzz laughed, bit Adam's chin and pulled out of his arms. "What's wrong, *Melvin*? Are we turning you gay with our hot manlove?"

"Never gonna happen, *Myron*," Jordan shot back with the practiced ease of someone who'd been doing it for years. "I'm happy with my girl." He grinned at Adam. "Jordan's my middle name," he said, answering the question Adam had thought but hadn't asked. "It's what everybody but my brother calls me."

Buzz shook his head in mock sadness. "One day, bro, I'm gonna turn you." Cupping his twin's face in both hands, Buzz planted a light kiss right on his lips. "We're out of here. Don't wait up, dude. Tell Tanya I said hi."

Adam managed a vague wave in Jordan's direction as Buzz grabbed his wrist and dragged him outside. *Twincest!* the not-Scarlett part of his brain screamed. *Oh my God, that's hot!*

Buzz gave him a knowing look. "You're thinking about me and my brother fucking, aren't you?"

Adam almost dropped his car keys. "Wh-what makes you think I was thinking that?" he quavered, managing to unlock the doors and slide behind the wheel. "I wasn't—"

"Oh yes you were." Buzz plopped into the passenger seat, his face fixed in a trouble-making grin. "Everybody seems to think that. Used to freak us out, but we got used to it. It's kind of fun to fuck with people's heads, you know? Make 'em think we're doing each other. I *totally* don't get it, but whatever. Gotta go with the flow, right?"

"Uh. Right." Adam started the car and backed out of the driveway. "So, where did you want to go? I'm easy."

Buzz slid a hand onto Adam's thigh. "I sure hope so."

"Oh, shit," Adam groaned, barely avoiding someone's barn-shaped mailbox. "Buzz, come on, give me a break. I'll wreck if you keep doing that."

Buzz pouted. His hand didn't move. "But I'm really horny tonight. I'm dying to touch you."

"Is there actually a time when you *aren't* really horny?" Adam squealed like a little girl when Buzz's fingers wandered higher. "Dammit, stop. Please."

Laughing, Buzz pulled his hand away. "I guess that means you don't want me to go down on you while you're driving, huh?"

The mental picture was nearly enough to make Adam soil his jeans. In his head, Scarlett shook her ringlets sadly. *Sugar, it's been way too long since you've bedded a man.*

Thanks for the newsflash, Scarlett.

"Buzz, after we go out and get to know each other better, you can do whatever you want to my body," Adam promised, and meant it. "But right now, I really want to live to experience it, so no, I don't want you to go down on me while I'm driving. Not that I don't appreciate the offer."

Buzz let out an exaggerated sigh. "Oh well, I tried." He turned sideways in the seat and grinned. "Hey, wanna drive over to the beach? We could hit the Purple Palomino."

"That's the gayest place on the planet," Adam said. He'd been before and hadn't hated it, but it surprised him Buzz wanted to go there. The man didn't seem like the type to enjoy the unabashedly flamboyant atmosphere of a place like the Purple Palomino.

"Yeah, I know." Buzz picked a thread from a hole in the knee of his jeans. "We can drink pink beverages with paper umbrellas in them, dance ironically to bad disco music and generally camp it up until we can't stand ourselves. What about it?"

Adam had to admit it sounded fun. "Okay, sure." He shot a quick grin at Buzz. "Too bad neither of us has a leather daddy outfit."

"How do you know I don't? Maybe I have a secret life as a Dom."

The idea was disturbingly exciting, but Adam knew better. No real leather daddy would beg to be fucked over the hood of a car. "Nice try. But hey, there's a shop just down the beach from the Palomino that sells leather gear. We could stock up before we go to the club."

"Happy Boy, I like the way you think." Buzz leaned back in the seat, stuck his hands behind his head and grinned. "Onward, Jeeves. The night's a-wasting."

Laughing, Adam turned the Viper off the narrow little street and onto the main road, heading across Mobile Bay to the beach.

ᏅᏅᏅ

The drive went by quickly. To his surprise, Adam found Buzz's musical tastes to be much more varied than he'd thought. As it turned out, they were both huge fans of Norah Jones and Patrick Wolf. They rolled down the windows and sang along with *Lycanthropy* as the Viper sped along the highway.

As usual, the public beach and adjacent stretch of clubs, restaurants and shops was crawling with people when they arrived. Adam parked in the public beach lot and they walked the block and a half to Daddy-O's hand in hand. Having never been in the place before, it was all Adam could do not to gawk like a tourist as they showed their IDs to the girl at the door and walked inside. He'd always secretly wanted to check the place out, though he'd never dared to go in alone, and had never felt comfortable enough with anyone else to suggest going. The fact that he was entering the store for the first time with Buzz felt a little surreal.

The shop was decorated in blues and purples, managing to give the impression of dangerous darkness in spite of the brightly lit shelves. Throbbing, percussion-heavy music played in the background, loud enough to set the mood without making conversation difficult. Groups, couples and a few lone shoppers mingled among the shelves. They all seemed just like anyone else Adam saw on the street every day.

"Wow," he said, gazing around. "This isn't exactly what I expected."

"Why, what'd you expect?" Buzz turned down a row of shelves containing various anal toys and lube. He ran his fingers over a package containing a realistic-looking rubber fist and forearm. "Dude, check it out. Bet that feels amazing."

Adam winced. "Ouch." Resting an arm across Buzz's shoulders, Adam led him around the corner to the next row. To Adam's relief, it contained nothing to make his anus clench in self-defense. "I don't know what I expected. Big guys in leather clothes leading around slave boys on leashes, I guess. Everybody in here looks like regular people."

"That's 'cause they *are* regular people." Buzz's eyes lit up. He snatched something off the shelf. "Dude, I am *so* getting this."

Adam looked. Buzz held a thick black leather collar with six silver D-rings set in it. *Oh my, now won't that look nice,* Scarlett lilted, reflecting Adam's thoughts almost exactly, if more coherently.

"Yeah, that's good," Adam said, wishing his voice wouldn't shake.

Buzz flashed an evil smile. "I'm getting this too," he added, picking up a long black leather leash. "I can be your slave boy for the night."

What a magnificent idea, Adam attempted to say. What actually came out was an embarrassing squeak.

Buzz pressed his body against Adam's and kissed his throat. "Oh yeah. You like that."

"Definitely," Adam answered, finding his voice at last. "Buzz, unless you want to get fucked right here in the store, you'd better stop it."

Laughing, Buzz flicked his tongue over Adam's pulse point, then pulled away. He swayed over to the other end of the row to peruse the available goods. Adam stared shamelessly at his ass. It was a damn fine ass, and Adam's hands itched to touch it. Seeing no reason why he shouldn't do just that, Adam walked over and planted his palms on Buzz's tempting posterior.

There was something small, flat and rectangular in Buzz's back pocket. Adam traced the outline of it with his thumb, wondering what it was.

Buzz smiled over his shoulder. "Fresh," he teased, wiggling his rear in Adam's grip.

"Yep." Leaning forward, Adam bit Buzz's neck. "What's in your pocket?"

Buzz turned and planted a quick kiss on Adam's lips. "I'll show you later."

Adam frowned. "But why—"

"Oh hey, here you go." Standing on tiptoe, Buzz plucked a black leather biker hat off the top shelf and tossed it to Adam. "You can't be a daddy without the hat."

Adam considered being annoyed at Buzz for not telling him what was in his pocket, but decided it wasn't worth it. He stared at the hat and cracked up. "Shit, I'm gonna look like such a fucking idiot."

"No way, dude, you'll look hot." Buzz draped his arms around Adam's neck and straddled his thigh. "I bet you couldn't look anything but smokin' hot if you tried."

To his supreme mortification, Adam blushed. He'd never understand why anyone thought he was hot. Buzz was hot; Adam, to his own mind, was cute at best. Not knowing what to say, Adam avoided the whole issue by kissing Buzz's seductive smile.

"Let's check out," Adam suggested. "I want to get to the club before the bar gets too crowded."

"Yeah, me too. Let's roll."

Buzz slid a hand down to Adam's butt, ignoring the threesome that wandered down the aisle at that moment. One of the men gave them a wolfish smile. Adam blushed harder and crowded closer to Buzz.

As he and Buzz left the aisle and headed for the register, Adam stole a glance at the threesome. "Buzz, those guys were checking you out."

Buzz gave him the sort of look you'd give a sweet but rather dim child. "Dude, those guys were checking *us* out."

Shaking his head, Adam got in line behind an expensively dressed silver-haired man carrying three huge dildos and what looked like a tub of Crisco. "Why would they even be looking at me? You're the sexy one."

"Why, sugar, you're both perfectly lovely young men. Why on God's green earth would you think gentlemen wouldn't be lookin' at you?"

Adam's mouth fell open. The world tilted on its axis. *Oh my God. No way. No fucking way.*

He forced himself to turn toward the honey-thick female voice coming from behind Buzz. A tiny woman in an ankle-length, high-necked black dress stood there, holding a copy of *Hog-Tied Lesbians* and a wicked-looking whip. She patted her lavender poodle perm and smiled at him.

"Pardon me," she said. "Didn't mean to pry. When you get to be my age, you tend to speak your mind and not fret about what folks think."

"Um. No problem." Adam clutched at the counter, relearning how to breathe. He was relieved to know he wasn't going crazy and even more relieved Scarlett hadn't somehow come to life.

Buzz grinned at the woman. "Lady, thank you for telling him he's hot. Because he is." He gave her a deep bow, causing her to titter behind her hand, then turned back to Adam. His brows drew together in a frown. "You okay? You look kind of green."

"I'm fine," Adam insisted, handing his biker hat to the clerk and digging a wad of twenties out of his wallet. "I just...I thought she was someone else."

Buzz gave him a curious look but kept quiet, for which Adam was grateful. He really didn't want to explain Scarlett just yet. Or, preferably, ever.

After paying for their purchases, they left Daddy-O's and started walking the short distance up the street to the Purple Palomino. A neon sign featuring a prancing purple horse graced the top of the large, sprawling building, which was also purple. Adam privately thought the half-naked cowboys and "ponies" painted on the outside walls were a bit much. But no one had ever accused the Palomino of being subtle, so he supposed it fit the general theme.

Since it was still early, the line to get in was relatively short. As soon as they took their place in line, Buzz tore the tag off his new slave collar and handed it to Adam with a grin. "Put it on me."

"Gladly." Adam buckled the collar around Buzz's neck, standing closer than was strictly necessary and brushing his fingertips against Buzz's silky skin as he worked. "There. Wow, that's hot."

Buzz didn't say anything, just pulled the price tag off the leash and gave it to Adam. His eyes burned. Adam gulped and clipped the leash to the collar. Buzz heaved a soft little sigh that went straight to Adam's groin. Unable to resist, Adam wrapped his arms around Buzz, bent and ran his tongue underneath the edge of the collar. The taste of leather and skin burst on his tongue, and he growled.

Buzz let out a breathless laugh. "Wanna find a private spot someplace?" His fingers toyed with Adam's hair, his neck arching to give Adam's tongue room to play.

"Yes," Adam said, nuzzling behind Buzz's ear. "But we bought this leather stuff, so we're damn well going in the Palomino to show it off."

"Yessir, Daddy." Wriggling out of Adam's embrace, Buzz snatched the leather hat from the bag, yanked the tag off and plopped it onto Adam's head. "There. All set."

Adam puffed his chest out and did his best to look menacing. "I need a mustache. Leather daddies have mustaches."

"You can use my pubes for a mustache, honey," offered one of the men in the group behind Adam and Buzz. He grinned and waggled his eyebrows. "Hey, hot stuff. I'm Larry. Want to lick my balls later?"

Adam rolled his eyes while Larry's companions roared with laughter. Lifting his chin, Buzz faced Larry with a stern expression. "Larry, nobody's balls but mine are going anywhere near my Daddy's face. Got that?"

Larry waved a dismissive hand at Buzz, nearly falling over in the process. "What*ever*. Don't get your panties in a bunch, sweetie."

Larry's friends burst into fresh peals of hilarity. "Ignore Larry, he's already drunk," gasped another member of the group, wiping mirthful tears from his eyes.

"No, you think?" Adam shot Larry and the rest a dark look. "Come on, Buzz. The line's moving."

He tugged on Buzz's leash and Buzz followed. Adam decided he liked having Buzz as a slave boy, even if it was only pretend. He wondered if Buzz would mind too much keeping the collar and leash on later, when Adam was fucking him senseless.

When they reached the head of the line, Adam paid for Buzz's admission as well as his own, silencing Buzz's protest with a look. Keeping a firm hold on the leash, Adam pushed open the padded purple double doors and led Buzz inside. A weirdly compelling mixture of sounds, sights and scents engulfed him. Sweat, smoke, liquor. Pounding music, laughter and shouted conversation. A crowd of men in various stages of undress danced under flashing multicolored lights.

For some reason he couldn't begin to fathom, Adam liked it. Maybe, he mused as he and Buzz made their way to the bar, it was the uninhibited atmosphere of the place. It was seductive in its own flaming way.

"Two tequila shots," Buzz shouted to the bartender. "With lime, not lemon." He turned a questioning look to Adam. "That okay?"

"Yeah, fine. Thanks." He reached into his pocket for his wallet, but Buzz stopped him with a hand around his wrist.

"I'm buying," Buzz told him.

"You don't have to."

"I know that, doofus. I want to."

Buzz gave Adam a smile that melted him into his Converse, then turned back to the bartender and slapped a handful of bills on the bar. Figuring he might as well let Buzz buy him a drink, Adam leaned an elbow on the bar beside his date—*your date!*—and took the shot glass in front of him. He licked the side of his hand and sprinkled salt on it, watching with undisguised lust as Buzz did the same.

"To daddies, slave boys and gay disco joints," Adam said, holding up his glass.

"Amen, brother."

They clinked their glasses together, licked the salt off their hands and tossed back their drinks. Eyes watering, Adam snatched up a piece of lime from the little plate the bartender had provided and bit into it, sucking out the tart juice. The corner of his brain not being mauled by tequila decided lime was indeed superior to lemon.

Before Adam had recovered enough to do more than stand there with his eyes crossed, Buzz let out a whoop and threw himself into Adam's arms. Adam caught him more by instinct than design, staggered for a second, recovered his balance and hung on. Buzz's mouth latched onto his in a deep, aggressive kiss, and Adam didn't even consider resisting. He closed his eyes and went with it, drinking in the tastes of tequila, lime and salt on Buzz's tongue. Buzz's scent sank into his brain, shampoo and skin and spicy cologne, more intoxicating than the liquor coursing through his veins.

Not for the first time, Adam marveled at the fact that this was truly happening. He was really here, making out with a sexy Goth boy in a gay disco. In a million years, he'd never have predicted it.

"We should move," Buzz breathed, running his tongue over Adam's lips. "Other people probably want to get to the bar."

Adam nodded. "Yeah. Want to dance?"

"Sure." Drawing back, Buzz gave him a brilliant smile. "Dude, you have no fucking idea how horny I am for you."

"Oh good. I hate being the only horny one."

Buzz laughed, and Adam laughed with him. Winding the leash around his wrist, Adam led Buzz into the writhing crowd on the dance floor.

Adam had been dancing before. He'd even been dancing at the Purple Palomino before. But this was different. His usual feeling of being awkward and out of place was gone, replaced by an effortless sensuality like he'd never experienced in his life. He and Buzz moved together with an almost frightening synchronicity. Adam didn't want to examine this new sensation too hard, for fear it would vanish like the dream he half feared it was. Maybe Buzz was always this graceful and intuitive when he danced, but it was a new experience for Adam and he intended to savor it as long as he could.

He had no idea how long they were out there, bodies moving to the music. Time seemed to have stopped altogether, holding them in an everlasting moment of heat and sweat and music that vibrated bone deep. Adam didn't care. He never wanted it to end. If the world stopped turning at that moment, he'd die a happy man.

When his favorite guilty-pleasure song came on, Adam thought he might explode with sheer sensual joy. To his delight, Buzz seemed to feel the same way. His hips rolled against

Adam's thigh, undulating to the languid, sexual rhythm of the music. *I want to touch you,* Buzz mouthed along with the sultry voice of the singer, *you're just made for love.* Adam felt the outline of Buzz's erection through his jeans, and that was all he could stand. Crushing Buzz's body to his, Adam kissed him hard and dragged him off the dance floor.

Somehow, they made their way to a shadowy corner at the edge of the club without unwinding themselves from each other. Adam slammed Buzz against the wall, one hand still gripping the leash and the other snaking down to rub Buzz's crotch.

"Oh fuck," Buzz gasped, thighs parting for Adam's hand. "God. Can't. Here. Not. Fuck, let's go."

"Where?" Adam glanced around, trying and failing to keep from humping against Buzz. "Oh, man. 'M gonna shoot."

Buzz's gaze locked onto Adam's, frantic and intense. "Don't you fucking dare. Save it for—" He stopped and bit his lip. "Just save it."

Utterly unable to speak, Adam nodded, thanking his lucky stars Buzz hadn't said "save it for my ass" like Adam knew damn well he'd been about to. Buzz flashed a dazed smile, grabbed Adam's hand in a death grip and headed for the exit with Adam in tow.

Outside, they made their way through the usual Saturday night throng without receiving more than a couple of knowing smirks. Most of the people frequenting this part of the beach on August nights were too caught up in their own hedonistic pleasures to pay any attention to two more gay boys with hard-ons hunting a private spot to fuck.

"Where are we going?" Adam whined when they reached his car. "I can't make it far."

"I know a place close by." Sliding into the seat, Buzz pulled the door shut and turned a weirdly serious expression to Adam.

"Turn left out of the parking lot, take the first right and go three blocks. There's an empty lot where the trees are really thick."

"That's a residential area," Adam said when his brain reached the end of Buzz's oral map. "Won't somebody see us?"

"I doubt it. There's new houses going up on both sides. No one living in either yet." Buzz yipped and grabbed the door handle as Adam peeled out of the parking lot on two wheels. "Whoa, don't do that."

"Oh, come on. I wasn't going that fast."

"You were, but that's not it." Buzz adjusted his position, teeth sinking into his lower lip. "It just shifted...something."

"What the hell are you talking about?" Adam glared at the bumper-to-bumper traffic. *Hurry the fuck up! Don't you idiots know I'm about to get laid?*

"You'll find out," Buzz proclaimed with a smirk.

Shaking his head, Adam took the right turn Buzz indicated and stepped on the gas. "How do you know about the houses beside the empty lot, anyhow? I don't think you come out here to get fucked every night." A thought struck Adam. "Speaking of which, do you have some rubbers? I've got some lotion in the glove compartment, we can use that for lube I guess."

"Never fear, dude, I totally came prepared." Lifting his hips off the seat in a way that nearly made Adam run off the road, Buzz dug into his front jeans pocket and emerged clutching a handful of Trojans and three individual packets of K-Y. He held them up, grinning. "See?"

Adam laughed. "Optimistic much?"

"Always." Buzz set the condoms and lube carefully on the console between them. "I've been to this spot before for fucking, but it's been a while. Me and Jordan were down here just the other day though."

"Oh really?" Adam leered, and was rewarded with a punch in the arm.

"Shut up, you perv. I was helping him find a house for Tanya's folks. They're coming down from Michigan for the wedding and wanted to stay at the beach. Tanya had to work so she couldn't come." Buzz's hand shot out to point at a tangle of gnarled pines between two partially built houses on the left side of the road. "There it is. Pull in between those two really fat trees in the front."

Adam slowed to a crawl, his need to get his cock inside Buzz warring with a horrific vision of scratched paint. "You sure it'll fit in that opening?"

Darlin', you really shouldn't be surprised, Scarlett chided while Adam waited for Buzz's howls of laughter to die down. *You made a funny, of course your young man is gonna laugh.*

Scowling, Adam crossed his arms and glared at the summer night outside. *Shut up and go away, Scarlett.*

Well! I never! Scarlett flounced deep into the dark recesses of Adam's subconscious. He hoped she stayed there and sulked the rest of the night.

"Yeah, yeah, it'll fit," Buzz gasped, wiping his eyes. "The space is bigger than it looks."

Biting back a smart-ass quip, Adam focused on easing his beloved Viper safely through the gauntlet of pines. To his relief, he found Buzz was right. He could've gotten his mother's Blazer in with room to spare.

When Buzz gave the word, Adam parked the car and killed the engine. He turned to Buzz, feeling suddenly nervous.

"So," Adam said. "Where do you... I mean, how... Um..."

Chuckling, Buzz leaned toward Adam and wrapped a hand around the back of his neck. "Dude. Shut up and kiss me."

That, Adam could do. He pulled Buzz closer by the leash he still wore and covered Buzz's mouth with his.

The kiss went from lazy to frantic in seconds, and the fierce lust Adam had felt in the club came roaring back. Winding his arms around Buzz, Adam dragged the man right over the console. Buzz yelped when his knee banged into the gearshift.

"Sorry," Adam mumbled, settling Buzz astride his lap.

"'S okay, I wasn't using that knee anyhow."

Buzz planted a hard kiss on Adam's mouth. Adam opened for him, and the kiss turned into a whole series of kisses, each deeper and more desperate than the last. It was damn good. Adam was tempted to stay right there, playing tonsil hockey and humping until he and Buzz both got off. But they could've done that in the club. Adam wanted more, and they were going to have to get out of the car for that. There was no way Adam was letting even a molecule of jizz touch his leather seats, even if it were physically possible to fuck in such a small car, which it wasn't.

Mustering every ounce of willpower he had, Adam grabbed Buzz's shoulders and pushed him back enough to look into his eyes. "Still wanna get nailed on the hood of my Viper?"

"Fuck yeah." Buzz licked the end of Adam's nose. "Outside. Now. Before I come in my fucking pants."

Adam fumbled for the handle and swung the door open. Snatching a condom and a packet of K-Y, Buzz wriggled off Adam's lap and stepped outside, setting the supplies on the car's hood. Adam followed him. The second the door was shut, they lunged at each other and fell into another devouring kiss.

Part of Adam wanted very much to take it slow, peel off Buzz's clothes bit by bit and explore every inch of lean, pale, gorgeous body as it was exposed. But his prick was screaming at him to get on with it already, and if his whimpering and shaking was any indication, Buzz was having the same problem. Promising himself they'd have a long, slow, delicious fuck later, Adam spun Buzz around and shoved him face down across the Viper's hood.

"Be careful," Buzz panted, turning his head to stare at Adam as they both fumbled to undo Buzz's jeans.

"Huh?" Adam tugged Buzz's zipper down and hooked his thumbs into the waistband of the jeans. "I'll get you ready, don't worry."

"No, I mean be careful with—Ah! Shit."

Good gracious! Scarlett shrieked, popping out of hiding long enough to render her opinion on what Adam saw when he pulled Buzz's jeans down. *What in the Sam Hill is that?*

Adam stared at the slim black wire snaking from the back pocket of Buzz's jeans to disappear between the cheeks of his naked ass. He had no answer, either for Scarlett or the more normal parts of his brain. Whatever it was, though, one end was most definitely lodged in the place Adam was dying to stick his cock. Which could be a problem.

"What the fuck's that up your ass?" Adam demanded, too weirded out to worry about being delicate.

Pushing up on one elbow, Buzz gave him a wicked grin. "That, Happy Boy, is why they call me Buzz."

Adam frowned, feeling like he was missing something. "I don't get it."

Buzz tore open the lube and handed it to Adam. "Put your finger in me. You'll see."

Since fingering Buzz was the second best thing Adam could think of to do at that moment, he didn't argue. He squeezed out a dollop of K-Y onto his middle finger, set the packet back on the hood and parted Buzz's ass cheeks with his free hand.

Staring at the black cord emerging from Buzz's anus and hoping the whatever-it-was in there wouldn't react badly to lube, Adam swirled the slippery gel onto Buzz's opening.

"Oh, yeah," Buzz breathed, settling his chest against the hood of the car and spreading his thighs as far as he could with his jeans still tangled around them. "Do it."

Drawing a deep breath, Adam pressed his finger against the dusky little hole. There was a moment of resistance, then Buzz sighed, the muscles relaxed and Adam's finger sank in to the hilt.

At first he thought the odd pulsing against his joint was Buzz's heartbeat. He'd never felt a guy's pulse in his ass, but that didn't mean it couldn't happen. Maybe Buzz just had a stronger heart than most people. Adam twisted his finger, grinning at the way it made Buzz whimper. Small rubbery bumps brushed against his knuckles as he moved. Underneath the bumps, something hard and oblong throbbed to a rhythm he now realized was far too irregular for a healthy heartbeat. In a burst of insight, Adam's mind connected the throbbing bumps to the black wire, and his mouth fell open.

"Jesus *fuck*, Buzz." Adam drew his finger out just enough to get another one in beside it, and began pumping Buzz's ass in earnest. The toy inside Buzz caressed his fingers with every stroke, making his skin tingle. "What is it?"

"It's an iBuzz." A sharp cry echoed from Buzz's mouth when Adam added a third finger. "I'll explain later. Just fuck me now."

Eyeing the black cord like it might bite him, Adam pulled his fingers out of Buzz's ass and snatched up the condom packet. "But what about the...the thing? How do I get it out?"

"Don't. Leave it." Twisting around, Buzz contorted himself enough to reach into the back pocket of his jeans and pull out something Adam's blood-deprived brain vaguely recognized as an iPod Nano. The black cord connected the Nano to the toy in Buzz's rectum. Buzz clutched the iPod in his hand and splayed himself across the hood again. "Fuck me with it in."

"But—"

"Dude! Trust me, will you? You can't even believe how amazing it feels on your dick."

He had a point. If the rhythmic pulse of it felt that good against Adam's finger, how mind-blowing would it be against his cock? He bit his lip. "It won't hurt you? Having both me and a toy in you?"

Buzz let out an impatient whine. "Adam, please."

The shock of hearing his name from Buzz's lips shattered Adam's indecision. Seized by a sudden frantic hurry, Adam ripped the condom packet open, rolled the rubber over his prick, slathered on the rest of the lube and shoved himself balls deep into Buzz's ass.

Well, it's about time, Scarlett sighed. Adam ignored her. He was gone, lost in a haze of delirious pleasure. Buzz's body squeezed him tight, the toy sending syncopated vibrations straight from his cock to his brain with every thrust. A tiny corner of Adam's mind wished he could feel it without the rubber. Another part of him was glad he had the latex sheath keeping him from experiencing the full effect. Something told him the pulsing of the toy plus the heat of Buzz's ass on his bare cock would make him shoot embarrassingly fast.

Buzz moaned and clenched his muscles around Adam's prick, sending a violent shudder through Adam's body, and Adam decided he'd just let it happen the way it wanted to and get over the embarrassment later. Hopefully with a long, slow, ego-repairing fuck in his bed. Clamping his fingers onto Buzz's hips in a bruising grip, Adam pounded into him as hard as he could.

"Oh, fuck yeah," Buzz growled, fingers flexing against the Viper's hood. "God, that's good."

"You like it?" Leaning forward, Adam grabbed the neglected leash between his teeth and tugged, forcing Buzz's head back. "Like me fucking you?"

His words were garbled by the mouthful of leather, but Buzz didn't seem to have any trouble understanding him. "Yes. God, Adam, yes."

The strangled lust in Buzz's voice made Adam burn. Rivers of fire crawled from his groin up his back and stomach and down his thighs, making him shake. The leash fell from his mouth and landed against Buzz's lower back. "Oh fuck, almost there."

"Yeah. Come on."

Adam let his gaze follow the line of Buzz's body, from that Goth-sexy hair down the lean spine under the tight T-shirt to that smooth, perfect ass. Buzz's hips hit the car every time Adam thrust into him. Adam saw Buzz's buttocks contract with each movement, and he gasped when the meaning of it hit him.

Holy fucking hell, he's humping my Viper. The realization sent a white-hot spike through him, and he came with a shout. Beneath him, Buzz shuddered, hands spasming as his hole contracted around Adam's cock.

The mental picture of Buzz's spunk splattering the side of the car wrung an extra pulse of pleasure from Adam's prick. All his strength ran out of him, and he collapsed onto Buzz's back.

"Oh. My. God." Burying his face in Buzz's neck, Adam drew a deep breath scented with sweat, sex and the nearby ocean. "I think I just got religion."

Buzz laughed, sounding breathless. "Told you. Feels amazing on your cock, right?"

"Mm-hm." Adam slipped a hand down to cup Buzz's balls. The man's cock was still semi-rigid, though it was deflating fast. Adam rubbed his thumb along the shaft, enjoying the satin softness of the skin there and the way his touch made Buzz squirm. "Damn, I went off so fast I didn't even get to touch you."

"Hey, I don't need a *hand* to get off."

Adam snickered. "I noticed."

Reaching back with the hand not clutching his iPod, Buzz stroked Adam's hair. "Dude, let me up. You're squishing me."

Reluctantly, Adam pushed away from Buzz's back and stood up. His cock slipped from Buzz's body, and he grabbed the edge of the condom just in time to keep it from getting lost on the way out. He tied it off and, not knowing what else to do with it, tossed it on the ground, promising himself he'd pick it up when they left.

"So tell me about that thing," Adam said, zipping up his jeans and watching Buzz peel himself off the hood. "That iBuzz thing. Where'd you get it?"

Buzz straightened up and turned around, shoving the Nano back into his pocket. His eyeliner was smeared, his eyes heavy-lidded and sated. Adam wanted to pounce on him and eat him up.

"A friend of mine at MIT sent it to me last year," Buzz explained, tucking his prick back into his jeans and pulling the zipper up. "It's actually a prototype of the product out on the market right now. Basically just a bullet that's tweaked to plug into an iPod and vibrate to the rhythm of the music. I have no idea how Toby got hold of it. I'm pretty good with electronics, so I fiddled with it some, fixed it up how I wanted it. I used it all the damn time, so my boyfriend started calling me Buzz. The nickname stuck."

Something cold and ugly curled in Adam's gut. "Boyfriend? What boyfriend?"

Buzz's eyes widened. "Dude, no. We broke up, like, eight months ago. I'm totally single."

"Oh. Good." Adam stared at the sandy ground under his feet. He had no idea where the sudden streak of possessiveness came from, but it scared him. Even if he was normally the jealous type—which he wasn't—he had no right to feel that way toward Buzz. One date and a fuck in a vacant lot did not a relationship make. Confused by his feelings and not wanting Buzz to see, Adam covered by yanking the car door open and grabbing a towel from behind the driver's seat. He swabbed the globs of semen off the side the car, keeping his gaze fixed on the ground, then picked up the used condom.

Buzz's red and purple sneakers came into view. Adam caught a whiff of the musky, spicy cologne Buzz wore. He looked up, and Buzz smiled at him. "One man guy, are you?"

Adam blushed. "I'm not usually like that. So jealous, I mean. Sorry."

"I think I like it." Pressing his body against Adam's, Buzz hooked an arm around his neck and kissed the corner of his mouth. "I like you, Adam. A lot."

The Scarlett part of Adam's mind swooned at the spark in Buzz's eyes. Thankfully, the rest of him was just manly enough to keep his cool. He wound his arms around Buzz's waist. "Want to come back to my place? I'll make some popcorn and we can watch movies."

Buzz snuggled into Adam's embrace. "Do you have *Texas Chainsaw Massacre*?"

"Of course. I have *A Nightmare on Elm Street* too."

"Cool."

"And *Night of the Living Dead.*"

"Dude, we can totally have a horror marathon."

"Hell yeah."

Laughing, Buzz laid a hand on Adam's cheek. "Kiss me again before we go."

Adam happily obeyed. He held Buzz close and let their tongues wind together. As they kissed, an unfamiliar feeling stirred inside Adam. A feeling that fluttered like a flock of butterflies in his belly. He wasn't sure what it meant, exactly, but he liked it. It felt like the beginning of something, and that was wonderful and terrifying and...good. It was good.

You'll have to tell your mama and daddy your big nasty secret, sugar, Scarlett pointed out. *If you start somethin' with this sweet thing, you'll have to tell them.*

I will. Later. Thus resolved, Adam pushed the issue to the back of his mind. It could wait.

Chapter Four

Adam tried to watch the DVD. He really did. *Return of the Living Dead* was one of his all-time favorites, and he and Buzz had agreed it was the perfect movie to follow the classic *Night of the Living Dead* in their personal mini-marathon of horror flicks. But the way Buzz moaned "coooooock" and grabbed Adam's crotch every time an on-screen zombie screamed for "braaaaaains" eventually became too much for Adam to resist. Which was why they'd abandoned watching the film about halfway through and were now making out on Adam's sofa to a soundtrack of screams, zombie groans and eighties punk music.

"Ooooh, my God." Sitting astride Adam's lap, Buzz arched his neck for Adam's kisses. "Let's fuck. This is making me horny."

Adam ran his hands up Buzz's back underneath the snug T-shirt. "What, the movie?"

"Oh yeah, brain-munching totally turns me on."

"I knew you were a pervert."

"Shut up. You know you're what's making me hard, not the damn movie." Grinning, Buzz ground his crotch against Adam's belly. "Hey, you wanna get kinky this time?"

Adam snorted. "You mean me fucking you with that toy up your ass while you're collared and leashed wasn't kinky enough for you?"

Buzz shook his head sadly. "Dude, you don't get out much, do you?"

Oh, honey, Scarlett chortled. *That boy has no idea what all you've done to him in your filthy little mind, has he?*

A blush burned its way up Adam's neck and into his cheeks at the reminder of some of his more creative fantasies involving Buzz. "I'm up for anything you want to try. What'd you have in mind?"

Buzz's eyes glinted with an evil light. "You're my leather daddy, and I'm your slave boy. You tell me."

Adam gaped. "What?"

Cupping Adam's face in his hands, Buzz stared straight into his eyes. "I. Am. Your. Slave," Buzz said, with—in Adam's opinion—an entirely unnecessary degree of enunciation. "Order me to do what you want."

Oh fuck. Adam licked his suddenly dry lips. "What if I want you to do something you don't want to do?"

Buzz shrugged. "Then I won't do it."

"I...I don't know anything about the leather scene." Adam squeaked when Buzz found his nipple and pinched it through his shirt. "I don't know what to do."

"Neither do I. But so what?" Dipping his head, Buzz bit Adam's neck hard enough to leave tooth marks. "Dude, relax. We're just playing, right? Enjoy it."

Adam's cock was already enjoying it. He canted his hips upward, rubbing himself against Buzz's denim-clad ass. "Uh. Yeah. Okay."

Buzz lifted his head and smiled, a lustful, dirty smile that stirred a hot glow in Adam's belly. "So tell me what you want, Daddy Adam." He leaned in and snagged Adam's lower lip between his teeth, tugging gently for a moment before letting go. "I don't have many limits, you know."

The raw lust in Buzz's voice gave Adam the courage to follow his desires. Winding the leash around his hand, he gave it a yank, forcing Buzz's head back.

"Get up and take all your clothes off," Adam ordered. The note of command in his voice startled him more than a little. He dropped the leash and held his breath, waiting for Buzz's reaction.

Buzz scrambled off Adam's lap, narrowly avoiding stumbling over the coffee table, and started stripping. In the background, a teenage girl screamed and ran from a dripping zombie clamoring after the contents of her skull. Unzipping his jeans, Adam took out his stiffening cock and stroked it while he watched Buzz get naked.

The sight was certainly worth staring at. Adam had, of course, become quite familiar with Buzz's bare upper body over the last month. But this was his first look at the rest of Buzz without clothes. Long, lean legs, firm little ass—which of course he'd already seen—sparsely fuzzed balls drawn up tight beneath a hard, flushed cock thick enough to make Adam's mouth water. Even the chipped black toenail polish looked sexy on Buzz. Adam bit his lip and groaned.

"What do you want to do to me?" Buzz's voice was low and rough, his eyes blazing.

Adam knew some of the things he wanted to do, but they seemed so...kinky. So dirty. *But that's what the boy wants, sugar,* Scarlett reminded him. *Speak your mind. He won't let you do anything he doesn't want.*

God, I hope you're right. Drawing a deep breath, Adam gestured at the coffee table where their drinks sat. "Drink the rest of your beer first."

Buzz turned and grabbed his Corona, one eyebrow raised. "Watersports? Dude, I had no idea you were into that."

It took a minute for Buzz's meaning to seep into Adam's lust-fuzzed brain. When it did, his jaw dropped. "Oh my God, no! Gross."

Buzz snickered. "Then how come you wanted me to drink all of this?" Holding Adam's gaze, he downed the rest of the golden liquid in a few gulps and wiped his mouth on the back of his hand. "You wanna watch me piss, is that it? 'Cause that's totally cool."

The mental image was strangely compelling. Maybe... Adam shook his head. He was *not* going there. "Just set the bottle down, get the rest of that lube out of your pocket and lie down on the floor."

With an amused look at Adam, Buzz did as he was told. Keeping his Nano clutched in one hand, he stretched out on his back on Adam's poorly vacuumed carpet and spread his legs. "You gonna get naked too?"

"Nope." Slipping off the couch, Adam knelt between Buzz's splayed thighs. "How do I get that thing out of your butt?"

"Just pull on the wire. I made sure it's strong enough." Buzz hooked his hands behind his knees and drew his legs up to his chest. His rosy little opening glistened in the low light. "Or you could stick your fingers in and fish it out."

Adam's prick decided the latter idea held the most appeal. "Hold your ass open."

Buzz obeyed, long fingers digging into his cheeks and pulling them apart. Fighting the urge to shove his cock into that inviting hole, Adam stroked the puckered skin with one

189

fingertip. Buzz groaned as his muscles relaxed and Adam's thumb and forefinger slipped inside.

"Oh, fuck," Buzz breathed, hips lifting as Adam probed deeper. "Say something dirty."

Startled, Adam stared at him. *Dirty? I don't know how to talk dirty.*

Why, of course you do, Scarlett soothed. *Just say what you're thinkin'. That's dirty enough for anyone.*

Adam tried not to think about the fact that the girl living in his brain was giving him advice on kinky gay sex. The idea was too disturbing for words.

"Uh, you like my fingers in your hole?" Adam blurted out, hoping that sounded dirty enough.

Evidently it did, judging by the way Buzz moaned and spread himself wider. "Fuck, yeah."

"You like toys up your ass, right?" Adam said, getting into the spirit of the game. He stuck a third finger in and twisted, grinning when Buzz yelped and trembled.

"God, yeah. Why, you got some?"

"Kind of." Forcing another finger into Buzz's rectum, Adam managed to grab the iBuzz and pull it free. He tossed the rubber-sheathed bullet beside the Nano now lying on the carpet, his gaze glued to Buzz's wide-open ass. "You were wondering why I wanted you to finish your beer. Well, that's why."

Buzz's head popped up off the floor, wide eyes glittering. "Dude, you are a kink-master. Do it. Oh, and hey, use the wide end, okay?"

Oh, wow. I was only thinking of the neck, not the bottom. Just the idea of Buzz's ass taking something that size was nearly enough to make Adam shoot without even being touched. Hanging onto his control with a monumental effort, he squeezed the entire contents of the open lube packet into his hand and began greasing Buzz's anus, using his fingers in a gentle massage until he thought Buzz was loose enough. He picked up the bottle and poised the wide, round base at Buzz's opening.

"Here we go," he whispered. "You ready?"

"Yeah." Grasping the backs of his thighs, Buzz pulled his legs up and apart. "Ready."

Biting his lip, Adam pressed the beer bottle steadily inward, slowly twisting it. He let out a surprised yip when it slipped easily inside. "Oh, my God. Wow."

The fact that Buzz whimpered instead of laughing or teasing told Adam just how much he was enjoying himself. "Adam, ooooh..."

Adam pumped the bottle in and out a few times, staring in awe at Buzz's asshole stretched tight around the clear glass. "Fuck, I'm gonna shoot. This is too hot."

"No, not yet," Buzz begged, panting. "More toys."

"But I don't—"

Buzz's hand shot out, snagging the swizzle stick out of Adam's drink and sending the empty glass tumbling to the floor. "Stick this in my cock."

Oh my. In the back of Adam's brain, Scarlett dropped into a dead faint. Adam was glad of it. Shocked to the core, he stared at Buzz. "That's hardly sanitary."

Buzz let out a dazed laugh. "Don't be such a prude. Just do it."

Adam thought about reminding Buzz who the daddy was in this scenario, but decided against it. After all, hadn't he fantasized about that very thing, alone in his bed with nothing but his hand and his imagination for company? He'd come to the mental image of himself sticking various toys into all of Buzz's orifices—his cock included—more than once in the past month.

Hoping he wasn't about to cause any damage, Adam opened the last packet of lube, took the swizzle stick from Buzz and dipped it in the K-Y. He watched Buzz's face as he took his cock in his hand and pushed the slim glass rod carefully into the slit.

Buzz's cheeks flushed pink, his eyes fluttering closed. "Oh, fuck. Yes."

Encouraged, Adam slid the rod in further, entranced by the way the flesh at the edge of Buzz's slit clung to the glass. "Jesus, that's hot."

Buzz moaned. "Wanna suck you off now."

Adam gulped. "But the toys—"

"Leave them." Lowering his legs, Buzz rolled onto his side, rose to his knees and shoved Adam onto his back. "Pull my leash."

Not knowing quite what to think about the whole thing, but finding it unbearably hot anyway, Adam obediently picked up Buzz's leash and gave it a sharp tug. Groaning, Buzz bent forward and swallowed Adam's cock whole.

Adam's last coherent thought was that someone somewhere had taught Buzz extremely well in the art of sucking cock. His tongue worked Adam's prick in ways he wouldn't have thought possible, and the grip of his throat was mind-blowing. The way Buzz moaned around his mouthful said he was enjoying it as much as Adam.

Lost in a haze of pleasure, Adam couldn't be bothered to feel embarrassed at how quickly his orgasm overtook him. He yanked Buzz's head up by the leash just in time to shoot all over Buzz's flushed cheeks and open mouth.

"Get me off," Buzz gasped, semen dripping from his chin. "Gotta come."

Clearheaded again after his orgasm, Adam lowered Buzz gently onto his back and pushed his thighs apart. "How? You want me to suck you?"

Buzz shook his head. "Just jack me. God, I'm so fucking close."

Sitting back on his heels, Adam took a second to drink in the vision of Buzz lying there with his legs spread, naked except for a collar and leash, with a beer bottle up his ass, a swizzle stick in his cock and spunk all over his face. It was, Adam mused, a disturbingly erotic sight.

"Dude, come on," Buzz whined. "Get me off."

Grinning, Adam tugged the glass rod carefully out of Buzz's cock and tossed it aside, then grasped Buzz's rigid shaft. "Come for me, slave boy."

Somewhat to his surprise, Buzz did, wailing and clawing the carpet as his cock spewed ropes of pearly white all over his belly.

The unguarded ecstasy on Buzz's face was irresistible. Straddling Buzz's body, Adam bent and kissed him. Strong arms came up to wind around Adam's neck, pulling him down into Buzz's embrace. He went willingly, letting his full weight rest on Buzz's body. He closed his eyes and breathed in the scent of sweaty, well-fucked male. On the TV, a zombie begged his terrified girlfriend to let him eat her brain, and Adam and Buzz both laughed.

"That was amazing," Buzz murmured, stroking Adam's back.

"Mm, it sure was." Lifting his head, Adam gave Buzz a loopy smile. "You hungry?"

"Starved." Buzz's mouth curved into a filthy grin. "You could've let me drink your protein shake instead of shooting it all over my face."

Adam groaned, his cock twitching. "Don't go there, Buzz. No swallowing or barebacking until after tests. That's the rules."

"Hey, I was just kidding." Buzz's expression turned solemn. He laid a damp palm on Adam's cheek. "I hope we can go there someday, though."

Not knowing what to say to that, Adam captured Buzz's mouth in a deep kiss. Bad enough, he thought, that he'd let his little head talk him into going out with Buzz in the first place. Even worse that the man had coaxed him into doing things he'd always thought to be shockingly—though deliciously—perverted. Now Buzz was making him think about long-term relationships. Maybe even the "L" word.

It scared him how right that felt.

I don't want to think about that right now. I'll think about that tomorrow.

Yeah. Tomorrow.

Closing his eyes and opening his mouth, Adam let Buzz's kiss carry him away. Tomorrow could take care of itself.

ᏬᏬᏬ

As it often does, tomorrow arrived before Adam was ready for it.

He woke with his face buried in Buzz's neck and Buzz's warm naked body in his arms. Cracking an eye open, Adam peered around his bedroom. Buzz's iPod and its associated sex toy sat atop Adam's dresser, where he'd put it before bending Buzz over said article of furnishing and fucking him again. Morning light leaked in through a gap in the dark red curtains, throwing a beam of gold across Buzz's sleeping face. His lashes cast lacy shadows on his cheek, and he was drooling on Adam's pillow. He looked adorable, curled on his side with one hand tucked under his chin and the other resting against his belly, the fingers laced through Adam's.

Adam smiled and snuggled closer, remembering the night before. They'd gone through three more condoms before finally falling into an exhausted sleep, sticky with sweat and spunk and not caring. The smell of sex still permeated the apartment.

A light tap on the front door answered Adam's half-formed question about what had woken him. He glanced at the clock just visible over the curve of Buzz's shoulder. Part of the display was blocked by the collar and leash draped over the bedside table and the leather hat which had fallen off the lamp at some point, but Adam could see it well enough. Eight a.m.

He scowled. His visitor was probably his friend Jimmy, who lived a few doors down. Jimmy had always been an early riser, and took sadistic pleasure in making sure everyone else was too, whether they wanted to be or not.

Moving carefully, Adam unwound himself from Buzz and slid out of bed. He kicked through the pile of inside-out clothes on the floor, found his boxer-briefs and pulled them on. Buzz mumbled something in his sleep and rolled onto his stomach with most of the sheet wadded underneath him. Taking a moment to admire the curve of Buzz's ass, Adam tiptoed out of the room and shut the door behind him.

The knock sounded again, tinged with impatience. "Coming," Adam called as loudly as he dared. Yawning, he shuffled to the door and flipped the deadbolt. "Jimmy, honest to God, I wish you wouldn't—"

Adam's complaints dried up in his throat at the sight of the Gucci-clad China doll on his doorstep. *Oh honey,* Scarlett chuckled. *You'd best think fast. No way to hide it from her.*

Adam gulped. "Hi, Mom. Wh-what are you doing here?"

Renata Holderman flashed a mouthful of expensive caps and patted Adam's cheek. "Do I need a reason to visit my baby?"

"Um..." Glancing over his shoulder at the bedroom door—which was thankfully still closed—Adam blocked the doorway in what he hoped was a subtle move. "No, but—"

"But nothing." Pushing Adam aside with one French-manicured hand, she sashayed inside. She wrinkled her nose. "Sweetheart, it smells terrible in here. Don't you ever clean?"

"Yeah, but Mom—"

"Just look at this mess." She plucked one of Buzz's socks off the back of Adam's sofa, holding it at arm's length between two fingers as if it were contagious. "Honestly, Adam. I brought you up better than this."

"I've just been busy, Mom." The lube-smeared beer bottle and swizzle stick still lay on the floor. Adam kicked them under the sofa before his mother could see and ran a hand through his hair. *God, I hope there's no come on me.* "Look, I'll scrub the whole place later today, okay?"

His mother smiled, the blue eyes Adam had inherited crinkling at the corners. "That's a good idea, honey. Now, since I'm here, why don't I make you some breakfast?"

Oh Christ no. No. "You don't have to do that, Mom," Adam said, trying not to sound as panicked as he felt. "I was gonna meet some of the guys at The Breakfast Barn later."

Renata waved a dismissive hand. "Nonsense. You need a good breakfast, not that greasy slop they serve at that place. I'll fix you something, it won't take a minute."

Before Adam could get a word out, his mother turned and bustled into the kitchen. Cabinets opened and closed, pans were pulled out and set on the counter. Adam heard her grumble a complaint about leaving yesterday's coffee grounds in the Mr. Coffee basket.

Groaning, Adam flopped onto the sofa and covered his face with his hands. Once his mother got into the kitchen, there was no getting rid of her.

Tell her now, Scarlett prodded. *Your young man's still asleep. Now's the time, before he wakes up and your mama causes a scene.*

Cold sweat broke out on Adam's brow at the thought. His hands shook. Could he really tell her? Just sit her down and say it? *Mom, I'm gay, and I just spent the night fucking the hottest guy I've ever seen upside down and sideways. As a matter of fact, he's still naked in my bed.*

"Nope," Adam muttered, glaring at his cock, which was twitching at the thought of Buzz. "Can't do it."

"What was that, dear?" Renata's highlighted blonde coif appeared in the kitchen doorway. "I couldn't hear you."

"Just talking to myself." Adam mustered a smile. To his relief, his mother smiled back and disappeared into the kitchen again.

At that moment, the bedroom door swung open. Buzz wandered into the living area, yawning and scratching his stomach. "Mm," he purred. "Do I smell breakfast?"

Adam stared at him, utterly unable to speak. The smell of bacon drifted from the kitchen. Adam could hear it popping in the pan.

"Uh..." Adam rose to his feet, torn between shoving Buzz back into the bedroom and ravaging him right there on the living-room floor. In spite of Adam's near-panic, the sight of Buzz standing there in nothing but jeans and love bites was nearly enough to destroy his good sense.

Buzz frowned. "Adam? Something wrong?"

"No, it's just..." Adam trailed off. Then inspiration hit. Lunging at Buzz, he grabbed him by the shoulders, spun him around and steered him toward the bedroom door. "Hey, why don't I bring you breakfast in bed, huh?"

Laughing, Buzz turned around again and wound his arms around Adam's neck. "Oooh, aren't you romantic?"

Adam squeaked when Buzz captured his earlobe between his teeth and sucked on it. "Um, yeah. Go back to bed, I'll be back in a few minutes."

Buzz smiled, eyes sparkling. "Dude. You're, like, the most awesome guy I've ever met."

Adam's insides melted into a gooey puddle. He couldn't have refused Buzz's kiss at that moment even if he'd wanted to. And he didn't want to. Pulling Buzz close, he closed his eyes and let Buzz fuse their mouths together.

A piercing shriek made them jump apart. Adam whirled around. "Mom! Oh, fuck."

Renata sank into Adam's battered old recliner, one hand pressed to her forehead. "Jesus help me!"

Buzz shrank closer to Adam. "Dude, what's going on? Why's she freaking out?"

Adam sighed. "She doesn't know I'm gay."

Much to Adam's irritation, Buzz chuckled. "She does now."

"Yeah, thanks for the newsflash."

In the chair, Adam's mother was busy wringing her hands and wailing. Adam gritted his teeth. "Mom, calm down, okay?"

Her mascara-streaked face snapped around, shocked blue gaze locking onto Adam. "Baby, why didn't you tell me this before?"

Adam's mouth fell open. "Huh?"

"Your sister tried to tell me you were...you know. Homosexual." She whispered the word, as if saying it too loudly would be scandalous. "But I wouldn't listen. I feel like such a fool."

"Whoa, wait just a minute." Adam stared at his mother, trying to read her face. "You mean you knew I was gay all this time? And you're not mad?" He thought for a second, and scowled. "And Cathy told you? Dammit, I'm going to kill her."

"Well, I didn't *know* until just now, and of course your father has no idea. But no, I'm not mad. And don't you be mad at your sister either, she was trying to get me to stop setting you up with my friends' daughters." She blinked, her expression radiating hurt. "What sort of person do you think I am?"

Adam blushed. "Well..."

Pressing a hand to her heart, she heaved a deep sigh. "I shouldn't be surprised, I suppose. No child ever thinks their mama can understand them."

Staggering over to the sofa, Adam dropped down beside his mother. "I don't believe this."

Shooting a withering glance at her son, Renata stood, visibly gathered herself, and marched over to Buzz. "Hello there. I'm Mrs. Holderman. And you are?"

Buzz grinned. "Myron Stiles, ma'am. I'm...uh..." He shot a pleading look at Adam.

Without giving too much thought to what he was doing, Adam stood, went to Buzz and put an arm around his shoulders. "He's my boyfriend, Mom."

The sudden tension in Buzz's body gave away his surprise, but he didn't say anything. Adam hoped that meant more than Buzz just trying not to embarrass him.

Adam's mother paled, but nodded. "Very nice to meet you. Adam, I have to go. Call me later, all right?"

"Sure, Mom." Moved by a sudden surge of affection, Adam wrapped his free arm around his mother's neck and kissed her cheek. "I love you."

"Love you too, sweetheart." With a halfhearted smile, she patted his cheek, turned and hurried out the door.

Adam stared after her. "Wow. I always thought she'd be upset."

"Looks like you were wrong, lucky for you. My mom had hysterics for a couple of years before she settled down." Buzz slipped an arm around Adam's waist. "Hey, Adam?"

"Hm?"

"Did you mean what you said before? About me being your boyfriend?"

"Yeah, I did," Adam answered, his voice only shaking a little. "Is that okay?"

"It's fucking awesome." Turning in Adam's embrace, Buzz kissed his chin.

A bubble of pure happiness expanded in Adam's chest. Laying a hand on Buzz's cheek, Adam kissed him. Buzz moaned, the sound soft and needy, and Adam's body responded. Cupping Buzz's head in one hand, he took the kiss deep.

Buzz hummed and licked his lips when they pulled apart. "Mmm. You make me so hot I can smell myself burning."

Adam started to say something, then stopped and frowned. The smell of something burning wafted through the air.

"Oh shit!" Adam broke out of Buzz's embrace and ran for the kitchen. Smoke curled from the pan where the bacon had charred black and fused to the Teflon.

Buzz slid his arms around Adam from behind. "Dude, I'm not eating that."

Switching the burner off and setting the pan aside, Adam leered at Buzz over his shoulder. "I've got something for you to eat right here."

"I bet you do." Laying a hand on Adam's crotch, Buzz curled his fingers around Adam's swelling prick. "Mmm, sausage. My favorite."

Laughing, Adam twisted around and swooped Buzz into his arms. "You know what?"

"What?" Buzz kissed him, tongue flicking out. "Tell me."

Adam rested his forehead against Buzz's. "I could see myself falling for you," he whispered.

Buzz let out a soft little sound. "You mean, like, forever?"

"Yeah. Like forever." It was a damn scary thing to say, but Adam felt its truth right down to his core.

A happy gleam lit Buzz's eyes. "Me too." Leaning forward, he nipped Adam's bottom lip. "Let's go back to bed. All this sweet romance is making me hard."

Adam snickered, but took Buzz's hand and led him toward the bedroom. "Can we play with your toy some more?"

"Sure." Buzz grinned. "You wanna catch a buzz this time?"

Letting go of Buzz's hand, Adam wrapped his arms around his lover and kissed him. "Looks like I already did."

About the Author

Ally Blue used to be a good girl. Really. Married for twenty years, two lovely children, house, dogs, picket fence, the whole deal. Then one day she discovered slash fan fiction. She wrote her first fan fiction story a couple of months later and has since slid merrily into the abyss. She has had several short stories published in the erotic e-zine Ruthie's Club, and is a regular contributor to the original slash e-zine Forbidden Fruit.

To learn more about Ally Blue, please visit www.allyblue.com. Send an email to Ally at ally@allyblue.com or join her Yahoo! group to join in the fun with other readers as well as Ally! http://groups.yahoo.com/group/loveisblue/

Look for these titles by *Ally Blue*

Now Available:

Willow Bend

Love's Evolution

Oleander House:
Book One of the Bay City Paranormal Investigation Series

Eros Rising

Hearts from the Ashes
(Paperback collection which includes Eros Rising)

What Hides Inside:
Book Two of the Bay City Paranormal Investigation Series

Firefiles

Coming Soon:

Twilight:
Book Three of the Bay City Paranormal Investigation Series

Untamed Heart

Closer:
Book Four of the Bay City Paranormal Investigation Series

Where the Heart Is

The Happy Onion

An Inner Darkness:
Book Five of the Bay City Paranormal Investigation Series

Nut Cream

Jade Buchanan

Dedication

Nut Cream wouldn't exist if my sister hadn't come up with the idea. Thank you Sarah, for always making me laugh with your crazy ideas, for making sure I don't lose sight of the small things, and for cheering me on at every opportunity.

Chapter One

"Hey, can you hand me the nut cream?"

Toby Madison whirled, startled by the deep voice behind him. *Nut cream? What the hell?*

The man standing in front of him wore a shit-eating grin, the corners of his full lips tilted up and the sides of his expressive baby blue eyes crinkled. Wonderful, just what he needed today—Cliff Bullen. The man could give a statue a hard-on. Too damn bad Toby wasn't interested.

He snorted—like hell he wasn't interested. He blushed when Cliff continued to grin at him.

Cliff towered over him by about half a foot. He was built like a linebacker—solid, ripped and all muscle. His black hair was cut short, just curling above his ears. He was dressed casually, in a pair of worn jeans and a black tee. Toby glanced down at himself, frowning at his pressed jeans and pale yellow golf shirt. Cliff's feet were bare, his toes long and elegant. Christ, why was he thinking about Cliff's toes?

"What are you talking about?"

"Nut cream... See?" Cliff teased, reaching over Toby to grab a bottle of lotion off the kitchen counter.

The bottle was white, the label clearly spelling out in large letters *Nut Hand Cream*. Toby blushed again, cursing his fair skin. He felt his cock start to stiffen just being so close to Cliff. Cliff's grin got wider and he chuckled.

"See, it has shea butter in it. It just makes everything so soft. Silky smooth," he murmured, brushing his fingers against Toby's heated cheek.

Toby shivered, backing up so they weren't touching anymore.

"What's taking so long, Bullen?" Mick, Toby's brother, called out.

"Just chatting with your bro," Cliff replied, staring down at Toby.

Toby muttered a goodbye under his breath, ducking under Cliff's outstretched arm to hurry to his room.

"Running away, Toby?" Cliff taunted after him.

Toby refused to turn around. He entered his room, slamming the door shut behind him. Cliff's soft laughter followed him, lingering in the small space. Toby threw himself on the bed. He couldn't deal with this right now. He willed his damn cock to settle down. His jeans pressed hard into his sensitive flesh, the rough material abrading his cock where it pushed insistently upward. He almost wished he had put on underwear this morning—at least the cotton would be soothing. His whole body was aching, throbbing at him to relieve the growing tension. He cursed the stupid mating phase that was hitting him. The last thing he needed was a phase that made him hard in the first five seconds of being around Cliff.

It would be so much easier if he could just find his mate, although to be honest he didn't want anyone other than Cliff. But there was no way Cliff could be his mate. Surely Cliff would have acted on it by now if he went crazy with lust every time he was within feet of Toby.

For years he had been in love with Cliff Bullen. The most popular guy at school. The most popular guy in the pack. It was ridiculous to be so affected by the man. It wasn't as if Cliff would ever look twice at Toby, so there wasn't any reason to even try to catch his interest. It would only end badly for Toby when Cliff rejected him.

Seven years older than Toby, Cliff had been best friends with his brother Mick for longer than Toby could remember. He used to trail after them, joining in whenever Mick let him, hanging on to every word Cliff said. He was pretty sure everyone knew he had a crush on the man. He just hoped they didn't know how bad it was.

He shook his head. Of course everyone knew he had a thing for the man. It was pretty obvious when they would be able to smell his arousal any time he got within five feet of Cliff. It wouldn't have been so bad if it wasn't the middle of summer. Now, faced with two months off from his teaching job, he had nothing to do but sit in the house, and try to avoid Cliff.

If Toby thought teaching fifth grade was bad, it was nothing compared to dealing with his brother and Cliff all summer. He couldn't exactly disappear while Cliff was over. Toby was only staying with his parents because he taught out of town and didn't have a place to go when he was inside the city limits. He supposed he could have spent the summer in his apartment in Turner Valley, but he wanted to be close to his family. He didn't know what was wrong with him. It wasn't normal for him to be acting like a horny, out-of-control teen who couldn't control his dick.

Actually, he should be blaming Mick for this one. Cliff was only over here so much because Mick was at home. He was in the process of building a house a few blocks over, but there was a delay with the construction so Mick had moved back home until everything got sorted out. Toby couldn't wait for Mick to be finished and then he and Cliff would stop bothering him. He couldn't turn around without seeing the two weres.

"Goddamn stupid werewolf senses," he grumbled. He stared at the stucco above his head. His sensitive ears picked up the sounds of Cliff and Mick in the other room. They were getting ready for the run they took every afternoon. Everyone who lived in this area was pack, so they didn't have to wait until dark to shift. The subdivision was in the south of Calgary, one of the older communities that was amalgamated into the city decades ago. The park that split the city in half butted right up against their community, something they were lucky to have. It wasn't easy being a were inside a city with over a million residents.

They lived on the outskirts of town, right where the park leading into Calgary began. Coyote and deer frequented the area, so Toby and his family blended in perfectly when they were spotted. He had even glimpsed a bear once. He had been driving past on his way to the university years ago when he saw the massive creature down at the river that bisected Fish Creek Park.

The sight of the bear had given him chills, and he'd felt cold for the rest of the day, even within the safety of the university campus. He'd phoned his dad the minute he got to school, but his dad and the others couldn't find the bear. Bears were the one threat to the weres in the park. In a one-on-one fight between a bear and a wolf, the bear would win every time, hands down. Every pup was brought up on the importance of staying away from them.

Since that morning, no one had seen a bear in the park. Everyone just assumed they'd moved on, which was a good thing for the pack. The weres liked to stretch their legs whenever they could, and it helped when they didn't have to look out for predators.

On the other side of their community was wide-open space. The nearby farms were all owned by pack, and they had the run of the land whenever they wanted it.

He turned at the knock on his door and Mick stuck his head inside. Toby had always seen Mick as a more grown-up version of himself. His body was bigger, his face more rugged, his hair a shade more brown than Toby's own reddish locks. He was more appealing, in Toby's mind. Why would anyone look at Toby, when they could see how much better looking his brother was?

"Sure you don't want to come with?" Mick asked.

"Have I ever gone with you?" Toby looked up at the oh-so-fascinating ceiling and ignored his brother. They'd been bothering him to go running since he came back home. As much as he wanted to, he was afraid of giving away his feelings for Cliff.

"Come on, Tobe. Live a little," Cliff said, popping his head into the room beside Mick.

"No thanks, maybe another time."

Mick shook his head, turning around to walk back to the living room. Toby waited for the door to shut. When it didn't, he glanced back to see Cliff standing in the doorway, an uncharacteristic frown on his face.

"It wouldn't hurt you to join in, Toby. We are all the same. No one is going to treat you any differently now that you're back again."

He huffed, twisting his body to lie on his stomach. It was rare for any werewolf to move outside the area. The pack tended to stay together—they were stronger when they were all in one place. There had been more than a few protests when he left Calgary to accept a teaching job outside the city, but he couldn't risk staying here and letting his feelings for Cliff get stronger. His parents might not have known why he was so adamant to move away this past year, but they supported his decision anyway. His dad had even butted heads with some of the elders over it.

Reaching over the bed, Toby picked up his headphones. He was terrified that Cliff would want to talk to him more. Every time he got near the man recently, Toby feared he would start to stutter, or say something infernally stupid. He didn't want Cliff to realize how far gone Toby was for him. He wasn't unintelligent, he was sure Cliff didn't have feelings for him. Hell, Toby'd never even seen Cliff with another man. He was probably as straight as could be. It would be better for all involved if he could just fall out of love and move on to someone he could actually get. He sighed in defeat.

"Fine, I can see I'm not going to change your mind today." Cliff shook his head.

Toby pointedly ignored him, jacking up the volume. He'd get the hint and leave, and then Toby wouldn't be surrounded by his appealing scent. The soothing sounds of the Traveling Wilburys filled his ears. He closed his eyes, resting his forehead on his bent arms.

He jerked when something hit his back. Trying to sit up, he was caught by the lean body that bent to keep him in place. Two tanned hands landed on the bed to either side of his face. Cliff lowered his body, sitting squarely on Toby's ass. He leaned his head in to smooth his cheek along Toby's.

Cliff neatly plucked off Toby's headphones, replacing the voice of Bob Dylan with his rumbling growl.

"I may joke around, I may even tease, but I will not be ignored. Is that clear?"

Toby nodded, breathing hard. Cliff shifted forward on Toby. He felt an increased pressure on his lower back, the slow rise of

Cliff's cock. Toby stayed absolutely still, stunned at the feel of the body on top of him. He smelled his own arousal decorating the air with the scent of his escalating passion. Cliff inhaled noisily. He ground his cock into Toby, causing him to squirm despite his attempts to stay still.

Cliff chuckled, scraping his teeth along Toby's jaw.

"Are you coming or not?" Mick's irritated voice interrupted.

"Not yet," Cliff crooned in Toby's ear. "But your brother is damn close."

"Jesus, Cliff. Enough," Mick barked.

Cliff snickered, pausing to brush his lips along Toby's cheek before gracefully arching up, swinging his leg over and landing beside the bed. Toby pressed his face into the covers below him, waiting until he heard the snick of the door closing. With a shuddering groan, he looked up. His brother and Cliff were gone. What the hell had just happened?

Chapter Two

"Are you done now?" Mick growled.

"Hell, Mick, I'm just getting started." Cliff chuckled at the look of irritation on his friend's face.

"If you're fucking with him, I'll rip your head off. And I damn well don't mean the one on your shoulders."

Cliff grinned, clapping Mick on the shoulder. "You have to admit how cute he is when he gets flustered and turns all pink and squirmy. Makes me want to just eat him up, one bite at a time."

"Jesus, that's my brother you're talking about. And I say he isn't ready for a relationship with you. He's just entering his mating phase. Don't push him. Do you hear me? 'Cause if you push him, I'll kill you next time we're at a worksite. I know how to bury a body so's nobody will ever find you."

Cliff laughed. Mick was always talking about how many different ways you could kill someone at a construction site and make it look like an accident. It was fun working with his best buddy. Made things interesting during the day, that was for sure.

Cliff continued walking to the door leading outside. Mick stepped in front of him, placing his hands on Cliff's shoulders and stopping him. Seeing the warning in Mick's eyes, Cliff turned serious. He didn't want to screw this up. Mick had been his best friend for more years than he could remember, but it was the youngest Madison who had been tying his stomach in knots lately. He couldn't get within five feet of the young pup without wanting to press him up against a wall...or a table...or the floor... Hell, he'd fuck him standing straight up or standing on his head if he could just get at that luscious body.

Toby was smaller than Mick, inheriting his human mother's stature and build. He was lean, lightly covered in solid muscle, but slender all the same. His shaggy brown hair was streaked with auburn highlights, just a tad too long, brushing his chin.

Cliff had realized months ago that Toby was coming into his phase. It had been right around Christmas, when Toby had come back to Calgary for the holidays. He should have gone through it years ago, but his mother's genetics messed up his werewolf genes. At twenty-six, Toby was a little old to hit what was basically his second puberty. Werewolf males hit an initial puberty in their teens like human males, but they didn't reach sexual maturity among their kind until their early twenties. Not that it mattered much. They lived longer than the average human.

Butch Madison, Toby's dad, had two children. Mick, a full-blooded were, and Toby, a half-breed. Mick was the result of one night of partying between a group of weres. Butch hadn't been mated to Mick's mother—it wasn't until he met the very human Charlene that he found the one person who completed him.

No one really knew what it was that attracted mates to each other. Regardless of whether they were male/female, male/male or even female/female matches, werewolf mates just knew they were meant to be together.

Fate was definitely a bitch, though. She didn't like to make things too easy, so quite often weres came across their mates in the weirdest ways. Take Butch and Charlene. They met one night when Charlene was on her way home from a party with some friends. Butch had found her, leaning out of a car, puking on the side of the road. Not the most glorious start to a relationship.

It was rare to mate outside the species, like Butch and Charlene, so the weres in the pack weren't exactly certain what would happen to Toby. He was one of the few half-breeds in existence. Most weres his age were already mated or searching for their mates, but Toby was different. His human blood was unpredictable.

Fortunately, when both mates were werewolves it was a little easier to find each other. The only problem for Cliff was that wolves didn't give off a mate scent until they reached their mating phase. It made sense, but Toby's scent had been driving him crazy for the past seven months. He kept popping a boner in the most unfortunate situations every time he scented Toby.

Cliff had never noticed Toby before, sexually. Toby had always followed them around, but he was just Mick's younger brother. Now, he knew that the younger Madison was supposed to be his, although he couldn't do anything about it until Toby was ready for a relationship. Lately, every time the pup had gotten near him, his pheromones intensified. He was positive Toby was ready for him, finally.

It was a good thing Toby was going to be his. Cliff had always been attracted to other men. It would have been horrible to have a female as a mate. What the fuck would he do with her? It wasn't unheard of for previously heterosexual couples to find same-sex mates. But, it definitely complicated matters. He didn't know if Toby was attracted to men since he'd never seen him with anyone, but the fact that Toby seemed to be responding sexually to Cliff's presence put things squarely in Cliff's favor.

To make matters more complicated, though, most werewolves weren't even interested in sex until they reached their mating phase. Unlike humans, when werewolves hit puberty in their early teens, they normally went through the physical changes but not all the sexual ones. In other words, even though Toby might be ready for a relationship now, he was still innocent compared to other werewolves. He would be completely fresh, his sexual urges not strengthening until recently. How did you seduce a man who was entirely mature emotionally, physically and intellectually, but still a virgin sexually?

Mick wandered outside, stretching in place, undressing and shifting to his wolf form. Cliff followed him, glancing to the copse of trees behind the house. He lived about four houses down, but they always got together at Mick's parents' place. He was glad that Mick hadn't moved into his home yet. Things were working positively for Cliff, with Toby's return to the city. He could come and go from Butch and Charlene's place without it seeming too strange, since the sweetest ass this side of the Rockies lived inside.

He grinned, peeling off his shirt. Rubbing his hand absently on his furred chest, he thought about which direction he wanted to run in today. He popped the buttons on his jeans, sliding them down his legs to stand completely nude.

Mick whined at his side, his shaggy coat a mixture of brown and gray. He danced in place, all four feet moving, anxious to be going. Cliff inhaled, breathing in the warm air. He loved summer, everything was just fresher somehow. He concentrated, his body shifting effortlessly. Standing on all fours now, he craned his neck and licked one of his black front paws.

Mick took off, loping toward the tree line. Cliff gave a happy bark, tearing after him. He needed to find some way to release his tension. If he couldn't find release with Toby, at least he could run.

ᏁᏁᏁ

Cliff panted, flopping down at the base of the tree in Mick's yard. Mick limped up the back steps, shifting in mid-stride before walking into the house. Smirking, Cliff remembered the chase that had resulted in that limp. It wasn't his fault that Mick had run just a tad too slow. It *was* his fault that he bit down on Mick's back leg, but it was too tempting to pay him back for the scratches that ran up his backside. Mick had nudged him right into a firepit and the damn metal grate raked across his ass before he realized what he had landed in.

He lowered his head, resting it on his front paws while he listened to the murmured words from inside. Charlene—who must have recently come home from work—was exclaiming over Mick's calf. His teeth marks were pretty obvious.

The porch door creaked open, shutting with a bang.

"What did you do to Mick?" Toby sauntered outside, stepping in a wide path around Cliff, careful to stay out of reach. He turned his head to glance at the trees that Cliff had viewed earlier.

Cliff studied Toby, raising his nose. The pup was leaking pheromones like crazy, the air rife with the tasty scent. He tensed his body, lifting up his hind end to crawl forward.

Toby turned back, and Cliff froze, settling back down. If Toby noticed that Cliff was now closer to him, he didn't say anything. Cliff waited, his neck stiff, until Toby glanced at the house where the muted conversation between Mick and

Charlene was still audible. Cliff took advantage of Toby's distraction and inched forward.

Toby twisted his head again, gazing at Cliff. He froze. This was gonna be fun. He smiled, allowing his tongue to drop and hang out of his mouth. *Harmless. Look at the cute, harmless wolfie. I'm not gonna hurt you. See how cute I am.* He wagged his tail, stirring the air.

Toby grunted. "You aren't fooling me with that act, so stop it." He couldn't quite hide the smile on his face. Cliff wagged his tail harder.

Facing him, Toby put his hands on his hips. Cliff bunched his back legs, waiting. Sticking out his tongue, Toby baited him.

Cliff pounced, pushing hard with his back legs, missing his prey by inches. Toby twirled in place, running flat out. He was wearing shoes—a serious miscalculation on his part—and wouldn't be able to shift. Lunging to the right, Cliff gloried in the happy laugh that Toby let out. Toby altered his path and started to run to the left. *Perfect.*

They hit the tree line seconds apart. Toby twisted, veering off the marked path. Barking, Cliff was pleased that Toby was heading deeper into the park. Lush greenery sprang up around them, peppering the ground, providing obstacles for Toby as he ran through the trees.

Cliff growled and snapped at Toby's heels, herding him in the direction Cliff wanted. They both knew he could have caught him at any time. He barked, and Toby slowed. Toby's chest moved unevenly. Weres didn't have the same stamina in human form. Toby turned, walking backward.

Cliff pounced, taking Toby off guard. Shifting back to his human form in midair, he slammed into Toby, rolling with him so that he was on the bottom with Toby cradled to his chest. Rolling again, he straddled Toby, pressing his hands to Toby's shoulders to hold him in place. Fragrant grass bent under their bodies, releasing a pleasant smell that hinted at wild summer nights.

"Damn it." Toby wriggled to get free.

Cliff moaned. His cock was between them, sliding against the rough fabric of Toby's jeans.

Toby bucked up into him once, before stilling completely.

Cliff chuckled. "Well, well. Looks like I have you right where I want you."

Chapter Three

Toby silently cursed himself. He couldn't believe he'd fallen for Cliff's chase through the park. Although, he did love the feel of Cliff's hard body on top of him. Speaking of hard, he wriggled—yep, that was Cliff's cock pressed against his. He couldn't see it from where he was pinned. He couldn't even breathe for looking at the expanse of smooth skin in front of his face. Cliff was completely naked, his sculpted chest perfection to Toby's eager eyes.

He felt the blush run up his neck and bloom on his face. Another mark of his human genes, the other wolves didn't blush nearly as easily as he did. He stilled when Cliff groaned again.

"God, baby. I can't believe I never noticed you before. To think you've been right in front of me for years when I could have had this."

Toby paused, unable to believe this was happening to him. He couldn't complain, but it just seemed so unreal. He wasn't sure if this was a good idea at all. If they had sex, Cliff was bound to reject him afterward. And sex was definitely where this looked to be heading.

"I don't think we should be doing this."

"Well, Tobe, we could sit here and debate what the next step is going to be, but there are way more pleasant things I would rather be doing right now."

Toby hesitated, more than ready to put a stop to this. Nevertheless, he was intrigued by the crafty glint in Cliff's eyes.

"What things?" he asked instead.

"Hmm, since you brought it up..." Cliff grinned wickedly, palming Toby's cock through his jeans. Groaning, Toby arched up into the pressure.

"This *thing* here seems like it could be fun to play with," Cliff teased.

Toby panted, close to losing it already. Cliff's rough hand grasped his cock tightly, pressing hard on his aching shaft. He needed that hand on his flesh, not just through his jeans. He squirmed, unable to form the words to let Cliff know what he wanted.

"What's wrong, Tobe? Do you want this? You want my hand on your dick? Tell me, baby. I want to hear those pretty lips form the words."

Toby struggled for breath, opening and closing his mouth. His whole body quivered, gasping pants escaping him.

"Please..."

"Please what, Toby?"

"Touch me?" His words formed a question.

Cliff ran his lips along Toby's jawline, catching his skin between hard teeth. Toby yelped when Cliff bit down lightly. His hand moved, sliding up to toy with the button on Toby's jeans. He hadn't worn a belt, and once the button was undone, there was nothing but one lonely zipper between Cliff's hand and Toby's flesh.

Cliff wormed his way into the opening, grasping the hard column of flesh in his tight fist. Squealing, Toby jumped, almost bucking Cliff off of him. Cliff released him, ignoring the hands that reached to hold him in place. He clutched Toby's shirt, caressing his chest through the yellow cotton.

"Are you real partial to this?" Cliff gripped the shirt in two handfuls.

Toby shook his head, confused by the question. Cliff was asking him to think? Now? His silence was rewarded by a hard yank, the shirt falling to pieces. Cliff obviously wanted him naked.

Toby felt his eyes widen and he gasped at the feral glint in Cliff's gaze. The bigger man lowered his mouth, sucking up a mark on Toby's chest. A part of him couldn't believe this was actually happening to him. What had set this off? And why was Cliff hitting on him now when Toby had been watching Cliff for years?

When Cliff twisted, they rolled in the grass, the blades caressing Toby's back. Cliff effortlessly maneuvered Toby, easing him forward until he straddled Cliff. His black hair contrasted with the vibrant green grass under him. The sun was shining down on Cliff through the trees, dappling his rugged features. His face tight with passion, his teeth were bared.

Cliff grasped Toby's hips hard, holding him down. Sprawling over Cliff's chest, Toby fisted his hands in the grass to either side of Cliff's face. Toby looked down, confused. He didn't know what to do, couldn't figure out what Cliff wanted next. Cliff moved, releasing Toby's hips and lifting one hand. Toby glanced down at the feel of the heated clasp against his cock. He gulped, seeing the tanned fingers on his shaft.

Cliff grunted, his only response before he let Toby go to hold his own cock in one large hand, pumping it once. It was massive! Bigger than Toby's own, the head was weeping slick fluid. Cliff ran his thumb over the slit, spreading precome over the glans and down the shaft. Toby bucked his hips, unable to keep still. His gaze was glued to Cliff's hand, unwilling to tear away from the sight in front of him.

He licked his lips. He'd dreamed of this moment and he couldn't get over the fact that he was here with Cliff.

Toby gasped when Cliff shifted under him, bringing them both into a seated position before pressing the two shafts together. Moving one big hand around both, he squeezed. Toby moaned, his mind clouding. He couldn't think of a single thing except the feel of heated flesh. The underside of his sensitive cock rubbed against Cliff's, sliding along the moist flesh, Cliff's precome coating his own shaft.

The air was filled with pants and sighs, both men rocking in time with each other. The warm sun shone down on Toby's back, his rough jeans abrading his balls where they were still confined.

He whimpered when Cliff turned them, and he landed on his back in the flattened grass. Cliff growled, grasping Toby's jeans in both hands and shredding them from his legs. Werewolf strength did come in handy at times. His shoes were dealt with in a similar manner, yanked off his feet and thrown over Cliff's shoulder. Toby couldn't muster up enough concern to figure out where they had landed. The two of them could always find the shoes later.

Cliff returned to him, laying his solid body on top of Toby. He undulated his hips, thrusting against Toby. With a move so fast Toby didn't really register it, Cliff shimmied down his body, ending up with his face inches from Toby's aching cock. Cliff wasted no time, opening his mouth and taking Toby deep in one long gulp. Toby cried out, held down by the hard, bruising hands at his hips. His eyes went blank, his sight gone. He threw his head back, slamming it into the ground below him.

Cliff paused, waiting for him to come back to earth before he swallowed, Toby's cock still held tightly in his mouth. He milked the head of Toby's cock with his throat, sending shock waves through Toby's body. He had never imagined it could be like this. His hand wasn't going to be enough ever again.

Backing off, Cliff released Toby's cock from his mouth with a pop. He smiled, the look on his face carnal. He flicked his tongue, pushing it into the slit at the head of Toby's cock. Toby hissed. Grabbing Toby's thighs, Cliff guided them up until his knees pressed to his chest. Turning his face, Cliff nuzzled one quivering thigh, biting into the muscle. He swiveled his head, repeating the gesture on the other leg. Toby mewled in response. He couldn't breath, caught up in what Cliff was doing to him. He wanted to pinch himself to actually make sure this wasn't a dream. What had he done to deserve this?

Sliding down Toby's body, Cliff ignored his cock, placing his mouth squarely on Toby's sac. He sucked gently, lapping at the sensitive skin. He mouthed each ball, putting one and then the other into his hot, wet mouth.

Toby closed his eyes, shivering despite the heat. Tensing his thighs, Toby shuddered at what Cliff was doing to him. Cliff's tongue was driving him mad, taking him closer to orgasm with every sucking pull on his balls. He'd never realized sex would be this intense. It was beyond his wildest dreams. Sure, he'd lain awake at nights, jacking off to his fantasies of Cliff, but that was nothing compared to the feel of Cliff between his legs.

Between one breath and the next, Cliff lowered his mouth, licking along Toby's crack. Toby made a sound that was suspiciously close to a gurgle, his eyes flying open. Cliff kissed up and down, teasing the puckered flesh. He paused, sucking hard against Toby's skin. Cliff continued to tease his anus, awakening all the tiny nerve endings, sending him flying. Toby couldn't believe what Cliff was doing.

Toby was terrified he was going to come, and how frickin' embarrassing would that be? Oh God, he wasn't going to last much longer.

Cliff arrowed his tongue, pushing it forward to lap inside Toby, moaning into his flesh. Cliff's stubble rasped against his sensitive skin, his fingers bruising on his thighs. Toby's legs were shaking, and he couldn't stop closing his thighs tight around Cliff's head. He didn't want the man to stop what he was doing. He might damn well die if he stopped.

"Please, oh God, please Cliff...don-don't stop, stop, don't stop, please..." he pleaded, desperate to come.

Cliff chuckled, flicking his tongue in and out. Toby saw stars. The ache was building in his lower back. His toes curled. God, he was going to come. Panting, Toby tossed his head to the side. He had a brief thought that he should warn Cliff he was close, but he couldn't form the words. Cliff released one hand from his thigh, curling it around Toby's cock, jerking once, twice. Toby screamed while arcs of come shot onto his stomach. Cliff didn't stop what he was doing, lapping at Toby's ass while he shuddered and moaned.

"Cliff, Cl-Cliff, oh, oh, oh God..." He wasn't even aware of what he was saying, babbling words to Cliff, anything to make the pleasure last. His breathing sped up again, unbelievably, and his cock started to harden once more.

Cliff finally released him, raising his head to meet Toby's eyes over his rapidly growing shaft.

"C'mon, baby, I know you can do that again." Cliff's fingers danced along Toby's shaft, toying with him, sliding up the veins and smoothing over the glans. He shifted, pushing Toby's legs down flat on the ground, straddling his thighs. He brought his own cock into contact with Toby's, jerking the two together.

"Fuck, yeah," Cliff moaned. "I'm almost there, Tobe. I need you with me, baby. I need you with me when I go."

Toby cried out, the pressure increasing in his balls. Cliff's eyelids were lowered, the look behind them heated and intense. It felt like Cliff was looking through him, right into his soul.

Toby shook, gasping out his release, his seed landing on Cliff's hand, dotting him with the white liquid. Cliff moaned, pumping harder, just shy of painful to Toby's sensitized flesh. Cliff groaned harshly, his come jetting out to fall on Toby's belly, mixing in with his previous release. Cliff panted, falling forward to collapse on Toby, thrusting his free hand out so he didn't crush him. Cliff rolled over, lying on his back. He shifted, settling Toby against his shoulder.

Toby curled into Cliff, placing a kiss on the skin in front of his face. He nuzzled against Cliff, so damn happy he didn't know what to say.

"Now, that's what I call nut cream," Cliff gasped, a smile in his voice. He brought his face to Toby's, kissing his brow. "God, I'm never going to get enough of you, am I?"

Toby smiled faintly, his breathing still rushed. "I hope to hell you never do."

Chapter Four

Cliff lay on his back, his little mate pulled up tight to his chest. Inhaling, Cliff smiled when he realized their scents were combining. Yep, Toby was definitely his mate. *Perfect.*

"We need to go back to the house," he whispered.

Toby shifted, tightening his arms around Cliff's chest. "Why?"

"'Cause we don't have lube, and I'm not waiting another day to get at this." He reached down and grabbed Toby's ass. He squeezed, pleased when Toby tensed his muscles. Nudging Toby to his feet, Cliff sprung up beside him. He smacked the delectable ass in front of him, causing Toby to yelp.

"Shit! I can't even put my clothes back on. Why'd you have to rip them?" Toby asked, completely adorable.

"I'll certainly keep that in mind next time. If you really want me to take the time to undress you first and hang up all your clothes so they don't get wrinkled, you just let me know." He tipped his head to the side, pretending to consider the idea. He had a feeling Toby wouldn't go for it. The little pup had taken to sex like a seasoned pro.

"Ummm...no, that's okay," Toby said, blushing.

He chuckled ruefully. "Good, because I don't think I can wait to be with you. I'll never get enough."

Grinning, Toby launched himself at Cliff. He caught the smaller man and hugged him tight, breathing in deeply. Curling his arms around Toby, he pressed his face into the side of his pup's neck.

"Crap, wait!" Toby pulled back, an alarmed expression on his face.

"What now?"

"I don't have any lube."

Cliff cursed, thinking quickly. Then it dawned on him. "Don't worry about it. I have something in mind that'll work just as well."

Toby smiled shyly, holding out his hand for Cliff. He took it, setting off at a casual pace. They walked back the way they had come, strolling through the sunny park, occasionally commenting on something around them but both content to remain silent.

The back of the house came into view, and Cliff sniffed to make sure no one was home. He exhaled noisily, grateful they were alone. *Thank God.* He didn't relish the idea of coming upon Butch Madison, completely bare-assed naked, smelling of his youngest son.

Cliff's clothes were still lying on the ground where he'd left them when he shifted to run with Mick. He'd have to remember to grab them later.

Padding up the steps, Cliff entered the kitchen. Cliff released Toby's hand, smacking his ass again just to see Toby jump in surprise.

"Go on into your room. I'll be there in a minute." He waggled his eyebrows at Toby.

Toby beamed, wriggling his hips while he loped into his room. Cliff paused to watch Toby, snorting when he realized what Toby was doing. God, Toby was innocent sometimes, but it looked like the devil inside him had come out to play. Cliff glanced around, finding what he was searching for. He stopped, studying the nut cream in his hand. He considered it, shaking his head and peering around for something else. It would work, but he wanted something a little more long-lasting. He wasn't going to let the pup go once he was inside of him.

He paced to the bathroom and threw aside the shower curtain. Spying the bottle of Nut Bath Oil, he grinned. He picked it up, retraced his path and walked into Toby's room, shutting the door behind him.

Toby lay on his back on the bed, propped up on his elbows. His hard shaft was waving gaily at Cliff, front and center. Toby twisted his hips, smiling sweetly. He had left the light off, but there was enough sunlight coming in through the open blinds that Cliff could see Toby clearly. The sun shone into the room, caressing Toby with its rays.

"What took you so long?"

Cliff felt his mouth flood with moisture. He ached to taste the body laid out before him, but he really didn't want this to end so quickly. If he got on the bed now, this wouldn't last nearly long enough. With a smile, he spied the large chair in the corner of Toby's room.

Sauntering over, he slumped into the chair, waving the bottle of nut oil at Toby. His pup's cheeks flushed bright red, the blush continuing down his body and spreading along his chest. Cliff was pleased he could affect his mate so well, seeing how Cliff was acting like an unschooled youth with his first crush. Cliff was afraid that it would be him coming at the merest brush of Toby's fingers if he wasn't careful. Being with Toby was like drinking the finest wine. It was going straight to his head. *So this is what it's like to have a mate.* Damn, he was lucky.

Toby gingerly sat up, sending a questioning glance his way. Cliff winked, patting his leg with his free hand. Smiling, Toby dropped to all fours and crawled across the bed. His movements were sinuously graceful, his were heritage obvious. When he reached the end of the bed, he tossed his head, letting his hair fall back. He rose up, climbing down to stand in front of Cliff.

He patted his thigh again, waiting for Toby to move. Toby's face was so red it looked painful, but nevertheless he crawled into the chair, straddling him. Cliff moaned low in his throat, the sound coming out in a rumbling purr. Grabbing Toby hard around the hips, he pulled him in until they were meshed together.

Cliff shifted lower in the chair, grasping their cocks with one hand. Toby brought up his arm, twining it around Cliff's neck for support. The other hand landed on Cliff's thigh, curving around near the bend of his knee. Toby's upper body was arched, and Cliff leaned forward and took one of Toby's delectable nipples between his lips. He pulled, sucking the nub into his mouth, desperate to drive his mate crazy with need.

He loved the feel of Toby in his arms—the younger man fit perfectly against him. Cliff inhaled, breathing in the scent of his mate and shuddering at the feel of Toby's hand on his thigh. Toby's fingers were opening and closing against his skin. The small movements coupled with the heady scent of Toby made his head swim.

He kept his hands at Toby's waist, holding him in place. Toby panted above him, twisting from the pleasure he was inflicting. Cliff released his nipple, licking across his chest until he reached the other. Biting and sucking, he worked the nub so it was as red as the first. Toby's cock was leaking profusely from all the attention.

He glanced up to see Toby watching him with wide, unblinking eyes. He was so beautiful. His mate was fucking gorgeous with his pale skin, dusted with the faintest blush on his cheeks. His eyes were completely guileless, and the most beautiful brown. They looked like melted chocolate and he knew he could get lost within them. Toby's lips were parted, rosy red with a sensuous curve to them. He realized that he hadn't yet kissed his mate. Now, how could he have overlooked that?

He arched his neck, offering his mouth up to Toby. He didn't want to pressure him—the pup needed to make his own choices here. Cliff wasn't going to force him into anything. Toby whimpered, closing the distance between them. Their lips met gingerly, testing each other. With a pained groan, Cliff increased the pressure, fusing their mouths together. He backed off, licking along the seam of Toby's mouth, encouraging him to open up and let him in. He slid his hands up along the lightly muscled contours of Toby's back.

Toby opened his mouth, making way for Cliff's tongue. He tasted like heaven, a combination of sweet ginger ale and pure male. Cliff could taste himself on Toby's tongue from their kisses earlier, and he groaned. He leaned his head back, releasing Toby. Cliff smiled tenderly at the younger man, stretching up to brush his hair back behind his ear.

He still couldn't get over the fact that he had his pup here with him. To be able to hold Toby, to caress his body was an amazing feeling.

"Is this what you want?" Cliff whispered.

"Yeah," Toby said quietly. "I've wanted this forever. I've wanted *you* forever."

Chapter Five

Cliff leaned in, brushing a kiss along his pup's shoulder. Reaching down, he grabbed the bottle of nut oil, popping the top with a snap. He held the bottle up, waiting until Toby turned to look. Upending the bottle, he poured a generous amount into his palm. The scent of nuts filled the room, complementing the pheromones that were coming off Toby and himself. He flipped the top closed, keeping the bottle in his hand. He smoothed his wet palm down his cock, making it glisten in the sunlight. Toby watched him carefully. Cliff couldn't take his eyes off the man.

"Your turn, baby," he said, his voice rough. "Have you ever played with yourself?"

Toby turned his head, grimacing. He couldn't quite hide the guilty expression in his eyes.

"Okay, now I need to know what that look means. What've you done?"

Toby hesitated. "Nothing major, I just... Sometimes when I'm in the shower, I-I've...you know..."

"What, Tobe? What've you done?" he repeated. He needed to hear the words, even though he was starting to have a good idea of what Toby was going to say.

"It's just been so hard the past few months... No, I don't mean hard! I mean... Well... Christ." He groaned, dropping his head to land on Cliff's chest.

Cliff couldn't stop the laughter that was building. He let it out, the sound startling in the room.

"Baby, you're just too much. Are you trying to say that you've experimented with yourself? You wanted to know what made you feel good? Is that it?"

Toby nodded, keeping his head down. His hair stroked across Cliff's chest, soft to the touch. Cliff wrapped his fingers in the silky strands.

"There's nothing to be embarrassed about. We've all experimented. I'm happy that you know what you like. It makes my job a hell of a lot easier." He tilted Toby's head, grasping his hair and pulling back until Toby met his eyes. "Now, when I ask you a question, I want you to answer me. I don't give a shit if you do it with a nod or a yes or no. Okay?"

Toby bobbed his head, staring at him with those big, trusting eyes. God, they made him feel like a king.

"Okay, first question. When you were in the shower, did you touch your cock? Wrap your hand around the shaft and jerk off?"

A second nod, timid, but there.

Cliff tried to hide his smile, not wanting to make this difficult.

"Second question. Did you ever touch your hole, smooth your finger around that tender bit of flesh? Maybe push your finger inside?"

Another nod, slow in coming.

"Good, Tobe. Did you ever insert anything bigger than your finger?"

234

A sharp negative shake.

"Did you want to?"

A hesitation, followed by a measured nod. Toby was grinning now, his lips tilted impishly. Cliff sent him an answering grin, glad that his mate was willing to play this game with him.

"Okay, what did you want to press into your ass?"

Toby smirked, shrugging and raising one eyebrow impatiently.

"Fuck. Fine, I'm supposed to ask you a yes or no question, right? Okay, did you think of me when you were in the shower?" he asked, going straight to the question that had been burning him inside.

Toby tilted his head, considering. He furrowed his brow. Cliff frowned, the beast inside him snarling.

"You little shit, don't tease me right now," he mock-growled.

Toby laughed, his face lighting up with a beaming smile. "Of course I was thinking of you. What? You actually need me to say the words? Okay, I thought of you then, I'm damn well thinking of you now and if you aren't inside me soon, I may burst from wanting you so badly. Is that clear enough for you?"

Cliff's chest tightened, his throat closing up and his body tensing.

"Get yourself ready for me, Tobe," he ground out.

Toby held out his hand, his face serious. Taking the bottle of oil from Cliff, Toby wet his fingers with it and reached his hand back. He lifted up slightly with the help of the two hands grasping his hips, Cliff taking his weight easily. Toby's eyes closed, his mouth opening on a long, drawn-out moan. Cliff strained his neck, desperate to see what Toby was doing with that hand. Cliff's pup had two fingers knuckle-deep in his ass, stretching the small opening.

Cliff made a sound, too damn close to a whimper for his liking.

Toby slid out his fingers, gliding the tips around his hole, massaging the tissue. He skimmed them forward, pressing against the bit of flesh behind his balls. He flexed his ass, wiggling into the hand Cliff had gripped on his hip. The damn pup was going to have bruises covering his body in the morning if he wasn't careful. Toby didn't look as if he cared.

A third finger joined the other two, forming a wedge, before Toby drove all three into his ass, bucking into his own hand. Cliff gasped, reaching down to touch the stretched flesh with his fingers. He couldn't take any more of this, he needed Toby *now*.

He urged Toby higher on his lap, pulling out the smaller man's fingers and replacing them with the head of his cock. Toby leaned back, anchoring his right hand on Cliff's thigh. Toby met his eyes, holding Cliff's gaze while slowly lowering himself over Cliff's cock. It was unbelievably erotic—he felt like he was connecting straight to Toby's soul. Cliff held him in place. The head of his cock breached the warm entrance, sliding in. Toby gasped, his eyes wide and unseeing.

"Shh, it's okay. Just stay still for a bit. Don't move, Toby," he crooned.

Toby shook his head, whimpering sharply. Without warning, he tilted his hips, relaxed his body. He bottomed out on Cliff's cock, his ass opening for him. A sliver of pain peeked out of Toby's expressive gaze.

Cliff moaned, unable to comprehend the feeling of being inside his mate. He was so damn tight that the friction was killing him. Toby's ass was against his groin—he had taken

Cliff's entire shaft. Toby's cock was flushed red, a deep hue, and curved up until it almost hit his stomach. Cliff blindly searched for the oil, grabbing the bottle when his hands closed around it. He popped the top. Not caring where the bottle ended up, he dropped it, squirted the oil into his hand and wrapped it around Toby's thick shaft. He tugged, urging Toby to raise himself. Toby gasped again, twitching his hips. His tiny, convulsive movements were driving Cliff crazy. He moaned, so fucking close to busting his nut inside his mate.

Toby let out a groan, jerking wildly while his seed splattered over Cliff's hand. His pup's ass squeezed on his shaft, the vise-like grip too much for Cliff. He shot off, releasing himself into Toby.

While he still had enough presence of mind, he lifted up, wincing when his spent cock slipped out of Toby's ass.

"Tobe?"

When he got no answer, he lifted Toby's head, staring intently down at his pup. Toby's eyelids fluttered shut and his lips curved into a sleepy smile.

Carrying his precious cargo, he slid into Toby's bed, turning Toby over to lie beside him. He slithered up behind him, pulling the smaller man tight. Closing his eyes, he breathed deeply, inhaling the scent of his mate. Toby let out a soft snore, completely lost to the world. Cliff smiled, tucking his head into the nape of Toby's neck and pressing a kiss to his skin.

Chapter Six

The slamming of the screen door woke Toby up. Panicked, he couldn't figure out where he was. Turning his head, he looked for Cliff. The man wasn't anywhere in sight. *Was it all just a dream?* Shifting, he winced at the ache in his ass. That was definitely real. So where the hell was Cliff?

He let out a little moan, burrowing deeper into the covers. The sheets smelled like Cliff, a woodsy scent that made him think of the outdoors. He curled up his knees, content to lie still and wallow in his memories for a moment.

Toby buried his head in the pillow, crying *yahoo* into the cotton. He heard a snorting chuckle from outside his room. Startled, he jumped up, ignoring the ache that made itself known again. He stumbled to the door, flinging it open.

"Cliff?"

"Jesus Christ on a crutch, I think I've gone blind! My eyes," Mick bellowed, sounding more like a bear than the wolf he was.

"Oh God." Toby slammed the door shut. He leaned his head against the wood, rocking back and forth. Well, that was humiliating. But it still didn't answer his question. Where the hell was Cliff?

A firm knock on the door interrupted his musings.

"Toby, put some goddamn clothes on and open this fucking door," Mick muttered.

Toby scrambled to his closet, picking up a pair of jeans and hurriedly tugging them on, hopping from one foot to the other. He scooped up a shirt from the floor and yanked it over his head. Opening the door, he realized he had his shirt on inside out and quickly pulled it off. Mick stared at him, bemused, while he waited for Toby to fix himself.

"Sorry, sorry," he gasped.

"In the kitchen with you."

Toby lurched after his brother, looking to the wall clock to see what time it was. He couldn't believe it was morning already. That meant he'd slept the entire evening and well into the morning. He had never slept so long before. Not even after he pulled an all-nighter marking report cards last month.

He stumbled to a stop, concerned when he spied the large form of his father seated at the table. He lowered his head, sniffing unobtrusively.

"Don't bother, you stink of that horny bastard," his father grumbled.

Toby felt himself flush, and he ducked his head to avoid everyone's gaze. He stood in the doorway, unsure of what to do. Used to being in control, Toby wasn't certain what to make of his sudden shyness.

His mom was at the sink, washing dishes, although she did turn to give him a sympathetic smile. Mick frowned, leaning against the counters to his left and crossing his arms along his burly chest.

"Dad?" Toby asked.

His father let out a sigh and pushed back from the table. He remained in place for a moment, propped against the surface. With another sigh, he turned, meeting Toby's worried gaze.

Butch Madison looked exactly like Mick. Tall, stocky, with thick brown hair piled on his head, he appeared wild and untamed. He was deeply tanned, courtesy of working outdoors at construction sites his entire life. His expressive eyes had laugh lines around them, and grooves framed his mouth. Butch was a man who felt strongly about his family and had no problem showing those emotions. His face was lived-in, like he had survived a long and eventful life.

"I didn't think this was going to happen, Tobias. I never thought you would mate because of the human blood flowing through you," he drawled.

Toby jerked in place, startled. "What are you talking about? I didn't mate! Shut up, Mick. It's not funny," he shouted over the sounds of his brother's laughter. He was acting undignified for a teacher, but his brother could piss him off faster than anyone else.

Mick was almost doubled over, snorting with glee.

"I'm pretty sure even the human in the room can smell the aftereffects of your *mating*, so don't try to hide it, Toby," Mick crowed.

"Hey, the human has a name," his mother said, frowning.

"That wasn't... I didn't mean... I was talking about... *Gah*," Toby exclaimed, frustrated when the words wouldn't come. "I just meant that I didn't mate in the werewolf sense of the word," he finally ground out between clenched teeth.

"Tobias, I hate to disappoint you, but I can smell you. Ah, wait for me to finish before you interrupt me again. I mean, I can smell your scent, and it's changed. For twenty-six years you've had the same scent. I could have found you anywhere you went it was so familiar to me. But your scent has changed since yesterday. You smell like him. The two of you mixed together. It means you've mated."

Toby froze, unable to comprehend the words he was hearing. He had always dreamed of this, of learning he was Cliff's mate. He couldn't believe it. *But...wait a minute...*

"You mean, Cliff knew? Cliff knew when he came to me yesterday? That I was his mate?"

"Cliff would have known months ago, when you first started going into your phase, that you were his mate," his father explained patiently.

"That ass! That big stinkin', hairy ass. I can't believe he did this to me. The fuckhead—" He was so angry. A part of him was appalled at his behavior but he couldn't seem to stop. What was happening to him? Was this because of the mating phase? He couldn't wait to get over it since it was making him act like one of his students. He was normally more reserved, not juvenile.

Hell, if anything, it should be Mick acting this way. Despite being older than him, Mick had a jokester streak a mile wide. He also had quite the temper. Toby couldn't wait for Mick to find a mate of his own. He'd been searching for years, but Toby was desperately praying that it would be someone who'd tie Mick up in knots. It would serve him right.

"Language, Tobias Edward Madison," his mother admonished, interrupting him.

"I don't see what the big deal is," Mick said, straddling one of the kitchen chairs. He tipped forward, resting the chair on two legs.

Toby had an overwhelming urge to kick the chair out from under him. Only the sure knowledge that Mick could beat his ass—not to mention the lecture he'd get from his mom and dad—stopped him. It was a pretty close call though. He fumed silently, gritting his teeth to keep still.

"If you don't understand it, then I'm not explaining it to you. Jackass," he couldn't help adding. "This is between me and Cliff."

"Well, if you're looking for Cliff, try following the path to the river. That's the direction he took off in when we got home. He told me you could find him there." Mick regarded him with curious eyes.

Toby hesitated, not sure if he wanted to talk to Cliff right now, before he realized that he had to talk to the ass sometime.

Nodding his thanks, he headed out the door.

He followed the path, kicking at the grass in his way. He was pissed and surly and Toby wasn't about to let the good weather get him out of his funk. How could Cliff do this to him?

He'd been panting after Cliff for years, so why now was Cliff showing an interest in him? Was it only because of the mate thing? Would Cliff ever have looked twice at Toby if he wasn't mated to him? He couldn't figure out what was worse. Having Cliff know for months that they were mated and not telling Toby about it, or having Cliff know that Toby had been getting a hard-on every time they were in the room together and ignoring the mating urges.

Toby had been freaking out every time he was within feet of Cliff, and apparently he shouldn't have. He didn't have to be so embarrassed and humiliated. He didn't have to hide his feelings. Why hadn't Cliff said something to him earlier?

It was bad enough that all the other werewolves treated him differently. Did they think he didn't know what they said about him? Yeah, he was half human, but he wasn't ashamed of that. It made him unique, although he wasn't lower than them. So what if he'd been a virgin at the ripe old age of twenty-six. Who cared if most weres lost their virginity when they hit twenty? It didn't make him stupid, or naïve or innocent.

"Okay, so I don't work in construction or in law, or something powerful. Yeah, I'm the first Madison to become something other than a laborer. Being an elementary-school teacher isn't exactly easy, and none of those fucktards would be able to do it. I'd like to see them face down a classroom of thirty kids, and still keep their so-called cool," he grumbled.

He just hadn't realized that Cliff was of the same mind as all the others.

"Hell, he came to my graduation. He was in the fucking front row, cheering me on when I accepted my degree."

He felt so incredibly dumb. When his father said that Cliff already knew, well that just put the nail in his coffin. He shook his head, depressed at the thought that Cliff felt he had to protect "poor, little Toby". Why else would he have hidden his mating urges for months? It had to be because he didn't think Toby could handle it.

"We should make all his decisions for him. Cut up his meat in case he stabs himself with the goddamn fork and knife," he sing-songed. "Fucking idiots."

He could smell Cliff before he saw him. The path bent up ahead, twisting before it met the bank of the river flowing through the park. His stupid fuckhead of a mate was waiting at the river for him, probably pleased as could be. Toby knew Cliff would realize he was coming. Cliff had a better sense of smell, he would have to, being full-blooded.

"Noo, it's just me, the stupid half human who can't smell anything. Can't smell my stupid mate, can't smell at all," he muttered to himself, kicking at a rock in front of him.

"You do realize I can hear you, right?" Cliff asked, appearing in front of him suddenly.

Toby yelped, cursing when he let out the sound. He cursed again when he realized he had cursed.

"Ah, fuck." He exhaled loudly, shaking his head.

Cliff had the good sense to turn his back, pretending to study something off the path, but Toby had already seen the smile that bloomed across his face.

"I don't want to talk to you right now. I'm mad at you, fuckhead," Toby said, refusing to hide his feelings. If Cliff was his so-called mate, then he better get used to how Toby acted when he was mad. Apparently he hung out with kids too much. He was starting to sound like one.

"What did I do, Tobe?" Cliff brushed back the hair at the side of Toby's face. He leaned into the caress before he realized what he was doing. He was supposed to be mad at Cliff. He jerked away from the touch.

Toby tried to walk past Cliff, but was hampered by the large hand that grasped his biceps.

"Toby, are you mad that I left this morning? I didn't have much of a choice. I didn't want to disrespect your father by staying in his house before I had formally approached him. As it was, I ended up talking to him bare-assed naked. Not exactly the way I always envisioned petitioning for mating rights." He chuckled ruefully.

Toby quirked his lips, amused despite himself at the image running through his mind. That would have been a sight worth seeing. He couldn't dream of having his dad walk in on them as Cliff was trying to make a getaway.

"What did he say?" he asked, shuffling his feet.

"He said that you deserved better than me," Cliff said quietly.

Toby opened his mouth to protest, shutting it when he remembered he was still mad at Cliff for hiding the fact they were mated. He remained silent.

"He also said that I needed to talk to you, explain what was going on. So, I think we should have that talk now, don't you? I'm not exactly sure why you're so put out. Do you want to explain it to me?"

Toby exhaled noisily, looking off in the distance.

"Come on, baby, let me in," Cliff cajoled.

"I'm mad at you because Dad said you knew months ago that I was your mate," he whispered. Cliff had to lean in to catch the soft-spoken words. "Why did you wait?" he finally asked, his anger giving way to simple hurt. "Did you think I was too immature to understand? So what if I was innocent, that doesn't make me stupid. I've got my goddamn degree in education, how stupid does that make me?"

"Enough!" Cliff snarled, startling him out of his rant. "If you ever call yourself stupid or immature again, I will turn you over my knee and blister your ass raw. You are the smartest man I know. You think I could have done what you did? Going to school and leaving town. No, you wanna talk stupid, how about the guy who just barely managed to get his high-school diploma. You have your fucking degree, Tobe. You sat through four years of university. I never could have done that. I think you're incredible for doing what you have. *So, don't you ever belittle yourself again!* Is that clear?" he growled.

Toby sniffed, trying to stop the flow of tears. He didn't know what to say.

"Tobe, I had to be positive. I've never felt this way before, so I had to be sure that what I was feeling was real. I needed to know that you were really my mate and not just some guy I popped a boner over. I couldn't figure out why I only saw your face in my dreams. Every night, I went to bed and dreamed of you. It didn't make sense that the man I had grown up with was tying me up in these great big knots. I didn't know why your

245

face was the last thing I saw before I went to bed, and the first thing I saw in the morning. Why, I couldn't wait to go to Mick's on the off chance that I might see you. Can you forgive me for making you wait until I figured out what I was going through?" he asked, holding out his arms.

Toby hesitated, long enough to see the crestfallen look on Cliff's face. With a smile, he jumped into his arms, unable to hold back. He had finally gotten his wish. So what if he had to wait a few months longer because Cliff needed to be sure. He still ended up with the man he was in love with.

Cliff shifted him higher, startling a booming laugh out of him. Cliff's laughter joined with his own, their voices blending together.

Cliff ran down the path, holding Toby high. Too late, Toby realized where they were headed. "God, Cliff, don't, stop. Please don't do this. I swear, if you drop me, I'll kill you..."

Cliff ignored his pleas, throwing him high in the air. Squealing, uncaring if he sounded like a little girl, Toby plunged into the water.

He erupted through the surface with a sputter, glad that the water was at least warm. Cliff stood on the bank, crowing with glee.

Toby pushed the sodden hair out of his eyes. "Well, if you wanted to get me wet, there are other ways of doing it."

Cliff immediately stopped laughing, a decidedly horny glint entering his eyes. His face appeared wanton, his smirk just shy of depraved. "I don't have to try hard to get you wet, Tobe, and we both know it."

Toby blushed, lifting his arms to pull off his soaked tee. He threw it to the bank, where it landed with a plop beside Cliff.

"Is that so?" He reached under the water for the button on his jeans.

He wrestled them down his legs, cursing the fact that he probably didn't look too hot doing it. There went his attempt to be sophisticated. When he glanced up again, he realized it really didn't matter what he did. The expression on Cliff's face remained unchanged—he was still aroused just by looking at him. Toby paused in wonder.

"I didn't think I would ever see that look on your face."

"It'll always be there when I think of you, Tobe. I promise you."

He started forward in the water, drawn to his mate. Cliff shook his head, holding out one hand to stop him.

"There was a reason I told Mick to guide you here. I have a little surprise planned for you."

Toby tilted his head, beaming at Cliff. "A surprise?"

"Yeah, call it your mate gift. I wanted it to be special. But you need to do a few things for me first."

"Anything."

"God, you do me in with your eagerness."

Toby bounced in place, bringing up handfuls of water to pour over his head. He tilted his head back, letting the water flow down his torso.

Cliff growled. "Don't tempt me, or you won't get your gift."

Pausing, Toby considered what kind of gift Cliff would get him. His curiosity finally outweighed his need to be fucked. He waited, fervently anticipating Cliff's next directions.

"Clean yourself off, Toby. I want you sparkling fresh."

He plunged into the water, scrubbing the residue from their night together off his skin. He would still be able to smell Cliff on him. Thank God, or he might never have washed again.

He came up to the surface, patiently waiting for Cliff to tell him what to do. Cliff grinned at him, tapping his chin thoughtfully. He was still fully dressed, wearing the same jeans and black tee he'd had on yesterday. Toby grimaced, realizing that his own clothes were even now somewhere in the park, ripped to pieces, where anyone could find them. Oh hell, who really cared?

"Now, I've hidden something for you. I'll give you one hint though. It sparkles, so you shouldn't have any trouble finding it."

Toby wrinkled his forehead, trying to think of something that sparkled that Cliff would gift him with. "Can you give me a hint to its location? Is it in the river or on the bank?"

Cliff smirked, remaining stubbornly silent. Toby huffed. So he wanted this to be a treasure hunt? He could find it, no problem.

He peered into the flowing river, struggling not to stir up the sediment on the bottom. It only took him seconds to realize that Cliff wouldn't have hid the gift in the river. He would have been afraid it might wash away in the current. His gaze went to the bank where Cliff was standing, his arms crossed over his chest.

"Hmmm... If you didn't put it in the water, what are the chances that you placed it close to you?" he mused.

"I love the way your mind works, Tobe. C'mon, smart guy, figure it out."

Toby hummed, his eyes not catching any glinting material. He swung his head around to the other bank, slowly moving toward the shore. He tracked his gaze along the bank methodically. Cliff wouldn't have made it too easy. Where was the fun in that?

Something caught his eye and Toby pushed through the water to get close to it. There was an item near the bend in the river, right where it curved out of sight.

"Aha!" He rushed toward the object.

He was intent on his goal, moving through the water until he reached the bank and waded up onto the ground. A small noise distracted him just as he approached the gold object. Swiveling his head around, he spied a small bear cub. *Bear cub? What the hell?*

He backed up, not wanting to startle the little guy. A larger noise sounded to his right, and he swung his gaze directly into the path of a large black bear.

Oh fuck...

Chapter Seven

Toby gasped, a high-pitched noise that had the bear swinging in his direction. Cliff panicked, unable to tear his gaze away from the danger to his mate. He reacted without thought, immediately peeling off his shirt and jeans, shifting even as he waded into the water. Toby was frozen, unmoving. He had to distract the bear long enough for Toby to get away.

The bear reared up, roaring at Toby, who lowered himself to the ground, obviously trying to make himself look small. Cliff made it to the other side of the river, shaking himself so his coat puffed up around him. He didn't take his eyes off Toby, crawling forward with his teeth bared.

Toby scooted back, pulling even with him. Cliff placed himself in front of Toby's body. They wouldn't win in a fight against a bear, Cliff wasn't that idiotic. Especially when the bear's cub was standing two feet away from them. They had to get out of there, now.

He backed up into Toby, moving him toward the water. Toby tripped, scooting backward. He suddenly stopped, reaching forward past Cliff and grabbing the gold chain from the rock it was resting on. Cliff would have shaken his head, but he was too concerned with the bear to worry about anything else. He waited until Toby was behind him again, before he started herding him to the river. Keeping his eyes on the bear, he ignored the threatening display it presented.

Attempting to appear harmless, he managed to get Toby into the water. The bear charged, coming straight for them. Cliff growled, snapping and snarling to warn the bear back. He didn't want to fight the bear, but he would protect his mate.

He sidestepped, trying to keep away from the slashing claws. He yelped when a fiery blow hit his shoulder. A loud bark sounded to his right, a small reddish-brown wolf distracting the bear. Damn it, Toby was supposed to stay out of this. The bear stopped in place, roaring before she dropped to all fours. Throwing himself to the side, Cliff bounded into the water behind Toby.

They swam through the water, hitting the other bank where their clothes were. Both wolves stayed low, waiting until the two bears left before they shifted back into their human forms.

"Jesus Christ, holy crap, I can't believe that happened," Toby panted. "Here, let me. Don't touch it. Just let me see how bad it is."

Toby gently maneuvered Cliff until he was seated in front of his little mate. He groaned when Toby probed at the claw marks on his shoulder.

"Damn, that hurts worse than that scrape on my ass."

"Do you want me to kiss it better?" Toby asked, leaning in and licking Cliff's jaw.

Cliff hummed, content to remain still. He looked up, making sure they were alone. "We should probably get out of here. I'm not entirely comfortable being this out in the open with a fucking mother bear around."

Toby stood, helping Cliff to his feet when he faltered. Toby bent down to pick up their clothes, his toned ass distracting Cliff from whatever he would have said next. Groaning, he reached forward and grabbed Toby's ass in both hands. "I'm not going to be able to wait long to get at this again, baby."

Toby turned and threw Cliff's jeans and shirt at him. He caught them deftly, holding them to his chest.

"If you're fine to make comments like that, then you must not be that injured. Let's go." Toby shook his head, smiling.

Following his mate, he scanned the area around him. He needed his mate, but he needed to keep him safe even more. They made sure to make a lot of noise walking through the vegetation, hitting the bushes lining the path. It would probably scare the bear away.

Finally, they came into view of Toby's house. Stopping his mate with a hand to his arm, Cliff pulled him aside.

"I think we're okay. The bear won't come this close to the smell of people. Especially with so many shifters around."

Toby immediately turned. He made several abortive attempts to reach out to Cliff, staring at his wounds and biting his lower lip. Dropping his clothes, Cliff pulled his mate into him, ignoring the twinge in his shoulder. He ducked his head, breathing in the warm scent of Toby. With a shuddering breath, he finally allowed his delayed reaction to set in.

"Oh God, I almost lost you. I could have lost you, Tobe," he ground out.

He nudged Toby, turning him around to guide him into the house. Right at this moment, he didn't give a fuck if the whole family watched them. He needed inside his mate. *Now.*

Hurrying in front of him, Toby whimpered slightly. He was shaking so hard he couldn't get the screen door open. Drawing in a breath, Cliff was relieved to discover that they were once again alone. He herded Toby into the house, not making it to his bedroom before pushing him down on the couch. He wasn't going to last very long this time. He would have to make it up to his mate later.

"Christ, we need lube. Why the hell don't you people have lube?" Cliff asked, mindless with need.

Toby whimpered, absolutely no fucking help. Cliff stood, stumbling to the kitchen and grabbing the nut cream off the counter where he had left it last night. Popping the top, he squirted some in his hand, wrapping it around his aching shaft. Returning to where Toby was sprawled on his back along the sofa, Cliff bent down, kissing him roughly. Toby moaned and arched up into him. He grabbed the nut cream again, wetting his fingers and pressing them against the tight pucker of Toby's ass. Rubbing his digits around the outside, he waited until Toby's backside relaxed before inserting both fingers in one thrust. Toby cried out, his cock long and hard from the attention paid to his ass.

"I'm sorry, Tobe, I can't wait. Is that enough? Can you take me now?" Cliff asked, near desperate.

Toby mewled, nodding frantically, grasping at Cliff.

With a last teasing touch, Cliff withdrew his fingers from the heated passage of his mate, replacing them with the head of his cock. Groaning, he thrust his hips, sliding inside in small increments. He was anxious, but he wasn't going to hurt Toby. He wasn't that far gone yet. When he was finally lodged to the hilt, gasping at the tight, hot clasp of his mate, he stilled.

Dropping his head, he moved to take Toby's mouth with his own. Both men pressed together, anxious to get as close as they possibly could. Toby raised his arms, entwining them behind Cliff's back, pulling him in close. Toby's legs wrapped around him, one heel resting behind his knees and the other drawn up to below his ass.

Cliff slid his hands up Toby's sides, grabbing his shoulders to hold him close. He withdrew his cock partway, opening his mouth at the mind-blowing feel of the silky passage. Toby flexed his ass, unwilling to let him go.

He thrust in, harder than before, making Toby buck in response.

"God, Toby, I need you..."

"Please, Cl-Cliff, again, again..."

He snapped, thrusting hard, taking them both closer to the blinding edge where they could lose themselves. He couldn't think past the fear of seeing Toby in danger. He needed to erase the sight from his mind, ensure himself that they were both safe...both alive.

Cliff lowered one hand, reaching for Toby's cock, determined to have them reach their release at the same time.

"I'm so close, baby. Come with me. Come on, Tobe, I need you now..."

Toby gasped, bucking his hips, fucking Cliff's hand.

They both moaned, finding their release seconds apart, tightening their hold on each other.

"I love you, Toby. God, I love you, baby..."

Chapter Eight

Toby sniffed, grimacing when Cliff smiled knowingly. He frowned at him. He couldn't believe they'd had sex right out in the open.

"We better move before we end up glued together on this couch." Cliff laughed, stroking his hands down Toby's sides.

Cliff shifted, stretching in place before sliding off the couch to stand beside it. Toby looked up at him, not wanting to get up, but knowing Cliff was right.

Footsteps sounded outside, Mick's scent intensifying as he came up the driveway.

Toby jumped off the couch and grabbed Cliff's hand. Tugging Cliff over to his bedroom, he got them both inside and slammed the door shut.

"What the hell?" Mick thundered.

Cliff snorted, loud in the sudden silence outside Toby's room.

Toby tried to stifle Cliff's laughter, desperately holding his hands over his mate's mouth to keep Mick from hearing.

Mick pounded on the door. "Goddamn it, Cliff. Get your own fucking room if you're going to fuck right out in the fucking living room where I watch TV, you fuckheads."

Toby had to admit, it was pretty funny to hear Mick rant.

They waited until Mick quieted, Cliff hugging Toby close to him.

"I think he's gone." Toby pressed his ear to the door, trying to hear if Mick was still lying in wait outside.

Cliff pushed open the door, quickly walking to the bathroom and pulling Toby in after him. Shutting the door, he leaned against the wood for a moment before he burst out laughing again.

"Shhh, it isn't funny! Mick's gonna kill me. He hates being here in the first place while his house is being built and now we just made it that much harder for him to sit around inside my parents' house."

"Trust me, your brother isn't bothered by that as much as he's bothered by the fact that he's not getting any tail right now. Besides, between Mick and myself and your dad, we can have his house ready as soon as he gets the lumber. It doesn't hurt that there's a whole construction crew around here."

Toby shrugged, leaning over to turn on the water, testing the temperature before stepping inside the bathtub. Cliff stepped up behind him, hugging him close once more.

"We need to check your wounds. I can't believe I forgot about it earlier," Toby said, frowning.

"It's not that bad, pup. I've had worse just from running around with your brother. It'll heal."

Toby shook his head, peering closely at the jagged edges of the wounds. It was bleeding sluggishly, his werewolf blood already healing it, but it still looked ugly and raw. It had to hurt.

Picking up a washcloth, he poured antibacterial soap on it and started to clean the reddened area around the claw marks. Cliff winced, jerking his shoulder away.

"Enough, Tobe, leave it alone."

Wanting to argue, but realizing it would be futile, Toby relented. They quickly shampooed and washed their bodies, unwilling to linger long. They stepped out of the enclosed space, toweling themselves dry.

They walked back into the living room, and were faced with three different expressions.

Mick growled at them, crossing his big arms against his body. His dad was sitting in a chair off to the side, his arm around his mate, who was sitting on the side of the chair.

His dad had a small smile on his face. Toby frowned. What was his dad smiling about?

"Thanks a lot. I can still smell my baby brother all over the fucking room. Do you think I really want to smell my brother and my fuckhead of a best friend? You know, I should be kicking your ass right now for corrupting him."

Butch snickered, a sound that didn't normally come out of him. Mick glared at their dad, and Butch coughed. "I'm sorry, Mick, but you should see your face."

Butch glanced at Cliff and Toby standing by the doorway. "You might as well come in the room. We all know what you've been up to. So maybe you can explain why I can smell blood in here."

Cliff shrugged, wincing at the pull on his shoulder.

"What the hell happened?" Butch exclaimed. "What did you two do?"

"We didn't do anything, Dad. It was an accident. The bear came out of nowhere."

"Bear?"

"We were down at the river. Toby was in the water, searching for something, and he got a little too close to a cub. I was distracted. I should have scented the bears before Toby got between them. It was my fault, Butch." Cliff squared his shoulders, ignoring the hand Toby placed on his arm.

"It wasn't anyone's fault, Cliff," Toby reasoned. He wasn't going to let Cliff take the blame. "I didn't scent them either. So stop beating yourself up about it. We're both okay."

Toby turned his head at a watery sniff. His mom was clutching Butch's arm, tears running down her cheeks. She stood, holding out her arms.

"I just need to check," she stated. "You're okay?"

Toby stepped forward, hugging her close to his body. Inhaling, he drew her familiar scent into his lungs. Turning his head, he watched Mick and Butch step close to Cliff, examining his wounds.

"Goddamn it, the woods are supposed to be safe. What would have happened if this was worse? How can you protect my son if you're going to be stupid enough not to check for bears when you play outside?" Butch ran his fingers over the wound, his lips pressed tight together. Toby knew part of it was just bluster. His dad was scared.

"I have to contact the elders. They need to know the bears are back in the area, so they can send someone out to scare them away. The last thing I want is for one of the pups to get caught by a bear." Butch frowned, his face grim.

Toby's mom released him, going to Butch and wrapping her arms around him from behind.

Satisfied that Cliff was all right, Mick stepped away, sprawling across the sofa. He sniffed, shaking his head.

"I can still smell you two, you bastard." He glowered at Cliff.

Cliff kept peering over at Toby, catching his gaze. It was going to take them both a while to get over that scare.

"What's this?" his mom asked, pulling his attention to her.

Toby looked over to see his mom holding the gold chain that he had rescued. Realizing that he had never actually had a good look at it, Toby bounded over, taking it from her when she held it out to him.

Delicate links formed a narrow mesh pattern. It appeared to be a small collar, but it was absolutely gorgeous. Delicate, but obviously strong considering the abuse it had taken in the last few hours. Toby ran the tips of his fingers over the links, glancing up to see Cliff's heated gaze on him.

"You bought this for me?" he asked quietly.

"A little while ago. I found it in a store downtown. I was passing on my way to a worksite when I saw it in the window. I just knew it would suit you. It looks like a thick chain, see. But it's a collar," Cliff said, rushing his words together.

He looked nervous. Toby stared at him, perplexed at this side of Cliff.

"You really bought this for me?"

"Yeah... If you don't like it..."

"No! I love it! I just can't believe that you bought it for me." Toby stepped forward.

Cliff met him halfway, reaching out to tuck a strand of hair behind his ear. "It looks perfect." He took the chain from Toby, undoing the clasp and fitting it around his neck. He re-clasped it, fiddling with it until it lay exactly the way he wanted it to.

Toby lifted his hand, running his fingers over the links against his skin.

"I love it," he whispered.

"I'm glad."

"I love you," Toby said in a stronger voice.

"Oh, Christ, gag me," Mick muttered. A loud slap was heard, followed by a startled yelp.

Toby couldn't take his eyes off Cliff.

"Ditto, Tobe," Cliff replied with a wicked glint in his eyes.

Toby blushed, aware of his surroundings again. His mom and dad were smiling indulgently at them, and Mick was grinning. Toby assumed that his brother would have something smart-assed to say before long.

Cliff pulled him aside, holding him close, ignoring the others in the room. He bent his head, rubbing his cheek along Toby's.

"Hey, Tobe?"

"Yeah, Cliff?"

"Can you hand me the nut cream?" he murmured, pitching his voice low enough that the others wouldn't hear.

Toby widened his eyes, unable to speak.

"I seem to have a partiality for it. It just makes everything so damn silky smooth," Cliff said, smiling widely.

About the Author

Jade Buchanan was born in the summer of 2006, out of a slightly shy but definitely warped mind. Jade's alter-ego spends her days working in the world of safety management consulting, but at night she lets Jade out to play. Preferring to live in the world of fiction in which she was born, Jade can be found wandering through fields of words whenever she can. Now if only she can find her dream man—a time-traveling Scottish laird who was born a werewolf that became a vampire and lived on a pirate ship, only to make his way to the new world and work on a ranch in Montana (with a brief foray in the Navy SEALS), before conquering the space time continuum and becoming a space marauding pirate and ruling the galaxy—she'd be a very happy lady.

To learn more about Jade, please visit www.jadebuchananbooks.com. Send an email to Jade at jade.buchanan@yahoo.com.

GET IT NOW

MyBookStoreAndMore.com

GREAT EBOOKS, GREAT DEALS . . . AND MORE!

Don't wait to run to the bookstore down the street, or
waste time shopping online at one of the "big boys." Now,
all your favorite Samhain authors are all in one place—at
MyBookStoreAndMore.com. Stop by today and discover
great deals on Samhain—and a whole lot more!

WWW.SAMHAINPUBLISHING.COM

HOT STUFF

Discover Samhain!

THE HOTTEST NEW PUBLISHER ON THE PLANET

Romance, fantasy, mystery, thriller, mainstream and more—Samhain has more selection, hotter authors, and everything's available in both ebook and print.

Pick your favorite, sit back, and enjoy the ride! Hot stuff indeed.

WWW.SAMHAINPUBLISHING.COM

GREAT
CHEAP
FUN

Discover eBooks!

THE FASTEST WAY TO GET THE HOTTEST NAMES

Get your favorite authors on your favorite reader, long before they're out in print! Ebooks from Samhain go wherever you go, and work with whatever you carry—Palm, PDF, Mobi, and more.